PASS IT ON!

In the [REAL LIFE] series, four girls are brought together through the power of a mysterious book that helps them sort through the issues of their very real lives. In each of these stories, the girls find the mysterious RL book exactly when they need it. Each girl leaves the RL book for someone else to find, knowing it will help the next person who reads it.

While the RL book is magical, this book could be left in the same way for the next reader. Maybe this book needs to be read by someone you don't even know, or maybe you already know of someone who would really enjoy this book. Simply write a note with READ ME on it, stick it on the front of the book, and then get creative. Give the book to a friend, or leave this book at your church, school, local coffee shop, train station, on the bus, or wherever you know someone else will find it and read it.

No matter what your plan, we want to hear about it. Log on to the Zondervan Good Teen Reads Facebook page (*www.facebook.com/ goodteenreads*—look under the Discussion tab) and tell us where you left the book or how you found it. Or let us know how you plan to "pass it on." You can also let your friends know about Pass It On by talking about it on your Facebook page.

To join others in the Pass It On campaign, pick up extra copies of the [REAL LIFE] series at your local Christian bookstores and favorite online retailers.

Other books in the Real Life series:

Motorcycles, Sushi & One Strange Book (Book One)

BOYFRIENDS, BURRITOS & AN OCEAN OF TROUBLE

[REAL LIFE]

book two

NANCY RUE

ZONDERVAN®

ZONDERVAN.com/
AUTHORTRACKER
follow your favorite authors

ZONDERVAN

Boyfriends, Burritos & an Ocean of Trouble
Copyright © 2010 by Nancy Rue

This title is also available as a Zondervan ebook.
Visit www.zondervan.com/ebooks.

Requests for information should be addressed to:

Zondervan, *Grand Rapids, Michigan 49530*

Library of Congress Cataloging-in-Publication Data

Rue, Nancy N.
 Boyfriends, burritos & an ocean of trouble / by Nancy Rue.
  p. cm.—(A real life novel ; bk. 2)
  Summary: As she struggles to recover from the fallout of boyfriend Preston's
abuse, fifteen-year-old Bryn receives help from her surfer grandmother and an
unusual book.
  ISBN 978-0-310-71485-9 (softcover : alk. paper)
  [1. Dating violence—Fiction. 2. Grandmothers—Fiction. 3. Surfing—Fiction. 4.
Christian life—Fiction.] I. Title. II. Title: Boyfriends, burritos and an ocean of trouble.
PZ7.R85515Bo 2010
[Fic]—dc22   2009054372

All Scripture quotations, unless otherwise indicated, are taken from the Holy Bible, *New
International Version®, NIV®.* Copyright © 1973, 1978, 1984 by Biblica, Inc.™ Used by permission of Zondervan. All rights reserved worldwide.

Any Internet addresses (websites, blogs, etc.) and telephone numbers printed in this book
are offered as a resource. They are not intended in any way to be or imply an endorsement
by Zondervan, nor does Zondervan vouch for the content of these sites and numbers for
the life of this book.

Published in association with the literary agency of Alive Communications, Inc., 7680
Goddard Street, Suite 200, Colorado Springs, CO 80920. www.alivecommunications.com

Cover design: *Rule 29*
Cover photography: © iStockphoto © Camilla Wisbauer 2009
Interior design and composition: Patrice Sheridan & Carlos Eluterio Estrada

Printed in the United States of America

10 11 12 13 14 15 /DCI/ 23 22 21 20 19 18 17 16 15 14 13 12 11 10 9 8 7 6 5 4 3 2

CHAPTER ONE

I didn't wish the car accident had killed me. But lying there on the table in the emergency room as that bald doctor with the tangled eyebrows shined his tiny flashlight in my eyes, I would have settled for unconscious. Just a nice coma so I wouldn't have to answer any questions. My few seconds of blackout didn't seem to count, because no one had stopped interrogating me since the paramedics had arrived on the scene.

The doctor—*Jon Wooten*, it said on his name tag—dropped the flashlight into his coat pocket and put his warm hands on the sides of my face. I tried not to shiver.

"So, you hit your head on impact?" he said, nodding at my throbbing forehead.

"No." I hoped what I'd learned in my drama classes would kick in as I faked a smile. "The air bag hit *me*. Those things are dangerous!"

"It got you right here."

He brushed his fingers along my cheek, and I winced.

"We'll clean that up and get you some ice for the swelling," he said. "It's an abrasion—it won't leave a scar."

I was *so* not worried about a mark on my face. What I was worried about was getting out of here before—

"All right, we're going to have you change into a gown so I can examine you."

Before that.

"I'll have a nurse help you." He nodded at my father, who was standing in the corner of the curtained cubicle where he'd been asked to stay. "She's definitely had a concussion. I may

5

want a CT scan to rule out internal injuries, but let's see if there's anything else going on first."

He motioned for Dad to follow him and then swept out.

Dad nodded, but he came to me and leaned over the table. His face was gray, his pale blue eyes wet around the edges. In the harsh hospital light, I saw lines etched in his face that weren't there when I left the house that night, as if he'd just gotten old that very minute. He had to be even skinnier now too, and the thinning place on top of his head made him seem somehow fragile. My father never showed much emotion except when he had to put a young dog to sleep. The way he was looking at me, I could have been a terminal puppy.

He was a veterinarian, but a doctor's a doctor. He couldn't be missing the fact that my heart was slamming at my chest and taking my breath away. "Bryn, this is serious," he said. "Don't downplay it—tell them everything, you hear?"

His Virginia-soft accent didn't usually affect me that much. Probably because he didn't actually talk to me that much. But right now it was doing me in. I swallowed back the sob that threatened to burst from my chest. At least he wasn't asking me what I'd been doing in a car alone with Preston.

"Brynnie?" he said.

"Okay," I said. "But I'm really not hurt."

Except for the pain in my stomach and the ache in my arm and the throbbing in my head, that was the truth.

As soon as he disappeared through the curtain, panic grabbed at my insides and climbed all the way up my throat and gagged me. I plastered my hand over my mouth and prayed I wouldn't throw up. Then I prayed that Dr. Wooten would learn about a sudden outbreak of the plague in Virginia Beach and forget about me, and Dad and I could go home and pretend to forget this whole thing happened.

But there was as much a chance of that as there was that once I was clad in a flimsy gown, that doctor wasn't going to see what was under it. I wasn't so worried about tonight's injuries. Those bruises wouldn't rise to the surface until at least tomorrow.

It was Wednesday's evidence I was worried about. I couldn't

6

let him see that. Not with Dad standing there. At least my mother wasn't here. At least there was that.

A nurse in turquoise scrubs and a messy ponytail slipped in through the curtain, a gown and a sheet over her arm. She looked at me like I was one of Dad's patients, recently brought in from a storm drain.

"Hey, girlfriend," she said. "I'm Cindi. How you doin'?"

"I'd be better if I could just go home," I said. "I bet you have people way sicker than me to take care of."

"Nope. You lucked out tonight."

She put her hand on my shoulder, and I tried not to cringe.

"I'm going to need you to take everything off and put on this precious gown." She gave me a winky smile. "It's not a good look for anybody, but it's all we've got."

If she was trying to get me to relax, it wasn't working. My mouth dried up, and I could feel my hands oozing sweat.

"Once you get that on you can lie back, and I'll cover you with the sheet." She tilted her head at me. "Are you cold?"

I was, even in my pink sweater, even though it was June and everybody else at the party had been in tank tops. It was pointless to pretend I wasn't shivering now. I could almost feel my lips turning blue.

"I'm going to go get you a blanket," she said. "If you even start to feel dizzy, lie down and I'll help you get undressed when I come back."

When she left I fought back more panic. Jesus, what do I do?

I wasn't swearing. I was really asking Jesus, just like I'd been doing for the last three months. I hadn't gotten any answers. I would have given up a leading role for one right now—because if there was any way out of this beyond a miracle, I wasn't seeing it.

I pulled the thread-thin blue gown to my face and breathed in the hospital smell and begged Jesus to make me disappear. Outside the cubicle, sneakers squealed past on the linoleum. I could either do it now or do it ten minutes from now or two hours from now. But they were going to make me do it, and the longer I put it off, the more suspicious they were all going to be.

I pushed the gown from my face. Okay—do it fast—like

it's no big deal. Make up a story about the bruises. Promise to be more careful with my bird-boned, five-foot-one self in the future.

I couldn't come up with anything else.

I pulled off the sweater, the one Preston said back in the beginning made me look delicious, and yanked the deeper-shade-of-pink long-sleeved tee over my head. The pain seared through me like I was being sliced with a bread knife, but I was now beyond crying. Fear steals your tears—I'd learned that. Still, I didn't dare look at myself as I fed my arms gingerly through the holes in the gown.

Tying the thing in the back was almost not worth the agony involved, but it might keep the doctor from seeing that part. Not that he would need to. The black-and-purple handprint around my bicep told enough of a story by itself. I was going to have to think of a better one and tell it with a sheepish smile. Assure them it would never happen again.

Please, Jesus—don't let it ever happen again.

Things were tangling in my head and I couldn't allow it. I put all my focus on wriggling out of the rest of my clothes and tucking the gown tightly around my legs and draping my hair over my shoulders. Maybe they'd believe some lame story because I was blonde. I was about to pull the sheet up to my neck when Nurse Cindi slid the curtains apart, already talking.

"Are we set?" she said.

Her lips stopped moving in mid-word. Even while I was retreating behind the sheet, I caught the flicker that went through her eyes. It was gone almost before it was there, a trick they must teach in nursing school. But it had lingered long enough for me to know she knew.

Any story I came up with was going to be perfectly useless. I buried my face in my knees.

"I'll be right back," she practically whispered. "No worries, girlfriend. We'll take care of this."

No. Jesus, please don't let them "take care of it." *You* take care of it. Make it go away.

He didn't. Instead, the curtain parted again, and I groped for my smile and the strands of my story. Everything on Dr. Wooten's face came to a suspicious point. Nurse Cindi wasn't even trying to hide the pity on hers.

"Where's my dad?" I said.

"Filling out some paperwork," he said.

I let go of a ragged breath that dragged through my ribs. Good. I didn't want him here for this.

Without a word, Dr. Wooten pulled back the sheet and examined my arms with only his eyes. I could feel him taking in the bruises—some of them pale blue and red, some dark purple, a few a sickening yellowish green. Cindi watched him, watched me, looked at him again. A whole conversation went on while nobody said a word. I had to stop it.

"Those are old bruises," I said.

"I know," he said.

"I got them playing football."

"I'm going to have you lie back for me."

"Seriously. I'm a double linebacker."

"There's no such thing as a double linebacker, Bryn."

"Single?"

Doctor Wooten pressed his hands on my abdomen and that's when I lost it all—my smile, my loser attempt at a story, my hope. The sucker-punch pain in my stomach throbbed worse now than it had when it first happened. I squeezed the sides of the table and cried without making a sound.

"This one is new," he said. "Were you wearing a seat belt?"

I shook my head and waited for the lecture. The doctor only frowned and pulled the sheet back up to my chest. Nurse Cindi smoothed and tucked and bit at her lip.

He rolled a stool close and sat looking at me long and hard. I should have seen it before: he had eyes you didn't lie to, even if you thought your life depended on it.

"Let's talk about how this happened," he said, "without the football scenario."

He put his hands on my neck and felt around, his eyes never leaving mine alone. He wouldn't find anything there. It never happened in a place I couldn't keep covered up. I didn't own any turtlenecks.

9

It was a random thought to have at that moment, but my mind was trying to leave my body. This doctor with the bald head and the intense brows and the eyes that saw everything must have seen that too, because he said, "Who did this to you, Bryn?"

"It was an accident," I said. My voice was so thin I could hardly hear it.

"Was it an accident every time?"

"He didn't plan it. He just got mad and it happened."

"And he hit you in the stomach."

I started to shake my head, but he went on. "You have a large hematoma that's rising even as we're looking at it. Probably a broken blood vessel in your abdominal wall, which could be serious. If you weren't wearing a seat belt—"

"Maybe I was—"

"Bryn. Who did this?"

His voice had gone soft around the edges. I closed my eyes and felt the tears slither into my ears.

"I'm sorry this has happened to you," he said. "We don't want it to happen again, so you need to tell us who's been hurting you."

"I can't." I opened my eyes and let them plead for me. "I'll make it stop, I promise."

"If you could have stopped it, you would have." His voice got firmer. "This is not your fault, Bryn."

"Yes, it is. Please—I'll take care of it."

He folded his arms and looked at me so sadly I thought for a minute he was going to let me.

"Your dad's *Doctor* Christopher," he said.

"He's a vet," I said.

"Does he have his own practice?"

"It's next door to our house." I didn't know where we were going with this, but at least it was away from my beat-up body.

"Is he under a lot of stress?"

"My dad?" I would have laughed if I hadn't been crying. My father was more laid back than Winnie the Pooh.

"Does your mom live with you?"

"Yes, sir, but she's away on a trip." Thank goodness.

"How long has she been gone?"

"Two weeks. She won't be back 'til the end of July."

I closed my eyes again. Suddenly I was so tired I could have faded away—if he hadn't said what he said next.

"I don't have a choice, Bryn. You're only fifteen. I have to report this."

My eyes sprang open.

"You're the victim of assault."

I tried to sit up, but I flopped back like a helpless fish. "He didn't assault me." I said. "He just—"

He just what? Was I going to tell them his eyes had gone wild and the veins in his neck bulged like purple cords and I knew he couldn't stop himself? That I knew it was going to be worse than last time because it always was?

Dr. Wooten stood up. "I'm going to send you down for a CT scan so we can be sure of what's happening with your belly. That will give you some time to think it over." He brushed my hand with his fingertips, like he knew that was the only place on me that didn't hurt. "I want you to know there's nothing to be afraid of, for you or your dad. He can get help—"

In spite of the breath-stealing pain, I sat right up on the table this time.

"My dad?" I said. "You think my dad did this?"

"No matter what you feel you did to deserve it, it's child abuse."

"You don't understand!" I grabbed for his wrist and caught a handful of his coat in my fingers. "My dad would never do this."

"Then who was it, Bryn? Because if you don't tell us, the police are going to assume it was him."

"The *police?*" I let go of his sleeve and shoved my hands into my hair. And then I let go of the words that were going to change my life forever and ever.

"It wasn't my father," I said. "It was my boyfriend."

CHAPTER TWO

For the next two hours, I tried to pretend it was all happening to someone else. I was usually good at pretending, but I couldn't quite pull it off that night. Everyone kept saying my name, like they didn't want me to think I was just another victim of abuse to them.

I was "Bryn" to the technician who did the CT scan, the woman who came in and took pictures of all my bruises for the hospital records, and of course Cindi, who kept telling me everything was going to be all right even though nothing was ever going to be all right again.

But to my father I was "Brynnie." He kept saying it from the minute Cindi brought him in, even when she stayed in my cubicle as if she'd been told to keep an eye on him.

He came straight over to the table, so I just pulled back the sheet. Everybody that worked at that hospital had already looked at my shame. Why shouldn't he?

He whispered "Brynnie" as he studied me. His face was no longer ash colored. He and I were both blushers, and he was now as red as he'd been pale before. I couldn't tell if it was from anger. I'd never seen my father mad until now.

"Brynnie," he said again. "Preston did this?"

If he'd sounded the tiniest bit like he didn't believe me, I would have said no. But it was more like a statement than a question, as if he didn't doubt my word for a minute. That broke my heart right in half.

"Did he?"

"Yes, sir," I said. "I'm sorry—"

"We're pressing charges."

He said it more to Cindi than to me, but it was still me who cried, "No!" Me who started to shake again, my head harder than anything else. Me who watched Cindi leave to get the police she said were still there, investigating the accident.

"Why can't we just leave it alone?" I said. "He's going away to swim camp next week, and I can change schools and never have to see him again—"

"Brynnie—"

"I did stupid things that made him—"

"Brynnie, stop."

I did. I had never heard him take that tone the whole time my sister Tara and I were growing up. My mother did the stern thing—the "that's enough," the "we're done." Not him.

He leaned on the table and put his face close to mine, where I could see his eyes swimming. "I don't care what you think you did to provoke this—or what you feel for this boy. It's wrong."

I didn't tell him I cared nothing for Preston Oliver. I just wanted this to go away. I wanted *me* to go away. I was nothing before I met him and I could be that again. But Preston was everything everybody wanted to be. Who were people going to believe?

Dad squeezed the bridge of his nose with two fingers. "I'm not letting him get away with this. I want you to tell the police everything."

I stopped arguing. I stopped crying. I realized for the first time ever that I didn't really know how to get my way with anybody. I did know how to pretend it didn't happen or that I could make it disappear, or that I was somebody else.

But like I said, I couldn't pull it off that night. I'd never experienced anything more real than having two police officers question me while I sat on a table wrapped in blankets. The shaking, the ice bag on my cheek, the pounding in my brain—there was no denying any of that.

The officer with the almost-shaved head and thick lips was the one who'd stayed with me at the accident until the paramedics got there, even though I'd told him I didn't need to go to the hospital. If he'd listened to me, we could have avoided all this. I already didn't like him.

The other one, an African American, had been with Preston. They had kept us apart, I remembered. I was glad. Until we'd heard the sirens, Preston had yelled at me, over and over, variations on, "Why did you grab my arm? Why did you—you made us crash! It's your fault!"

It was always my fault.

"I'm Officer Day," the black cop said now. "This is Officer Garrett."

I didn't care what their names were. But like everybody else, they seemed to love saying mine.

"Bryn, we're going to need you to tell us about the abuse, starting with the most recent incident. Take your time. You can stop and rest whenever you need to."

No way. I was getting through this as fast as possible.

"We were at a party for Preston's birthday," I said.

"Preston Oliver."

"Yes, sir. It was a big thing because he turned eighteen."

They looked at each other like that was important somehow. Behind me, Dad made a deep sound in his throat, like he was suddenly in pain.

"What happened at the party, Bryn?" Officer Day said.

He was obviously going to ask all the questions while the other one wrote everything down, which was fine. He had kinder eyes. Maybe he wouldn't make me tell every detail. Maybe he'd believe I was telling him more than he needed to know.

"This girl—Josie—from my drama class came up to us and started talking about what a great job I did on my final monologue and how Mr. Chadwick—that's our drama teacher—said I had a real future in the drama department. Preston got mad because I'd promised him I wasn't going to do theater anymore, and he grabbed my arm and took me out the front door."

"Did anybody see him do that, do you think?"

I nodded. How could they not have? Preston had acted like he didn't care whether anyone saw him drag me across the room. My kitten heels didn't even touch the floor.

"Where did he take you?" the officer said.

"To his friend Andrew's car. The party was at his house."

14

The other officer flipped back the pages on his notepad. "Was that the black Mazda RX-8?"

I nodded again. "Preston didn't have his car there. I don't go anywhere with him in his car anyway."

I said that for Dad's benefit, so he wouldn't think I'd completely turned into some rebellious stranger-daughter who didn't follow her parents' rules.

"What happened at the car?"

"He made me get in—"

"How did he make you?"

"He threw me in," I said to my lap. "On the passenger side. And then he got in on the driver's side and started yelling about how I was a liar and did things behind his back and he couldn't trust me." I squeezed my eyes shut, but I couldn't block out the scene. "I should have just let him yell until he was done, but it was like something popped in me—"

Just get away from me, I'd yelled back at him. *Just get away.* Because in that instant, I knew I couldn't be with him anymore. Ever. No matter how much he cried when he apologized.

I'd turned and fumbled for the door handle, but I'd never been in Andrew's car before, and by the time I found it, Preston had me by the back of the neck, like he was trying to squeeze my spirit out of me. He wrapped his other hand around my wrist and wrenched me to face him, and I knew. I knew he was going to hit me again, and he did—only this time it wasn't just a jab in the arm or a knock into a wall. He grabbed a flashlight from the dashboard and jabbed it into my stomach, so hard I had no breath.

He didn't look like he was going to stop there—but somebody yelled something from the front porch. He dropped the flashlight and let go of my shoulder, but his eyes held me for a cold, hard moment. The same silver-gray eyes that used to devour my face and make me feel like I was one person with him were paralyzing me in the seat. I already knew by then that they could change from one to the other the way a thunderstorm interrupts a picnic. I just hadn't learned to tell what was going to make it happen.

I was still trying to breathe again, otherwise I might have gotten out the door. But before I could even try, Preston pulled

Andrew's keys out from under the seat and started up the car. I went for the door handle again but by then Preston had us squealing out of the driveway. He had scared me before, but until then I didn't know I could be so terrified that I couldn't swallow or scream or do anything to save myself. I felt the pain when my forehead slammed against the side window as he took the first corner too sharply. I hadn't even had time to fasten my seat belt, so I smacked against him after he made the turn and grabbed his arm to stop myself. The wheel jerked and he couldn't get it back. As if it were suddenly in slow motion, the car went sideways. I closed my eyes then, so I only heard the smack of metal and felt the air bag smother me and scrape the side of my face. Only later when they got me out of the car did I see that we'd hit a parked car. Before then, all I knew was that the whole thing had been my fault. Preston kept screaming that at me until I believed it. Like I always had.

"Do you have enough to go on for now?"

I blinked and looked over my shoulder at my father. His face was washed out again, as if I'd just said all of that out loud.

"I think so," Officer Day said.

So I *had* said it. I was glad Dad had stopped me then, or I probably would have gone on to say I'd even been glad Preston said it was my fault he'd wrecked his best friend's car. Maybe he'd break up with *me*, and I could go back to playing parts on stage instead of the ones he made up for me.

But then the sirens had threaded their way through the night, and I'd gotten the shakes. The sound of fire engines and ambulances always made me shiver, but that was the first time I'd ever heard them coming for me. I could feel the whine across my skin and down in my stomach and up in my throat, and I couldn't stop trembling. Preston got his arm around me and cried, sobbed that he was sorry. That was how the police had found us. These same two officers, who were now looking at me as if I couldn't possibly be talking about the same contrite young man they'd seen comforting me in the wreckage. Nobody else was going to believe it either.

"That should do it for now." Officer Day stood up. "We have enough to take him in, but if you want to go further with it—talk about any past incidents—you'll need to contact the DA's office."

Officer Garrett closed his notepad and handed Dad some kind of card. If I hadn't been trying once again to lift myself above what was happening around me, I would have snatched it and chewed it up and swallowed it. *Go further with it?* Hadn't we gone far enough?

Evidently not. Officer Day smeared his hand over his mouth and looked at me with his kind eyes again.

"Two more questions," he said. "One—can you prove any of this?"

"Excuse me?" Dad said. "She just told you—"

"We just need to know if there were ever any witnesses, anybody who can corroborate your story."

"No," I said. "He never did it in front of anyone."

"Her word isn't good enough?" Dad said.

"We're just trying to get all the information we can." The officer looked at me again. "I also have to ask—has Mr. Oliver sexually abused you?"

"No!"

His eyes shifted to Dad.

"I'm not just saying that because my father's here. I haven't had sex with Preston or anybody else!"

"We're not accusing you of anything, Bryn," said the other officer, whose name I had already forgotten. "But he's eighteen, and you're a minor. It would be considered statutory rape."

"Rape!" My voice was so shrill it hurt my own ears. "There was no rape—there was no—nothing!"

I plastered my hands over my face so I wouldn't tell them that I would always rather have Preston smile at me than kiss me. Nobody could smile like Preston when he was happy—like when he hoisted himself out of the pool after a race and looked at me like I'd won it for him. I would rather have him look right into my eyes and let one side of his mouth turn up and then let his eyebrows rise like the sun coming up and then the other side of his mouth until it was all about me. I would rather see that than touch him.

"Brynnie?" Dad said.

"I'm telling the truth! I might be stupid, but I'm not a slut—"

"Nobody is saying that."

Dad put his hand on the back of my hair, and then he pulled it away like he was afraid he would hurt me. As far as I was concerned, he already had. I hugged my arms around myself and turned my head from him.

"We can have them do a rape kit," Officer Garret said.

I forced myself not to ask what that was. I could hear my father breathing.

"No," he said finally. "I don't think we need that."

"If you don't, you won't have any evidence should she change her mind down the line."

"No," Dad said.

At least there was that.

"We'll put this together and have you come down to the station in the next couple of days and sign it," one of them said.

I didn't know if he was talking to me or not and I didn't look to find out. Dad followed them out of the cubicle, and I could hear them muttering beyond the curtain, probably trying to convince my father that I'd been raped too—as if being slapped around wasn't bad enough.

There was no rape. Preston did push me too hard too fast. He was already trying no-things before I even got to enjoy yes-things. I liked holding hands and hugging and flirting and even sweet-kissing. He got past all of that the first week. He said he wanted me breathless. I liked the way that sounded. I just didn't like the way it felt.

I could never figure out why he didn't leave me for some girl who wanted to be breathless. Heaven knew there were enough of them at Tidewater Prep drooling for their chance. He just kept saying I was so innocent, not like the girls he'd dated before. So if he liked me innocent, why didn't he want to let me stay that way? He would push too much, and then I would cry, and then it was like he enjoyed brushing away my tears and kissing my face until I smiled at him again. That wasn't the issue that made him hit me.

"Brynnie?"

It was Dad, outside the curtain. I told him to come in.

"We're going home," he said. "You go ahead and get dressed, and I'll meet you in the waiting room."

I was already off the table. I didn't care how much it hurt or how disgusting my clothes looked and smelled. I had them back on almost before the curtains closed behind him.

Before I could get out, though, Nurse Cindi came in, face long and sympathetic.

"I'm really glad you're pressing charges," she said. "Too many girls let guys get away with this stuff. You're very brave."

I didn't tell her it had nothing to do with bravery and everything to do with having no choice.

"I know you're still in shock," she said, "but take this to read later." She handed me a white plastic bag that felt like it had brochures in it. "Materials on relationship abuse. There are names of a couple of really great counselors in there. One of them even has a group for battered teens."

"Battered?" I said. "Like a battered wife?"

Cindi nodded, more tendrils of hair dripping out of her ponytail. "It's just as bad as domestic violence. If you get good help now you can avoid ever having to deal with this again."

The only help I wanted was in getting out of there.

"Could you show me where the waiting room is?" I said.

Dad wasn't there yet when Cindi left me—reluctantly—in a chair, and I breathed the closest thing I could to a sigh of relief. My stomach still hurt; the doctor said it would for a while even though the pressure inside the skin had cut off the bleeding on the inside—or something like that.

I didn't think that was why it hurt. The pain was the memory of that look on Preston's face—a face that didn't belong to the Preston everybody followed like he was the Messiah. That man-gorgeous face with the sun-bleached eyebrows that made him seem intense, like you could lean on him, like you could trust him to know things. The strong jaw I liked to run my finger down because it seemed like it would make me feel safe. Sometimes my touch melted him. Sometimes it made his cheek muscles harden like strips of steel. Again, I could never tell which it was going to be.

Why couldn't I know? Why couldn't I just look at him and know?

And then I *was* looking at him.

Preston was coming through the doors that swung out from the emergency room, flanked by the two officers. He was looking hard at the floor, but I didn't miss the jaw muscles this time.

Frantically, I looked around for something to hide behind. There was a worn-out-looking leather book on the table next to me. I snatched it up and opened it in front of my face. He wouldn't see me. He wouldn't even think to look for me, not when he was being ushered to the door by the cops.

I kept the book there and listened for voices, but there were none. The whole waiting room seemed to be holding its breath. I kept hiding until I heard the automatic doors sigh open and closed. Even then I kept the book in front of me—only now my eyes actually focused on the few words printed on the page.

If you've found me, you need me. I was left for you for a reason. Read and discover what that is.

I got a chill and slapped the book shut. I'd had enough shaking for one night.

People in the waiting room were all staring out the glass wall. Without thinking I let my eyes go with them. I was just in time to see Preston twist his head to look back over his shoulder. He found what he was looking for, because his gaze stopped on me, and the hatred on his face paralyzed my soul.

I didn't move until the officers had deposited him in the police car parked outside the door. I was still huddled there hugging the leather book when my father appeared above me and said, "Brynnie?"

"Can we please go home?" I said.

CHAPTER THREE

I woke up the next morning to the sound of a motor running in my ear. It took me a full fifteen seconds to realize it was our cat, Copper, purring in my face. It took less time than that to remember that my whole life was basically over.

I tried to pull the pillow across my eyes but Copper had his fat self ensconced on it like a furry orange Henry the Eighth. Moving him was out of the question. So was rolling over, as I found out when I yawned. Every cell in my body screamed, "Lie still! You're killing us here!"

I groaned at Copper, who blinked without sympathy.

"I know Dad fed you," I said.

His answering purr bordered on a low growl, which clearly meant that made absolutely no difference to him. All Copper thought about was food.

I wished that was all I had to think about.

What *I* had to think about was talking Dad out of going after Preston. He'd said it again on the way home: "He won't get away with this, Brynnie. He'll be prosecuted to the full extent of the law."

I sat up now and was sure the muscles in my arms were tearing into strips. Dad hadn't seen the look on Preston's face when he left the hospital with those policemen. What if I was the one who wasn't going to get away with it?

"I can't go there," I said to Copper. "Come on—I'll feed you again."

He led the way to the kitchen.

The coffeepot light was on, which meant Dad was up. He was probably out running like he did every morning. I looked at the sunburst clock over the table in the corner. Almost eleven. No—he'd been back for hours.

Copper complained from the counter and looked pointedly at his dish, which as I'd suspected was licked clean.

"You should get a Golden Globe Award for that performance," I said.

I pulled the bag of dry food out of the cabinet and dumped some into the bowl. He sniffed at it and glared at me as if I were trying to poison him.

"Best Performance in a Dramatic Role goes to Copper Christopher," I said. "But I'm still not giving you any wet food."

He proceeded to rub his head against my arm.

"Okay," I said, "but don't tell Dad."

Copper all but crossed his white chest with his paw.

I opened the cabinet again to grab a can of Fancy Feast. "No wonder you look like Jabba the Hutt," I told him. "You think they have Jenny Craig for felines?"

I thought for a second that he actually answered me, until I realized it was Dad's voice I was hearing. It was coming from the sunroom on the other side of the house, just off the living room. I couldn't hear what he was saying, and I needed to. Only one subject would make his tone that grim.

I left Copper meowing indignantly at the unopened can and tiptoed across the tiled entrance hall and into the living room, where the wood blinds had been opened and a shaft of sun shot across the yellow rug. I might as well have been standing in a spotlight. I was tempted to hide behind the ficus tree, but Dad's voice was so focused, he probably wouldn't notice if I went in there and planted myself right in front of him.

Besides, it hurt to stand up any longer. I curled into the corner of our sunset-colored couch and hugged a throw pillow and listened. Maybe he was talking to a client about her sick shih tzu, although he never did business on the house phone—

"I know, Windy," he said. "It boggles the mind."

So much for that hope. "Windy" was my grandmother. No wonder his voice sounded like somebody was pinching it off.

This was outstanding. Now he was telling the relatives that I was a "battered teen." People I hadn't seen since I was ten.

22

"From what the doctor told me," Dad said, "this wasn't the first time. In addition to the hematoma, the CT scan showed a partially healed fracture on the left side, ribs six and seven. They couldn't make an exact determination of the age, but judging from the various bruises, this has been going on for at least a month."

Two months. The bruises from the first few times had already healed. They hadn't been as bad. Preston had only grabbed my arm and twisted it when I went to an Arts Festival rehearsal during lunch instead of eating with him. When the practice I had after school the next week ran long, he'd shoved me against the wall outside the theater and bruised both shoulders. The weather was just turning warm then, and I'd had to wear long-sleeved tops just to make sure nobody saw. Preston promised me he'd never do it again, and I promised I'd never make him feel like he came second to my acting again. He didn't know that was when I *started* acting with him.

"It won't surprise you that Kate was determined to cut her trip short and come home," Dad was saying now. "Uh-huh ... right, she's a mother bear ..."

Please, Jesus, no. I might be able to talk Dad out of this, but never my mother. She had a blazing temper about things like university politics and the mistreatment of women in the Middle East and the newspaper guy who kept throwing *The Virginian-Pilot* into the birdbath. If she weren't in Central America someplace, Preston would have been a candidate for one of her blowups for sure. It wasn't that I didn't think he deserved it. I just didn't want things to get any worse than they already were. Although, I didn't see how they could.

And then they did.

"No, she's not," Dad said. "It took some doing, but I convinced her I have it under control. She has that whole group of graduate students with her ... Yeah, Tara went too. They've been planning it for a year ..."

I was disappearing into guilt. It might actually be nice to have my older sister here to help me turn Dad around. She was twenty and had a lot more experience with that than I did, being the push-the-envelope type. But if she had to miss out on the chance to explore Aztec culture with my mother and have it to put on her resume for getting into grad school herself, I would be ruining her life as well as mine.

My stomach hurt and I realized I had the pillow jammed against it. I let go and tried to breathe. Maybe I should pretend to be asleep so if Dad saw me here, he wouldn't make me talk to Mim.

That was what the grandkids called my mom's mother. It hadn't been my choice. Our boy cousins had been born before Tara so they got to name her. Since they couldn't pronounce *Grandma*, she ended up with Mim. If it had been left up to me, she would be Grandmama, with the accent on the last *ma*.

Actually, it hadn't mattered that much, because my grandfather died when I was a baby and Mim married a Hawaiian guy when I was about five and moved to Honolulu. I'd only seen her one time since I was in kindergarten, and even that was one time too many. I was pretty sure my dad felt the same way about his mother-in-law, which was why it surprised me that he was even talking to her.

"I didn't think about calling you," he said.

He was closer to the doorway, so I closed my eyes and tried to breathe deep and even. It felt like I was dragging barbed wire through my midsection.

"No ... I would think this would be your busy time of year at the camp ... yeah, Kate told me you have a full staff now ..."

So this was Mom's doing. I wanted part of my mother here—her silky voice, her touch on my hair. But this was the part I didn't want: the part that would suggest that my grandmother could be helpful.

Behind my closed eyes I had a clear vision of Mim when Mom, Dad, Tara, and I were visiting her and her husband in Hawaii. She didn't care that I was ten and wanted to curl up under a palm tree with *The Lord of the Rings*. She thought I should be bodysurfing and boogie boarding with her and Tara, who was eating it up with a spoon. The waves scared me to death. I didn't tan—I just burned and peeled no matter how much sunscreen she slathered on me, acting the whole time like it was my fault I had pale freckly skin like my father. For the whole first week I woke up every morning dreading what she had planned for me. The day she made me go snorkeling I burst into tears when they put the mask over my face, and I guess she got disgusted with me, because she stopped trying to turn me into a beach bunny after that. We definitely didn't bond.

Maybe I wouldn't have prayed for us never to visit her again if she'd moved to someplace like Ohio when Grandpa Paiana died three years ago, instead of to California. She could be fun when she wasn't trying to train you for an Ironman competition. But San Diego? That just sounded like more bodysurfing to me. Maybe even parasailing ... bungee jumping ...

My father's voice filtered into my vision of myself falling to my death at the end of a frayed cord. "That'll work," he said. "Just let me know when you book a flight, and I'll pick you up."

Pain ripped through my back as I sat straight up on the couch. Mim was coming *here*?

"No, don't rent a car. You can use Kate's ... I'm off until Monday ... no, that's great, Windy. I'm glad Kate had you call me ... Right, I'll tell Bryn."

Tell me what? That if I'd been concentrating on playing soccer or something, like girls were evidently supposed to, this wouldn't have happened to me?

Dear Jesus, please, please don't let her come here. Just — please.

I heard the phone conversation peter out and I slumped down, eyes closed again. I must have truly been losing my touch because Dad said from the doorway, "So you're awake."

He passed through to the kitchen and came back with two Tylenol and a glass of juice. We exchanged some awkward sentences about how I slept — fine — and how much pain I was in — not that much — and whether I needed anything — nothing. He was asking me questions he already knew the answers to and I was telling him lies. It was all about avoiding what neither one of us wanted to talk about.

When we'd finally run out of pointless conversation, Dad sat on the edge of the Aztec-print chair facing me and studied his hands while I studied the spot on top of his head. From pictures I'd seen of him when he was young, I knew his hair used to be blond like mine. Instead of going gray as he got older, it went ash brown and thinned out. My mother always said his bald place was sweet, and she'd kiss it and then he'd blush. I'd grown up thinking that was the way couples were supposed to be with each other.

"Mim's going to come help us out while your mother's gone," he said.

"Aren't we doing okay?" I pretended to gaze at the tidy living room. "The place looks fine to me—"

"You know what I mean, Brynnie."

His voice was weary. More guilt piled on, and I bit my lip.

"I talked to your mom last night and she suggested it."

Suggested it? She arranged the whole thing.

"Mom's hating it that she hasn't been able to hear your voice. She's going to try to get to Mexico City today, where there's better reception, so she can talk to you. She kept cutting out last night."

I didn't bother to suggest that maybe he'd misunderstood Mom—that she hadn't said Mim should come here at all. Even I couldn't pretend that. The only reason my mother wasn't coming home to take Preston down herself was because she knew my grandmother could do a better job of it.

"Is she mad at me?" I said instead.

"Who?"

"Mom."

Dad's eyes drooped into the bags that had formed under them overnight. "Why would she be mad at you?"

"Because of this whole mess."

"You didn't make the mess. And I'm going to get it cleaned up—make no mistake about that—"

"Then why do we need Mim?"

Dad nodded at the glass of juice on the coffee table. "I want you to drink that. Then we'll think about breakfast." He tried to smile. "Or maybe lunch."

"I'm not hungry."

"That's why we need Mim." I watched the doctor thing kick in. "You experienced a trauma, and you need somebody to take care of you—make sure you eat and rest."

And do aerobics before dawn.

"I keep telling you it's not that bad," I said. "They wouldn't have let me come home if it was." I tried a smile of my own. "I promise to eat—and I have 'rest' down to a serious art form. I can take care of myself, Dad."

My father was no actor. He couldn't mask the look that came over his face, the look that said, "If you could take care of yourself, we wouldn't be in this situation."

"Okay," I said, "I'm going to go rest."

*

I spent the afternoon in bed but I didn't sleep. Every time I closed my eyes I saw somebody's face—Nurse Cindi's full of pity, Officer What's-His-Name's tight with suspicion, Dad's old and daughter-weary.

Preston's.

As much as I didn't want to talk to anybody, I was halfway glad when Dad brought me the phone around two o'clock. At least I wouldn't be able to see Mom's expression.

But just as Dad handed it to me he whispered, "It's Tara."

I started to cry the second I heard her voice—smooth like our mother's but warm—golden silk instead of silver.

"Is Dad in the room?" she said.

"No," I said.

"Is your door closed?"

"Yes."

"Then tell me the truth—are you okay? I mean, seriously?"

"No," I said. And then we had to wait until I stopped sobbing. Something about finally telling the truth opened me up like a faucet. That and my vision of my tall, latte-tanned sister sitting on some adobe wall with her long legs draped on either side, listening to me with the space between her dark brows drawn into a single vertical line. Her hair about the color of cherry furniture would be slapped into a ponytail and still look ready for the cover of *Cosmo*.

"So is this jerk the same guy that saw you in *The Wizard of Oz* and said you were his dream woman?" Tara said.

"*Alice in Wonderland*," I said.

27

"What happened? Did he hit you when he was drunk or what?"

"He doesn't drink," I said. "He doesn't do drugs."

"He just beats up girls. So what was it, jealousy?"

"Kind of."

"Some other guy looked at you and he flipped out?"

"He was mostly jealous of theater."

It was the first time I'd said it out loud and it sounded lame, even to me.

"You're not serious." Tara gave a thick grunt. "Let me get this straight: he sees you playing a flower in a play—"

Actually, it was the Ace of Hearts.

"—and he, an upperclassman, supposedly falls in love with you—a lowly freshman—because you are perfection on stage—"

He'd said I was even beautiful in a card costume.

"—and then he decides the thing he loves about you is also the thing he hates."

"Yeah," I said. "He said it took away from our time together."

"I'm not buying that," she said. I imagined her deep-blue eyes sizzling. Unlike my pale ones, hers could burn down a room. "Did he spend twenty-four/seven with you?"

"No—"

"Didn't you tell me he was this major swimmer? Tried out for the Olympic team?"

"He pulled a muscle the day before the tryouts and he missed the cut by five-hundredths of a point."

"So did he give up swimming totally?"

"No. He's on the school swim team, and he wants to try out for the US Team again. It tore him up when he didn't make it."

"Which means he's training every spare minute—am I right?"

She barely gave me a chance to say yes.

"Which means he was allowed to do his thing but you weren't allowed to do yours."

"He wanted me to come and watch his practices," I said.

"And when you didn't, he slapped the snot out of you."

"No. I went."

28

In the pause I heard Tara gasp.

"You are *not* serious!" Her silky voice twisted into a hard knot. "You watched his swim practices instead of rehearsing for your plays?"

"Only after the Arts Festival was over." I knew I was winding up into defensive mode, but I couldn't help trying to explain it to her. "He knew that was a huge deal and I *had* to rehearse for it a lot. We were the only group picked from Drama I, and it was a piece from *The Outsiders* so we had to get all this stage combat right. I was Ponyboy, which was one of the main parts—"

"Do you hear yourself?"

"I'm just trying to tell you—"

"What you're telling me is that theater is who you are. You actually sound like you're alive when you talk about it. And you let this jackal take it away from you?"

"What was I supposed to do, Tara?" I said. "He came to the performance and when he saw me with the other actors, the guys, in the fight scene, he freaked out."

"Define 'freaked out.'"

I suddenly didn't want to tell her anymore, but I was too far in now. I spewed it out as fast as I could. "He dragged me by my hair out to the dumpster behind the school and slammed me against it and pinned me there until I promised I wouldn't do theater again."

"Was that last night?" she said. "Before the accident?"

"No," I said. "That was two weeks ago."

"You kept going out with him after that?" Tara's voice was so shrill I had to pull the phone away from my ear.

"He said he'd kill himself if I broke up with him."

"And you believed him."

"Why wouldn't I? He was crying and punching himself in the chest—"

"Was this before or after he punched *you*?"

I didn't give her an answer. She didn't seem to need one. I could almost hear a door in her brain slamming itself on any explanation I gave her. She wouldn't have heard the rest of the story if I'd told it to her—how Preston said he was sorry but that

29

I was *his* and the sight of some other guy putting his hands on me made him so crazy he couldn't control himself—

"You should have told him to go ahead," Tara said.

"Go ahead and what?"

"Kill himself. Bryn—guys like that don't commit suicide over girls. They're too narcissistic—all they care about is themselves and their petty little insecurities. I can't *believe* you couldn't see through that. No—yes, I can. Everything's a fairy tale with you."

And she apparently saw herself as the Evil Stepsister. While I willed myself not to cry another tear, she went on about how I should have seen the warning signs and walked out on him immediately and never looked back. I didn't hear much of it. I was too busy vowing that I was never going to talk to anyone about this ever again.

It wasn't hard to keep that vow five minutes later when my mother's voice flowed through the phone. Once she got past, "Are you sure you're all right, darlin'?"—because apparently nobody believed Dad could report the damages accurately—and "Are you upset that I'm not there for you? I'll be on a plane tonight if you need me—," she did all the talking herself. I didn't care that it bordered on a lecture, as long as there wasn't going to be a test at the end.

"Bryn," she said, sighing her way into the sentence, "I thought when you asked your dad and me in February if you could date Preston we agreed to certain rules." I could picture her counting them off on her slender, smooth-nailed fingers. "No car dates. Only group outings ..."

I remembered that conversation. It was like most of the "discussions" I had with my parents, where she had already decided everything and told my dad and had him there to nod while she told me.

"I thought we were clear on that."

"We were," was all I said. She didn't wait for more.

"I want you to hear me—I am *not* saying this was your fault. This boy obviously has some serious issues, and if this isn't taken care of, I *will* be on the next flight." I could hear the "but" being shaped. "But if you'd stayed with the guidelines, it might

30

not have been so easy for Preston to pull this off. Again—not that you were in any way to *blame*, but—can you see what I'm saying?"

"Yes, ma'am," I said. I could also see, in my mind at that very moment, Preston being able to get me alone before I even realized everyone else had dissolved from the scene. He was magic that way. The seas parted when Preston Oliver walked through. One look from him and people either ran to do his bidding or cleared the room.

"Well, lesson learned, yes?" Mom said.

"Yes, ma'am," I said.

"What's important is that we get you healed now."

Which could start immediately if everyone would just leave me alone.

"Bryn?" Mom said. Her voice had softened.

"Ma'am?" I said.

"I know this has been a lot for you to deal with, but we're doing everything we can to fix this. You realize that, don't you?"

"I know."

I also knew she was pulling herself up to her full perfect-posture five foot ten—a trait I didn't inherit—and closing her jewel-blue eyes to gather her thoughts. Her hair would be pulled up into a dark curly thing on top of her head, making her look even more like Tara, and probably making every person in the cantina she was obviously standing in glance at her at least twice. I'd figured out at about age six that I was never going to be like her so I'd never even tried. I was sure most of her students and colleagues who met me for the first time thought, "This can't be Dr. Christopher's daughter." If they knew what was going on right now, they'd stake their lives on it.

"I just hate that your first experience with a relationship had to turn out like this," she said. "I knew you were too young … well, lesson learned for me too, yes?"

I wouldn't have known how to answer that even if she'd given me a chance. Since when didn't my mother know all the lessons already? It seemed like *everybody* had the answers.

Everybody but me.

CHAPTER FOUR

By Sunday afternoon, I was feeling better—at least enough so that I didn't want to stay in bed any longer. But there wasn't anywhere else I could be. Every time I came out of my room my father pushed food in my direction and looked at me like I was going to fall apart before his eyes. I was actually afraid I was, and I didn't think either one of us would know how to pick up the pieces.

So mostly I stayed in there and scratched behind Copper's ears and tried to imagine what life was like for fifteen-year-old girls who had never heard of Preston Oliver. Those were the only two things I could do without practically having a panic attack.

I couldn't re-read one of the fifty-plus fantasy novels on my shelves or memorize another Shakespeare monologue just in case I was suddenly called in to audition for something. I couldn't use any of the escape routes that used to take me to places where I could sort myself out before I met Preston. Maybe there was no self left to sort anyway.

I definitely couldn't get anywhere close to a mirror. Every time I saw myself I grew more hideous. The place where the air bag scraped my face looked like a package of raspberries had been smashed against it. A dark-blue knot had formed on my forehead where I collided with the car window before we even crashed. It hurt to raise my hands over my head so I hadn't washed my hair, and it lay matted to my head, an attractive look I didn't have the energy to cover with a ball cap.

But even if I'd had a makeover, I couldn't have erased the way my mouth refused to smile or my eyes refused to meet themselves for more than a second in the glass. With the dark smudges under them and the humiliated hang of my head, I looked exactly like what Nurse Cindi said I was. "Battered."

Basically all I could do was sit in the yellow corduroy bowl chair in the corner of my room and try not to go crazy. I had to move a bunch of stuff first—the collection of brochures from Cindi, which I dumped into the trash can, and the beat-up leather book that I'd accidentally brought home with me. I thought I'd read in it that I was supposed have it, but I didn't open it to check. I wanted nothing to do with anything that happened that night.

So I was actually grateful when my cell phone beeped that I had a text message. I wouldn't have cared who it was—but I was surprised when I saw it was Regan.

CN WE MEET? it said.

My thumbs shook as I texted back that I was practically on lockdown. Regan had once told me I was the only person she knew who spelled out every word and typed complete sentences when I texted.

HOW BOUT YR HSE? she sent back.

I hesitated for a second. I should probably ask Dad, although I was pretty sure he'd say yes. He'd asked me no less than five times if there was anybody I wanted to talk to.

Even as I texted back COME ON OVER, I realized I hadn't thought of Regan at all when Dad had asked me. We were friends—though not kindred spirits the way Emma and Isabel and I were when I lived in Newport News. Regan was Andrew's girlfriend, so I'd seen a lot of her in the past three months. She was a junior and had her own car and credit card and was in student government and on the dance team. Basically, she had a life about ten notches above mine.

But she was decent to me—always talked to me at their table at lunch, told me how into me Preston was, did my hair for his party Friday night. She had other girls on her level that she was close with, including Claire, Preston's girlfriend before me, but she didn't make me feel like I was a lame freshman she didn't have time for. Even though I knew she never would have given me a second thought if I hadn't been Preston's girl, she had kind of become a mentor for my new career as one of the popular kids.

I watched her and did what she did, and they accepted me. Not that they wouldn't have taken in anybody Preston told them to, but still ...

And yet as I watched for her through the sunroom windows, anxiety seeped in. She was going to want to hear the whole story, and I didn't want to talk about it. She'd want to hear what I planned to do, and I'd have to tell her it was totally out of my hands. How lame was that going to sound to somebody who seemed to run her own life?

It was going to sound as lame as it was.

When she pulled into the driveway in her white Mustang, I almost asked Dad to tell her I'd taken a turn for the worse and couldn't see her, but he had the door open before she even got to the front steps. I heard him introduce himself and then, in a voice I obviously wasn't supposed to hear, say, "Would you mind if I went over to the office for about fifteen minutes?"

Regan was no doubt blinking her enormous violet-blue eyes by then.

"Uh, no," she said.

"I just don't want to leave Bryn alone."

I could feel my face turning the color of a canned beet. "I'm fine, Dad," I called to him.

He led Regan into the sunroom, looking like I'd caught him reading my diary. She had obviously recovered from "are you *serious?*" because she smoothed the pulled-back sides of her dark hair with her fingertips and gave him a smile as reassuring as a middle-aged babysitter from one of those agencies.

"She'll be okay with me," she said.

When Dad finally mumbled his way out of the house, her face crumpled into a near-laugh that she neatly covered with her hand. "Can you say 'overprotective'?"

"He's just freaked out," I said.

Regan folded her arms over the pale purple babydoll tunic she seemed to have forgotten to button. Matching earrings dangled from her lobes, but nobody—at least no male—was going to notice those. Not with that much cleavage showing.

She dropped her Coach bag onto the glass-topped table and joined me on the window seat. Her legs, clad in denim shorts she'd poured herself into like a pitcher of cream, folded on the cushion. Never once, even as she peeled spangled flip-flops from her tanned feet and let them slide to the floor, did she take her eyes off of me.

"I guess it runs in the family," she said.

"What does?" I said.

"Freaking out." She shook her head like she didn't want to go there yet and openly stared at the raspberry wound on my cheek. "That looks horrible. Does it hurt?"

"Not that much," I said.

"That's from the accident." She pointed to my forehead. "And so is that."

They weren't questions so I didn't say anything. I wanted to squirm but I willed myself still.

"Preston said you grabbed the wheel and that's why he hit that car."

I felt my eyes bulge. "You talked to Preston? Where?"

"He's not in jail if that's what you mean. His dad posted bail, of course."

My stomach clutched at itself, but I still didn't say anything.

"Andrew and I went over to his house yesterday. He's, like, wrecked over this. The cops treated him like some kind of criminal. You know what they charged him with?"

I shook my head.

"Aggravated assault."

"I didn't mean to aggravate him," I said.

Regan rolled her eyes and flipped her hair off her shoulders with an impatient hand. "That isn't what aggravated assault is. It means you said he hit you with a weapon."

She waited, waxed eyebrows lifted, as if I were supposed to fill in the blank.

"A flashlight," I said.

"It's a *felony*," Regan said. "Do you know what *that* is?"

"It's—"

"It's some serious—" She put up her hand as if to stop herself and glanced over her shoulder. The rest of the house was still quiet. "It means if he gets convicted, he could go to prison."

I pressed both hands over my mouth and closed my eyes.

"Yeah. Because you did your little drama queen thing. It was a car accident—which *you* caused—and you turned it into a *court* case. Happy birthday, Preston."

I opened my eyes. The mentoring junior who had modeled how I should act at the elite table had disappeared. Judge Judy had replaced her.

"You can't do this," Regan said, eyes boring into me from the bench. "In the first place nobody's going to believe Preston hit you. I never saw him do it, and neither did Andrew. How do you plan to prove it?"

To my own surprise, I slid the sleeve of my sweatshirt up my arm and exposed the set of bruises that were at their blackest and bluest. Like everybody else, she sucked in her breath.

And then, slowly, she shook her head. "That was from the accident."

"No, it wasn't," I said.

"Fine. Then somebody else did it."

"No—"

"No—you listen." Regan leaned forward until her face almost touched mine. I could see the tiny blood vessels in her eyes, smell the cinnamon gum she always chewed. "Preston didn't do it. That's what you have to say. You made a mistake. It happened some other way."

"But it didn't," I said.

"You don't get it. We're not gonna let you do this. You can't ruin Preston's life—he can't try out for the Olympics again if he has a criminal record."

"I'm not trying to ruin his life!"

I heard the tears in my voice and so, apparently, did Regan. She pulled her face back and softened her eyes and put her hands over mine.

"Look, Preston's your first serious guy, right?"

If you didn't count Lance from Newport News who played Romeo to my Juliet in eighth grade, yes. I nodded.

"So you have no experience with the way relationships work—and that's why I'm here." She resituated herself on the seat, tossing the hair off her shoulders again and still holding onto my hands with her cold ones. "Look, guys can be stu-

36

pid—it's in their contract. Andrew will start to ignore me and I'll do something to get his attention and then he'll get all ticked off and, I don't know, he'll twist my arm or pretend like he's slapping me in the face."

I stared at her. She talked as if she were describing a casual conversation at the drinking fountain.

"I can see how you could take that the wrong way," she said. "You're, like, all innocent, and you have the whole drama thing going on. But it's not 'assault.' It's just boyfriend and girlfriend stuff. You and Preston can work this out. I'll even take a message to him for you if you want." She checked over her shoulder again and let a sneer form on her face. "Obviously your daddy isn't going to let you talk to him."

"I don't *want* to talk to him," I said.

"Fine. I'll tell him you guys are over—but you have to drop the charges."

"I didn't bring the charges in the first place," I said. "My father did."

Regan let go of my hands and threw her head back to look at the ceiling like she was trying to find a way to make this moron understand. When she looked at me again, her eyes had a cold, hard look I'd seen somewhere else before.

"What *I* don't get is why you told anybody Preston gave you those bruises. Even if he wasn't your boyfriend, that's just, like, flipping on one of your own. You just don't *do* that."

"I had to," I said. By now the tears were streaming down my face, burning the wound on my cheek. "I had no choice—they accused my *father* of doing it."

"So you're protecting Daddy."

"Yes—no! There's nothing to protect him from—"

"You are so screwed up I can't even believe it." Regan unfolded herself from the window seat and stood up. Her breathing threatened to bring her entire chest out of her top. "Okay, I didn't want it to come to this, but I said I'd do it if I had to."

"Do what?"

Regan's eyes narrowed until they almost crossed. "I'm

supposed to warn you. Drop this whole thing and say Preston didn't do it, or you'll be sorry."

"Why?" I said. "What's going to happen?"

"I guess you'll find out, won't you?" she said.

As she gave me one last glare, I knew why that cold, hard look was familiar. I'd seen it in Preston's eyes.

*

The clinic was silent when I burst through the door and shattered the quiet with my stomping through the cage-lined back area and into the surgery where Dad was savagely cleaning a stainless-steel table with disinfectant. From one of the cages a cat wailed, but not nearly as loudly as I did.

"We can't do it!" I said.

Dad dropped his rag, and the color drained from his face—not surprising since I had never raised my voice to either of my parents before. Not even when they told me we were moving from Newport News to here. I'd had no choice then, either. But I had to have one now.

"What's going on?" he said. "Where's ...?"

He was obviously groping for Regan's name, but I didn't supply it. I leaned on the table, smearing its shiny top with my sweaty palms, and continued to cry the way I'd been doing since Regan walked out the front door.

"I don't want to press charges—please—let's just drop the whole thing."

Dad's face colored up again as he came around the table toward me. I backed away, though I had no idea why because he had never so much as smacked my hand my whole life.

"What happened?" he said. "Did that boy call you? Did he threaten you?"

"No!"

"If he does, if he comes near you again, he'll go straight to jail. The police told me to stay away from him, or I'd—" I watched him swallow. "I got a restraining order. You don't have to be afraid, Brynnie."

"It isn't that! I just don't want to do this—"

"You need to sit down."

Dad reached for a stool but I backed away from that too.

"I'll never see him again, I swear," I said. "I'll change schools, I'll do anything, but please, I can't do this."

I couldn't go there.

"Is it Mom?" I said. "Is she making you do this?"

"No, Bryn."

He looked stung, and I didn't care.

"This is my decision," he said, "and it's the only one we have. Your mother backs me up. We're both backing *you* up." I watched him swallow again as if it hurt all the way to his ears. "You don't have to do anything, Brynnie. I'm taking care of it."

"Don't!"

I actually stomped my foot, and that was a step too far. Dad's eyes watered, but his jaw set so hard I could almost hear it. It was a sound I didn't know.

"I have to," he said. "I don't know how to make you see that."

"You can't," I said.

And then I walked out on the first fight I'd ever had with my father.

CHAPTER FIVE

Dad made me go to the airport in Norfolk with him late Monday afternoon. He didn't have to use much force because I saw him now as the Borg in *Star Trek*. Resistance was futile. The only thing I knew to do with that was not talk to him at all.

So during the ten-mile ride to Norfolk International, we might as well have been in a hearse. In the back. In the coffin. The silence gave me way too much time to envision my upcoming reunion with Mim, though it was hard to predict what her approach was going to be. Would she interrogate me like the cops? Offer me educational materials the way Nurse Cindi did? Do the Dad thing and go legal? Take Tara's approach and tell me what an idiot I was?

NO—this was obviously going to be my mother's method: decide what needs to be done and then do it without asking anybody else. Mim was probably worse, since she was the one who taught my mother. Either that, or Mom learned it in self-defense, something I myself had never done. Didn't matter. The point was that now, more than ever, I was no match for my grandmother.

Dad pulled into the drop-off zone. "I'm going to let you out here and go park," he said—the first words he'd spoken since we left the Beach. "Her plane should've landed—you want A concourse—"

Coward, I wanted to say to him. I was starting to believe that the only brave people were the ones who didn't have any other choice. I climbed out of the Tahoe and seriously considered making a run for it.

But where was I going to go?

As I crossed the terminal I tried to ignore the quick stares at my face, followed by even quicker looks away, as if it made people nauseous to look at the scab on my cheek and the midnight blue lump on my forehead, neither one of which I'd been able to cover with makeup. I draped my hair and tried to keep my head down and found the waiting area. The security officer guarding the entrance gave me the shivers. I was sure he was going to come over and interrogate me.

Actually, everything was making me shake. This was my first time out of the house since Friday night, and the whole world seemed to have changed since then. Had people always formed judgments on their faces like this? A twentyish woman curled her lip from behind her magazine. A man with a belly roll folding over his belt shook his head as if I were a lost cause. A four-year-old stopped swinging on the bubblegum machine and gaped openly at me, nose running, until his mother pulled him away like abuse might be catching.

I was actually relieved when I caught my grandmother's unmistakable confident walk down the wide hall. At least I'd be getting out of here soon.

And then what? I blinked back tears. It wasn't going to matter where I went. Until my face healed, people were going to stare at me and make assumptions that were mostly true. I vowed to stay home until it did.

All eyes were now on the passengers approaching us. I watched Mim stride among them and remembered the one word that always came into my head for her: straight. Even though she wasn't tall like my mother, she stood as if she were. She also looked directly at people and talked right through a subject without taking any turns. My mother always said you couldn't get Mim off on bunny trails. That was one of about twelve things that had my heart throbbing in my neck.

Another was that the closer she got, the clearer it was that she still ought to be on the cover of *Sports Illustrated*. She still looked younger than fifty-nine, still had skin that resembled a well-taken-care-of leather handbag, was still thin the way runners and skiers and bicyclists are thin. I was surprised she wasn't carrying a tennis racket.

When she got about two steps in front of me, she stopped and looked into me with eyes like blue topaz stones you'd choose for earrings. They made me afraid to even think for fear she'd read what was going through my mind—which was, *Please, Jesus, don't let her yell at me*.

"Bryn Christopher," she said. "I want to look at you."

I closed my eyes. She could look at me all she wanted, but I didn't have to watch her do it.

She pulled me straight into her chest and held onto me. "You're beautiful," she said.

Lying wasn't even among the options I'd looked at for her. I felt myself rocking sideways, and she steadied me with her hands. A groan escaped from my throat.

"Still pretty tender?" she said as she pulled away.

"It's okay," I said.

It's a lot of things, Bryn, but "okay" isn't one of them. That was what I expected her to say. But she didn't. She didn't say anything except, "Where's your dad?"

"Parking the car," I said.

She lifted an eyebrow, which disappeared beneath the honey-brown bangs dipping from her bob.

"He'll meet us in baggage claim," I said. "Can I carry something for you?"

She only had a slouchy canvas purse and a laptop bag, but it was all I could think of to say. Mim shook her head and pointed me toward the baggage sign.

"My rule is if I pack it, I have to carry it."

Of course. Which left me without a topic. Fortunately, Dad was already there when we reached the carousel. He didn't seem to have much more of a clue than I did what to say to her, but at least it was on him now. They exchanged kisses on the cheek, and Mim asked how things were going at the clinic—

"It's picking up."

—and told him the running agreed with him.

"Thanks."

I watched Dad's face grow redder with every exchange, which was fine with me. He was the one who told her she could come.

"Are you hungry, Windy?" he said as we made our way

across the traffic to the parking garage. "We can go some-place for supper."

I almost froze in the middle of the street. He was actually going to make me sit in a restaurant where people could feast on my face along with their entrées?

"You know," Mim said, "I think I'd rather go on to your place and get settled. I can always run out and get something for us later."

I felt her looking at me. When I looked back, in spite of myself, she said, "Does that work for you, Bryn?"

"Yes, ma'am," I said.

"You still have those nice Southern manners," she said. "I always loved that."

You could have fooled me. I remembered her making fun of Tara's and my "no, ma'ams" and "yes, sirs" when we were in Hawaii. Tara had immediately stopped doing it. I had just stopped talking all together.

*

I sat in the backseat and pretended to doze while Dad and Mim made conversation in the front. I couldn't have repeated anything they said—all I knew was that it wasn't about me or Preston or police or doctors or any of the things I expected them to discuss as if I weren't there. Still, long after I showed Mim to the guest room and ate the Chinese food Dad went out for, I hadn't stopped waiting for the other shoe to drop.

But while I watched the sun sink into pink through the living room window so I'd know when I could get away with saying I was going to bed, Mim just sat, legs curled under her, in a corner of the couch and told us about her new life. Living in San Diego, adjusting again to being a widow, running some kind of camp for women who'd had cancer.

"Their courage is amazing," she said. "I'm inspired by them every day."

Dad—who was perched on a straight-backed chair near the doorway as if any minute he was going to think up a canine emergency and flee—gave a little laugh that sounded like he was clearing his throat.

"I'm sure it's the other way around," he said. "It's hard to be sick around you."

Then his face headed toward cranberry. I was pretty sure that hadn't come out right.

Mim looked at him through the steam rising from the cup of tea she was sipping — the same tea she'd set in front of me, which I hadn't touched.

"Should I ask you what you mean by that?" she said. "Or should I just take it as a compliment?"

"Oh, a compliment — absolutely!"

By now Dad was drowning in an entire cranberry *bog*. I kind of felt sorry for him. The real Mim was emerging.

"Well, just so we're clear," she said. "I don't want it to be hard to be sick around me. I want it to be easy. That makes the healing easier." She started to take a sip and stopped before she added, "At least, that's been my experience."

Huh?

She looked straight at *me* now and for a piercing moment I thought I'd said it out loud. But she just nodded at my teacup, still on the coffee table.

"I suggest you drink that," she said. "It's chamomile. It'll help you relax."

The only thing that was going to help me relax was for her to go ahead and get the lecture over with. That was also the thing that was going to tie me further into knots, because in there somewhere was going to be her plan for me. She had to have one. Everybody else did.

She was still just looking at me, so I picked up the cup and acted like I was taking a sip. A little tea touched my lips. It did actually taste kind of good. She was *still* watching. I took two gulps.

"Well ..." Dad stood up and glanced at his watch as if he hadn't been checking it every ten seconds since we finished supper. "I need to check on a few things in the clinic and then I'm turning in."

"You do look tired," Mim said.

No, he didn't. He looked like he wanted to escape. I'd have gone with him if I thought I'd get away with it. He was going to leave me alone with Mim, and *then* it was going to come out. I didn't feel sorry for him anymore. At all.

"'Night, Brynnie," he said to me.

"'Night," I said without looking at him. Then I regretted it. As soon as he was gone, she was either going to ask me what that was about or tell me my father was just trying to help me and I better straighten up.

"How's that tea?"

I jumped, slopping some of it onto my wrist. She handed me a napkin.

"It's good," I said.

"Why don't you take it to your room with you—sip on it while you're getting ready for bed."

There was no point in trying not to stare at her.

"It's all right, Bryn," she said. "You'll talk when you're ready."

Then she stood up and stretched and picked up the tea tray. "I think I'll turn in myself."

I watched her go all the way into the kitchen before I came to my senses and hightailed it to my room in case she changed her mind. Copper, who was bathing himself on my bed, looked up as if he were surprised to see me.

"Yeah, tell me about it," I said, as I eased my still-hurting self down beside him. "There's no way that just happened."

I even waited for Mim to tap on the door, or just burst right on in and say, "All right, enough pussyfooting around. Let's get real."

She didn't do any of that. I heard her feet pad down the tiled hall, listened as her door closed, strained for the slightest hint that it would open again. Nothing.

I let out a long sigh of relief, but it left me empty. The loneliness suddenly ached worse than the hematoma and the abrasion and everything else that was wrong with my body.

"I need somebody," I said to Copper.

He stopped licking the back of his leg and narrowed his yellow eyes at me.

"I mean somebody who can talk back," I said. "And not about this whole evil mess. Just talk. About anything else—and make me forget."

The ceiling blurred as I stared at it. There were only two people in the world who could do that, who could always do that. If Emma and Isabel lived here instead of twenty miles away on the other side of the Hampton Bay, they'd be in my room right now, taking me away from words like *battered* and *aggravated assault* and *you'll be sorry*. They would waft me to another world, full of beautiful vocabulary—*kindred spirits, mists of mystery, compassion's kiss*.

Although—if Emma and Isabel lived here, I probably wouldn't have gotten involved with Preston in the first place. I wouldn't have gone out with him out of loneliness from the move last August, away from everything I knew and loved, everything that let me be who I wanted to be. I would have spent every lunch, every after-school, every spare minute rehearsing with them, getting ready for auditions, running lines. If I'd even hinted to them that I might let some boy take away the one thing I lived for, they would have kidnapped me and held me hostage until I regained my sanity.

I dabbed at a tear before it could slip under my scab. I would even be willing to go back to the way we three used to be, before we discovered Shakespeare Club in middle school. Back when we watched Harry Potter movies and then reenacted them in their backyard while our mothers, both PhD students then, had study sessions inside. Back when we had fantasy names for each other—Castiel and Aurora and Katalina. Back when any problem could be solved simply by killing off the dragons and dancing with the king.

Why couldn't back then be right now?

I reached for my cell phone, which was still on the floor by the bed where I'd left it when Regan texted me. I hadn't talked to a person my age in forty-eight hours. The sisters' number was still in my phone, even though I hadn't called them in weeks. I swallowed down the guilt and pressed CALL.

"Bryn!" Isabel, when she picked up. "Is it really you?"

Among the three of us, Isabel always had the strongest sense of the dramatic.

"'Tis I," I said. I hadn't talked like that in forever. It was all I could do not to sob.

"Em, it's Bryn," she said. "Pick up the other phone. Bryn, how *are* you? We thought you were trapped under something heavy."

She laughed the pattering laugh that always reminded me of rain. At least she wasn't mad at me for not calling. At least there was that.

"Are you calling to tell us you're coming home?" Emma's voice was heavier than her sister Isabel's, rich like velvet. You didn't even have to see them to know they weren't identical.

"I wish I were," I said. "You have no idea."

"What's going on?" Emma said. "You sound vexed."

Isabel shrieked. "'Vexed'? Did you just say 'vexed'?"

"Yes. Is that a problem?"

"No—I love it. I'm going to try to use it sometime in this conversation."

Emma grunted. "Have fun with that. Meanwhile, I'm going to try to find out what's up with Bryn. Is everything okay—how did your Arts Festival thing go?"

Had it been *that* long since I'd talked to them? Before the hitting really started? Back when I was still somebody else?

Suddenly I wasn't sure I should be trying to talk to my oldest friends at all. But Isabel was pattering out another laugh and saying, "I'm totally vexed because you get to be in an amazing private school theater program while we're still slogging it out in a lame drama club led by losers who all want to act in soap operas. How was that?"

"It's not really *that* bad, Bryn." I pictured Emma shaking her fiery ball of red frizz. "We're both auditioning for community theater—they have this summer thing. Forget the high school program."

"Can you say 'lame'?" Isabel put in.

"No, but I can say 'inane,'" Emma told her. "I love that word."

I let them chatter and floated in it the way I always had. I wanted, in fact, to float all the way back.

"You're not talking," Emma said.

"I was just thinking," I said. "Remember when we called ourselves the Kindred Spirits?"

"Ohmigosh!" Isabel's voice reached new heights. "From *Anne of Green Gables!*"

"And then we got into fantasy and gave each other names?" I said.

Emma squealed, a thing I'd loved about her from the first time I met her when we were nine years old. "What was mine — Aroma? Adora?"

"Aurora," I said.

"I was Katarina — no — what was I?"

My heart was sinking. "Katalina. I was Castiel. You called me ..."

I paused but no one filled it in.

"Tiel," I said.

"We were such strange children," Isabel said. "It's a good thing we found theater or we would have been the social outcasts of Christopher Newport Middle School."

"We *were* the social outcasts of Christopher Newport Middle School." I knew Emma was once again shaking her frizz. "We just didn't know it because the three of us were in our own little world: Bryn and the Twins. Don't you think Shakespeare Club was just a more acceptable way to be geeks?"

"I wasn't a geek," Isabel said. "Was I?"

"You still *are.* Bryn was the first one to break out of that. Speaking of which, so what about the guy you were seeing? Are y'all still together?"

I was no longer floating. My soul had sunk like a lead bauble. We couldn't go back to what we were — and I didn't know how to be anything else with them. Certainly not the battered woman.

"You still there?" Isabel said.

"Yeah," I managed to say, "but I've gotta go."

"Not before you swear we'll get together this summer," Emma said.

"We'll make our parents bring us to the Beach."

"Okay," I said. I hung up just before I started to sob.

Jesus, what do I do? Why am I alone in this? Where did you go?

I pulled the pillow out from under Copper and smothered my head with it while I cried and prayed. The praying stopped first.

48

Because it occurred to me as I lay there in every kind of agony there could possibly be that I had been praying to Jesus for five months — ever since the first night Preston took me to Young Life, the night I had the vision.

Young Life was where all the really cool kids from our school went on Thursday nights. The really cool kids and the ones who wanted to be really cool kids. I was there because Preston took me, but I loved the whole thing. They sang, which I adored, and they did skits, which I could do without even thinking about it, and that first night they had that speaker — I couldn't even remember his name now. But he talked about having the Lord to go to when everything gets messed up. My life wasn't even messed up yet then. Preston was still being Prince Charming. I'd been in *Alice in Wonderland* and the kids in the drama program were actually starting to talk to me. They'd even invited me to sit at their lunch table, but I had to eat with Preston. Still, it appealed to me, having this unseen figure I could go to anywhere, any time.

Preston had told me he did it — went to Jesus. He'd already filled me in on the Olympics disappointment. How he was still screwed up over it until he met me and I made him feel sane again — which I found hard to believe, but it was heavenly to hear. He said he knew I was the answer to the prayers he'd prayed at Young Life. I watched him with his eyes closed while we were all singing and I got swept up in it. I mean, completely. Suddenly I was seeing Jesus holding out his arms to me and I could feel myself running to him. It was like a dream, only I was awake. I heard Preston say, "Hey, Baby, are you okay?" It was gone then, but I wanted it back. I would try to meditate at night, but it was always just out of my reach.

Still, from that night on, I prayed to Jesus all the time. It wasn't like I'd never heard of him before. We had kind of belonged to a church in Newport News, but it didn't mean that much to me. It seemed like it was all about "don't do this" and "don't do that," and I didn't feel like I needed that. I couldn't even remember the last time my parents had to ground me for anything. We never got around to finding a church in Virginia Beach, with Mom starting the professorship at Old Dominion and Dad taking over the animal clinic from the old vet that retired. Young Life was the first thing that ever really felt like church to me, even after I figured out that Preston was actually there to be seen more than anything else. I never told him about my vision. My dream that we were going to pray together and get baptized side by side popped like a bubble. But I kept begging Jesus to change things. I kept hoping for the vision that would take me up somewhere, above all the stuff, someplace where I could maybe be a mystic or something.

My face was hurting, and I pulled the pillow off of my face. A piece of my scab came with it. Another chunk of myself falling off. Like the dream world I grew up in with Emma and Isabel. Like the stage where it was so easy to be someone else. I stared at the scab as it tumbled listlessly onto the sheet. Maybe that was all Jesus had been to me — just another dream to keep me from what was real.

Because I couldn't handle real.

All my tears had been used up by then, so I cried without them — dry, heaving sobs. Even if he were real, why would he care about me? He obviously didn't, or he would've stopped Preston from hurting me. He wouldn't let Regan threaten me. He wouldn't allow everybody to ruin my life.

That was it then. No more praying. No more counting on Jesus to come to me in a vision when it was clear he wasn't going to show up. No more dreaming. No more acting. From now on, I was just going to be Bryn Christopher.

And then I cried myself to sleep — because I had no idea who that was.

CHƏPTER SIX

The other shoe didn't drop on Tuesday. I stayed in bed until noon and only got up then because Copper was using my scalp for a scratching pad. Mim was in the kitchen when I emerged to feed him, but she didn't comment that I was sleeping my life away, like she had in Hawaii when I'd slept in until eight. She didn't say much of anything, apart from suggestions about what I should eat.

She *said* they were suggestions. It was more like she put things in front of me and I ate them because I didn't have the energy to argue. All healthy stuff. When Dad brought in pizza for dinner, I expected her to at least scowl at it, but she cut up raw veggies to go with it and filled a bowl with ranch dressing.

I knew she was always looking at me — when I was staring at the DVD I wasn't actually seeing or pretending to take a nap in the hammock with Copper in the sunroom. I guessed she was waiting for me to talk. What I couldn't figure out was why she was making it so easy for me not to.

Before I went to bed Tuesday night, she brought me the usual cup of chamomile tea, which I had to admit I liked, and a tube of something.

"This is a vitamin ointment," she said. "I think it'll help your face heal more quickly. A lot of the women at the camp use it when they get scraped up."

I didn't ask how they got scraped up. Maybe it had something to do with chemotherapy? She *had* said they were cancer survivors.

"Thanks," I said. I tucked the tube into the pocket of my hoodie and groped for something to fill the awkward silence. "What's the name of your camp?"

"*Lugar de Curación*. That's Spanish for *Healing Place*. So how are you feeling—physically, I mean?"

I hadn't thought about it much, and when I did now, I was surprised. "I'm not actually in any pain now," I said. "I'm mostly tired."

Mim patted her stomach. "The hematoma is healing?"

"It's not sore anymore. I'm really fine."

"You come from good stock. Let me know if you like that ointment. I have more."

I headed for my room, where I immediately went to my laptop and got on the Internet. Googling *Lugar de Curación* got me an immediate result, once I figured out the right way to spell it. There was my grandmother with two very short-haired women, all three of them holding surfboards.

I should have known.

I scrolled down, read women's testimonies about how learning to surf with Windy Paiana had helped them conquer their fears and find the confidence that cancer had taken away. "Catching my first wave did as much for my healing as radiation, I know it," one woman said.

In all the pictures, Mim looked so kind and caring, she was practically Mother Teresa in a swimsuit. Except in the old—way old—photograph of her back in the sixties, taken when she was a teen in California. She had a knockout body then that put Regan and Claire to shame, and her hair ran long and sun streaked over her shoulders. Weirdly, in that shot she looked more like the Mim I remembered than she did in the recent pictures. There was something sort of hard and haughty about her back then, like she was saying, "If you can't keep up, get out of the way." This lady on the website, just a few years later, was a softer version.

Still, as I logged off I was glad I wasn't recovering from cancer. She would probably make me surf my way back to health.

*

My stomach was growling when I woke up Wednesday morning, so I got up even though it was only nine. Copper glared at me from the other pillow and went back to sleep.

Mim greeted me in the kitchen with a yogurt parfait and a spoon. "They make these at camp," she said. "It's the first time I've done one myself."

She sat across from me at the tile-topped table and watched as I scooped some into my mouth.

"Good?" she said.

I nodded and chewed.

"You look much better today," she said. "I suggest we get out of the house for a while."

I stopped chewing.

"That doesn't appeal to you," she said. "But have you looked in the mirror this morning?"

I didn't tell her that I was avoiding mirrors like the swine flu.

"I think you'll be surprised. Your cheek is still red but the scab has all but disappeared. You tried the ointment."

"Yes, ma'am."

"Some sunlight would do you a world of good. Do you have any makeup with sunscreen in it?"

I shook my head.

"I do. It'll be a little dark for you, but you're welcome to it until we can get you some in your skin tone." She tilted her head at me, sliding her bob against her cheek. "You have a beautiful fair complexion like your dad's side of the family."

Maybe my being so stunned by the compliment was the reason I didn't see sooner where it was all going. I agreed to getting out, applied the SPF 45 makeup, even pulled my hair into a French braid and put on actual clothes. Long sleeves with my shorts, yes, but at least not sweats, which I'd even worn to the airport. I didn't ask where we were going.

I should have.

As we pulled out of the driveway in my mom's Corolla, Mim said, "I thought we'd go to Dick's Sporting Goods. That's on Lynnhaven Parkway, right?"

Why would I have any idea where a sporting goods store would be?

"I guess I should have asked you instead of assuming—" she said.

Really.

"—but you don't have a one-piece swimsuit, do you?"

What?

"I'm sure you look adorable in a bikini, but you're going to want a one-piece—"

"For what?"

I put my hand to my lips, but it was too late. Mim didn't look surprised.

"You might enjoy a swim in the ocean," she said. "And I thought I'd treat you to a one-piece suit so you don't have to worry about your bruise showing."

This time I restrained myself. I didn't blurt out, *I would NOT enjoy a swim in the ocean. I would enjoy going home and—*

Doing what? Staring at TV shows that made no sense? Trying not to think about what was happening with Preston? Hoping I would magically disappear? What difference did it make what I did?

"Okay," I said.

Thankfully, when we got to the store Mim bypassed the snorkels and swim fins and other implements of torture and headed straight for the swimwear. Even though it was all for women, I could feel my panic rising being that close to things members of swim teams wore. I'd sat at the side of the school pool afternoon upon afternoon watching bodies in Speedos thrash through the water, wishing I were somewhere else, and knowing if I were, I'd pay for it.

"You look a little pale," Mim said. "I have a granola bar—"

"I'm fine." To prove it, I shoved some hangers aside and gazed at a plain black suit with a white stripe up the side.

"I don't think you wear a size fourteen," Mim said. "Not that there's anything wrong with that, but we want it to actually stay on your body."

I shifted to the section she pointed to and thumbed through the rack. Mim wandered over to the flip-flops. What? She wasn't going to pick one out for me and "suggest" I buy it?

Certain that was next, I took a closer look at the selection and found one in pink with flowers across the top. Preston said I looked delicious in pink.

I shoved that one aside and felt the shaking start. The next one was lime green. I grabbed it and said, "I like this one."

Mim looked up from the shoes and nodded. "Very cute. You should probably try it on."

There was no point in arguing. I was going to have to put the thing on eventually for our "swim in the ocean." I locked myself in the dressing room and wriggled out of my clothes and into the suit. I tried my best not to look in the mirror, but I was surrounded by them. One glance and it was like watching a train wreck. Of course I'd seen myself briefly when I took showers and changed my clothes, but I'd tried to keep my eyes closed or look away fast. Now I couldn't take my gaze away from the collage of yellow and green and blue and black that covered my arms and shoulders like tattoo sleeves. The fading scrape on my face couldn't hold a candle to all of that.

"You want to model for me?" Mim said outside the door.

No. I wanted to throw up.

I actually thought I might, and I didn't want to do it in the dressing room. That was the only reason I opened the door, my shirt in my hand—so I could make a run for the restroom.

But when I saw my grandmother staring at me, I couldn't move. She looked even sicker than I did. Both hands went to her mouth and she, too, seemed unable to pull her eyes from the sight of my beaten-up body. Slowly she shook her head, and then she let her eyelids drop.

"I'm so sorry, Bryn," she whispered. "I am so, so sorry."

She managed to recover and told me the suit was darling on me. Then she took the tag and went to pay for it, suggesting I just put my clothes on over it. She couldn't possibly think we were still going swimming, could she?

She could. We drove to 46th Street and parked and strolled down to the beach as if I didn't look like I actually *had* been in a train wreck. Mim didn't say much except to describe the offerings in the cooler and suggest I put on more sunscreen.

By then my mind was screaming so loud I knew I'd say something horrible to her if I didn't get some of it out. Kind of like poking a hole in your smashed thumbnail to let the pressure off.

"Do I really have to go swimming—like this?" I said.

Mim set the cooler in the sand and brushed away a strand of hair that had escaped from my braid and blown into my face.

"You don't have to do anything," she said. "But I think you'll be fine if you keep the shirt on. It looks cute with your suit."

It doesn't look cute. It looks like I'm trying to cover something up. Which I am.

But from who? It was still only ten in the morning and there was no one else on the beach except one lone woman scouring for shells. Even if I took the shirt off I wouldn't scare any little kids or have old men shaking their heads at me.

"Okay," I said, for what must have been the tenth time that day. I'd lost count.

"Shall we?" Mim said.

I tried to follow her to the water, but she kept slowing down for me to catch up and walk beside her. She herself was in a brown and orange one-piece that made her skin glow. How many other teenage girls in America were at that moment worrying about how they looked in their bathing suits next to their grandmother? I guessed zero.

Mim let the water splash up to her calves and gave a husky laugh. "It's cold, but it's nothing like the Pacific. I'll never get used to that again after living in Hawaii. Most of our gals at the camp wear wet suits when they first start off."

At least she hadn't gotten me one of those. As long as I didn't develop breast cancer, I was safe.

Cold or not, Mim suddenly just dove into the surf. If I didn't do it too, she was going to tell me I "might enjoy" trying it, so I sucked in some air and plunged in after her.

It wasn't that I didn't like to swim. I'd always loved going to the beach as a kid. Swam like a dolphin every chance I got—Tara and I both did. Even after our evil trip to Hawaii, I learned to love it again when Emma and Isabel and I spent summer afternoons in the pool at our apartment complex pretending to be mermaids. I actually still did that in my mind on our family vacations when we'd stop at hotels. Now—since Preston—not so much with the swimming.

I came up to find Mim close by, watching me. That seemed to be her new career.

"You're a strong swimmer," she said. "You want to go out a little farther so we're not battling the waves so much?"

I nodded and dove into another one, emerging near Mim,

who was lying on her back, lazily kicking her feet. The sun-sparkled water gathered its bubbles around her like it loved her.

"Salt water is so healing," she said. "I love to watch our women soak it up. You can almost literally see them getting better right before your eyes."

"Does it actually heal their cancer?" I said.

"No." Mim looked into me. "It heals their souls."

We bobbed with the pre-breakers for a while. Mim kept asking me if I was tired, which I wasn't. I got more tired than that going from the couch to my bed. Finally, she said, "I think I'll ride one in."

Here we go with the lessons. I could feel my throat muscles tightening.

"I'll meet you there," she said.

She swam casually away from me toward shore and waited, watching an oncoming wave as if it were speaking to her. Suddenly she broke into a hard kick, and the wave almost crashed into her—and then it lifted and carried her all the way to the beach.

Lifted and carried. Too bad waves couldn't lift and carry you in the other direction, away from everything. Still—it sounded so peaceful.

I swam away from the calm sea to where I'd seen Mim look back for a wave. There was one practically on top of me. I broke into a desperate crawl with the churning foam hovering above. It did not, however, lift me and carry me to the beach. I was suddenly tumbling end over end like a shoe somebody put in the dryer. When I hit the sand, it was flat on my back with my shirt shoved up under my armpits.

That was why I didn't try athletic things. And that was why I took my time heading up to the cooler where Mim was shaking a smoothie in a covered plastic tumbler. Let the instructions begin.

"You're not allergic to strawberries, are you?" she said. She put a smoothie in my hand. "The water takes it out of you. You up for a little more shopping?"

"I don't have any dry clothes," I said.

"Where we're going they don't care."

"Where are we going?"

"I'd like to go to the Surf Shack. Do you mind?"

I shook my head. Mim was looking out at the water.

"This isn't the best beach for beginners," she said. "Where the camp is, we have long, consistent rollers, nice gentle breaks. It's perfect." She gave the lacking Atlantic Ocean another look. "But this would do. This would do just fine."

I didn't ask for what. I didn't have to—not after we arrived at the Surf Shack on 17th Street and she asked the guy behind the counter if she could look at his longboards. Not after he asked her if she needed it for a beginner and she said yes, possibly.

Possibly?

No, IMpossibly. Because unless she knew somebody in Virginia Beach I was not aware of, I was the beginner in question. And that was *not* happening.

Mim put her hand out to the guy—who looked like he was about nineteen—and shook his firmly.

"Windy Paiana," she said.

"Shaun McKenna. So—tell me—"

I didn't want to hear whatever it was she was going to tell him. It didn't matter. I wasn't doing it. Why was I such an idiot not to have seen this coming the whole time? Mim hadn't changed. She just used different tactics now. But it all led to the same thing: her making me do things I was totally incapable of doing. Just what I needed when I already felt like a world-class loser.

So while Mim and the surfer dude chatted it up as if they were on the beach at Maui, I went to the far corner of the shop and got myself behind a rack of wet suits. I would have pretended to be interested in the stuff they had for sale, but I had no idea what any of it was, except for the boards standing up in slots and hanging from the ceiling. They all had graphics of lightning bolts and dragon backs and wicked-looking logos on them. The rest of the items were foreign and scary and I hated it all. I closed my eyes, but I could still hear the voice on the DVD they had playing, talking about somebody named Archy who was "built for speed." I was not. I was built for getting out of here, back to Copper and the hammock, which I never should have left in the first place.

"So—you're Bryn?"

I jerked and rammed my elbow into a display of sunglasses. Shaun—was that his name?—caught it before it could crash to the ground and adjusted a pair that swung precariously from its perch. Shaun's own shades hung by an earpiece on the front of his Surf Shack T-shirt.

"That's in a bad place," he said. "People knock it over all the time."

I was sure they didn't. Guys lied.

"So—I just want to say I have a lot of respect for what you're doing."

I jerked again, but this time my arms were hugged around me so none of the merchandise was in danger. Mim had told him about my "situation"? I thought they'd been talking about making me surf.

"Windy says you're not into sports," he said, "and I just think it's cool that you're getting out there and trying this anyway." His eyes, brown as a pair of Hershey Kisses, danced across my face and didn't land on my reddened cheek. "A lot of girls would be like, 'Ooh, no, I don't want to look stupid.'" He grinned, tucking in his chin. "You're gonna look—well, not stupid, maybe a little funky at first. But I like that you don't care."

I do care! I wanted to scream at him. *You people have no idea!*

But all I could do was look up at him—at his happy face and his spiky dark hair and his sprung eyebrows that seemed to be waiting for something very cool to happen any minute. If he wanted to think I was that self-confident, let him. He wasn't going to have a chance to find out otherwise once I left there. And the sooner the better, because every muscle in my anatomy was now clenched into one big frightened fist.

"So the boards you're looking at," he said, "are shortboards which, in my opinion, are the coolest—"

Was I looking at boards?

"The only thing is, they're for people who know how to surf already." He grinned like it was no effort at all—like nothing was an effort. "They're kind of like the sports cars of surfing. You don't put somebody who doesn't know how to drive behind the wheel of a Corvette the first time out, right?"

"I don't know," I said. "I don't know how to drive, either."

"I hear you," he said. "I just got my license a couple months ago." Grin. "I was too busy surfing."

This time I just nodded. Maybe if I didn't answer, he would stop talking to me and go away before he saw that I was starting to shake.

He didn't.

"A lot of people our age don't want to go out on a big clunky board when all the experienced surfers are hopping on shortboards, but since you don't care about that ..." He shrugged his slender shoulders. "We have some cool-looking longboards. We'll find you something you like."

I didn't like any of them.

"We won't even look at anything shorter than nine feet. It'll handle more steadily on a wave—let you learn to paddle easier, catch a wave quicker. Plus, you can ride smaller waves at first. You won't have to do that for long, though."

He'd been leading me toward a rack full of standing-up surfboards that were three feet taller than him and almost made two of me. I followed, but I was breaking into a sweat even under my still-wet long-sleeved T-shirt.

"The only drawback is that it's kind of big to drag down on the beach, but there are two of you so you can switch off." He grinned again and shifted his eyes to the other side of the store. "I bet your grandmother could carry it all the way to North Carolina."

"Yeah," I said—eloquently.

"Since she doesn't have a rack on her car, I told her you guys could just store it here since you're renting from us."

Tell me, Shaun, I wanted to say. *Will it hurt her bad if I hit her with it?* Anger was getting the upper hand over panic. I couldn't do this. I couldn't.

"So—these are the rentals." He pulled out a white board with long, wide red stripes running down it. He looked at it and shook his head. "Doesn't look like you."

I shook my head too.

He frowned at the selection, eyebrows crowding toward each other. The long muscles in his arms stretched against tanned skin—not at all like Preston's muscles that bulged even under his shirts. Shaun was taller than Preston. Skinnier. Not as handsome in the Abercrombie and Fitch way.

My chest seized up. Was I going to compare every guy I

60

ever met for the rest of my life with the one who made me think I loved him and then punched me? And was I going to freak out every time one talked to me?

"I don't see pink for you."

I jolted back to the surfboard Shaun was putting back in the rack in all its pinkness.

"No, I don't do pink," I said. "You know what—it really doesn't—"

"Okay, this one is ridiculously cool. It wouldn't work for everybody but—check it out."

He produced a gleaming white board with slender blue-green swirls that seemed to accidentally form a cross at the top.

"Yeah?" he said.

"It's pretty," I said, once again displaying my way with words.

"I know it's not like you're buying it, but if you're going to be using it for however long, you want it to be a good fit."

Everything in me wanted to say, *No surfboard is ever going to fit.* Maybe I would have if Mim hadn't popped her head around the corner and smiled up at Shaun's choice.

"Is that the one you picked out?" she said to me.

And then they both looked at me, faces shining and expectant, like they'd gone in on a Christmas gift together for me and were going to live or die by whether I liked it. With one word, with one shake of my head, I could wipe away those expressions. I'd been doing a lot of that lately: taking previously peaceful faces and creasing them with worry lines, pumping them with sleep-deprived bags, slitting their eyes down to places that made them ugly. I was starting to hate myself for it.

"I like it," I said.

"Perfect," Mim said. "So you'll hold it for us, Shaun?"

"Absolutely," he said. "I'll have it waxed for you if you want."

"Not completely. Bryn might want to learn how to do that."

Sure.

Bryn will do anything anybody tells her to.

CHAPTER SEVEN

It still wasn't over. Mim then had to ask if Shaun knew of a good Mexican restaurant in the area—she wanted burritos. Shaun didn't know, so he called in another guy from the back to consult. We stood there for five more endless minutes while Shaun, Mim, and a long-haired kid named Goof—I'm serious, Goof—discussed Guadalajara vs. El Tapatio, and I let my illusion that I had any control over anything drain out of my head.

"I don't know, man," Goof was saying. "I heard they used cats in their tacos down there."

"Who does that?" Shaun said. "Nobody does that."

"Just kidding." Goof flipped his bushy, bleachy hair out of his face and looked at me. "So you're gonna learn to surf?"

"Um," was all I got out before he said, "You're gonna hate it."

"Dude—shut up!" Shaun said. "What are you doin'?"

"Just kidding."

That seemed to be his favorite phrase, and it was the right one for this situation as far as I was concerned.

"I just said that because you're probably going to be really good at it, and then you'll be out there competing for the same waves as us."

"I don't *think* so!" I said.

"Hey, you can never tell, right?" Shaun said.

He shrugged and grinned happily, and I decided he was a goof too.

"You're a kook right now," Goof said to me.

"I think you'd better define that for her." Mim gave me a nudge. "It's not as bad as it sounds."

"You better let me do it." Shaun squinted at Goof and then

turned his brown eyes to me. "So—a kook's just somebody who won't even try surfing because they don't think they can or whatever. That doesn't apply to you."

Goof let his lower lip hang. "That's not what it means."

"Shut up, dude," Shaun said. "That's what it means today."

"And on that note," Mim said, "we're going to find some burritos. See you tomorrow morning—if Bryn's up for it."

"Look at her—she's ready."

Shaun gave me the grin, but I just couldn't grin back. His was fading as I turned to follow my grandmother out the door.

*

Guadalajara wasn't what Mim had in mind. She sighed over the burritos and said, "Well, I think they're doing the best they can. I'm spoiled in San Diego."

I poked a hole in a tortilla and watched something reddish-brown ooze out. I tried not to think about cats.

"Did you want to go home for lunch?" Mim said. "I'm sorry—I should have asked you."

"It's fine," I said. "You wanted Mexican."

She lowered her voice, and her eyes twinkled. "I think we would have done just as well at Taco Bell. Shaun seemed like a nice boy."

I felt my eyes widen. Okay, that was random.

"He looks Mediterranean. I'm thinking the south of France. It's hard to believe he's only seventeen."

Despite my effort not to respond, I said, "Really?"

"The other one, Goof, is twenty and acts like he's twelve. You can never tell with men."

No, you never can. The thought was so depressing I put down my fork.

"Do you know what I think, Bryn?"

I looked up to find her watching me, as usual.

"I think we're in for a sea change. Not just the tide going in and out—the media uses the phrase all wrong in my opinion." She folded her hands under her chin and once again looked into me like she saw something in there I didn't know about. "It's going to be a real transformation. That's a sea change."

"Yes, ma'am," I said. And speaking of definitions . . . "What is a 'kook,' really?"

Mim laughed and sat back in the booth. "A kook is a beginner. A lousy surfer—because every beginner is lousy."

"Oh," I said. So Shaun was just trying to make me feel good. Goof really was the one who got me.

"So, shall we blow this taco stand?" Mim said. She laughed again. "I always wanted to say that."

*

I was finally alone that afternoon, except for Copper sitting on my chest giving himself a pawdicure. Not having to talk to anybody didn't feel that much better, so when my cell phone rang, I picked it up without checking to see who it was.

"Bryn—how's it going?"

I sat straight up, tumbling Copper off onto the bed. It was Andrew's voice.

"Don't hang up," he said. "I know Regan told you a bunch of stuff—but it's not true, okay?"

"Okay," I said, though I had no idea why. My mind was reeling like I'd just gotten off a theme-park ride. Andrew was calling me? Andrew Upton had never called me in his life. Preston would have ripped out his larynx. And he was saying Regan lied to me? Regan? His "woman," as he called her?

"Look, I just want to talk to you," he said. "Can I come get you and we'll go to Sonic or something?"

"I thought your car was totaled," I said. I was saying things that hadn't entered my mind until they came out of my mouth. It was like someone else was doing the talking for me.

"I don't even want to go there," Andrew said—coldly.

Oh. So that was it. He was mad at Preston for wrecking his car. Did that put him on my side?

"I got a Camry. It's not my RX-8 but I'm cool with it, I guess." He so wasn't.

"So, like, can I pick you up?"

"It's not a date, is it? I mean—I'm just saying—my parents won't let me—"

The color of my face was by now probably making my father look absolutely ghostly on his most embarrassed day. But Andrew didn't laugh in my ear. He actually sounded understanding when he said, "No, I know. It's just to talk, okay? I need to process some of this stuff. I thought you'd get it."

I was glad he wasn't there to see my mouth fall open. None of that sounded like it should be coming from Andrew. I knew him as the kind of guy who did stuff just to get Regan to throw things at him. The kind who called other guys by their last names and said things like, "Are you *stupid?*"

But maybe that was because the only time I was ever around him was when Preston was there. Maybe I wasn't the only one who hid themselves because of Preston.

"When?" I said.

"You rock, Bryn. See you in ten?"

"Yeah," I said.

As I hung up, I looked at the time on my phone. It was three. Dad would be at the clinic until five. Not that he wouldn't let me go with Andrew, but asking Mim would be easier. She seemed to want me to get out of the house.

I was right. When I told her I was going to Sonic with Andrew, she smiled and told me to have a good time and went back to typing on her laptop. I waited for Andrew on the front porch.

He pulled up in a beige Toyota and started to get out, but I hurried down the steps and climbed into the passenger side. I really didn't want Mim meeting him and then analyzing what part of the world his ancestors came from.

"You look good," he said as we backed out of the driveway. He sounded surprised. Regan must have told him I was more on the order of Godzilla.

He actually looked good too. I'd never thought he was all that cute, but that was probably because next to Preston nobody was that cute. He was a shade paler and a degree smaller. His hair was blonder but it didn't have that rich look like Preston's. He couldn't wear it the same way because it was too thick and curly. Even his eyes were like a lesser version of Preston's. They were gray-green and could be just as cold, but they never got that bedroom look going on, even when he was with Regan. With her he was kind of, "Do this, woman," which I guess a lot of girls liked.

Right now, though, he didn't seem so sure of himself, and

that made him easier to look at. His mouth wasn't in a hard, I-have-to-say-something-cool-now line, and he wasn't looking around like he had to make sure somebody was watching. Like maybe Preston. He was jittering his fingers on the steering wheel and trying to make conversation with me.

I tried too. It pretty much amounted to:

"You seem okay—"

"I am. So do you—"

"Thanks for comin' out—"

"Thanks for asking me."

We finally pulled into a slot at Sonic. By then Andrew couldn't seem to keep his hands still at all. He played them on the wheel like piano keys, rubbed his thighs, folded them at the back of his neck. If he wasn't nervous, then he was on speed or something. It started to make *me* nervous. That and the fact that we weren't ordering.

It occurred to me that I might not have any money, and I was digging into my purse when Andrew opened the door on his side and got out. Preston slid in to replace him.

My shaking started from the inside out. I twisted toward the door but Preston said, "Two minutes and I'm gone. Two minutes."

Something somewhere in my mind told me I should know what to do, but I didn't. Nothing I had ever done before had worked. Why should it now?

So I nodded. Preston didn't touch me, but he didn't let go with his eyes. His jaw muscles twitched before he opened his mouth again. I waited with my teeth clenched together so they wouldn't shake themselves loose.

"Regan gave you my message," he said.

I nodded again.

"So, what—you just decided to ignore it?"

"No," I said.

"Then ..." Preston drew up his shoulders, held out his palms. He looked at me like I was incredibly stupid. "Why haven't the charges been dropped?"

"I tried—"

"Not hard enough, evidently. Did you actually say, like, 'Preston never hit me. I lied'?"

I at least had the self-respect to say, "No! You did hit me!"

"That was between us. We could've worked it out." He licked his lips and jerked his head to look through the windshield. "Look, you knew I was stressed out about swimming. You knew I needed you to be there for me—and you weren't."

"I *was*!" I said. Stupidly. Because when he looked back at me, his eyes had already turned to stone.

"I don't even care about that now. Or you. What I care about is that you made it a big deal, and now you have to undo it."

"I can't—"

"Yes, you *can*!"

His fist came down on the dashboard. "You're such a drama queen." His voice dropped into a dangerous place. "But the act's over. I don't care what you have to do—you get those charges dropped. Or you're gonna find out what pain really is."

There was a knock on the glass behind me and Preston craned his neck to see around my head, his eyes annoyed. They sprang open as the person knocked again.

"Bryn, get out of the car," that person said.

It was my father.

Preston turned toward the door on his side. I fumbled with the lock and somehow got myself out. Dad put me behind him with one hand. The other one was closing his cell phone.

"Don't go anywhere, son," Dad said. He jabbed his finger over the top of the car at Preston, who was looking around, obviously for Andrew. "You just stay right *there*."

In spite of the threat in my father's voice, I don't think Preston would have stayed if a police car hadn't appeared and pulled up right behind Andrew's car and blocked it in. Preston threw his hands up and his head back, the way I'd seen him do when somebody on the swim team blew a relay while he was watching. How could they be so stupid—these people who didn't get it?

He wasn't afraid at all. And that frightened me more than anything.

*

It seemed like hours before I was back home, curled up on the couch with a blanket around me and Mim's chamomile tea

67

in my hands. The soup she'd heated up for me had gone cold on the coffee table. So had Dad's. It's hard to eat when you're pacing.

He'd been walking back and forth across the living room ever since we got home from Sonic, where I'd sat in the back of a police car for an eternity saying over and over that this time Preston hadn't touched me. Dad himself hadn't asked me anything, but I knew it was coming. Either that, or he was going to have a stroke. Mim seemed to be watching for that too.

Finally Dad pulled the Aztec chair closer to the couch and sat on the edge of it, and looked at me with eyes ringed in red and frustration.

"I don't understand you, Bryn," he said. "Why did you go with him when you knew there was a restraining order?"

"I didn't go with *him*," I said. "I went with Andrew."

"His best friend."

"He said he was mad at Preston and he just wanted to process it all with me. I didn't know Preston was going to be there."

"Would you have gone if you'd known?"

"No!"

I put the cup down and pressed my hand over my mouth but I couldn't keep the sobs back.

"Brynnie, I'm sorry," Dad said. "I know you wouldn't—I guess—I don't even know what I know anymore." He got up and paced again. "He's an arrogant kid, I do know that much."

"You think?" Mim muttered.

"Did he actually believe you wouldn't say anything if we hadn't caught him?"

"Probably," I said, and then I covered my whole face. Please, please—don't ask me if I would have. Please.

The phone rang and Dad went to the kitchen. Mim picked up my teacup and handed it to me.

"More?" she said.

I nodded and took it, but I couldn't drink. I was still crying.

"This boy is powerful," she said. "What are his parents like?"

"I don't know. I only met them once, at a swim meet."

"Your father came in right after you left and asked me where you were. I didn't go out to the clinic and inform him."

I watched a tear fall into my tea. Why was she telling me this?

"I just want you to know that I trust you, Bryn," she said.

Then she just watched. I took a sip, but I couldn't stand the silence.

"I really didn't know Preston was going to be there today."

"Why would you? Most boys wouldn't have taken that kind of chance. I think we have some narcissism going on." Her eyes lifted as Dad came back into the room.

"They've upped his bail for violating the restraining order," he said.

He leaned on the back of the chair, hands pressed into the fabric. Their squeeze made me think of Preston with his fingers around my wrist. Was this ever, ever going to go away?

"I was hoping they'd rescind his bail completely and put him in jail. Somebody has some influence, I think." Dad said that more to himself than to me, and then he leaned farther over the chair. "This means we have to be very, very careful, Brynnie. I hate that you have to be punished for somebody else's crime, but I don't see that we have a choice."

I didn't understand, and it must have shown on my face.

"I can't let you leave the house with anybody except Mim or me—even friends you trust. He could show up anywhere, and we can't risk that. He obviously thinks he's above the law."

Dad tilted his head at me, his eyes sad, but I just shrugged. What friends did I have to go anywhere with anyway? Even the theater kids I'd started to hang out with before Preston—I hadn't really talked to any of them since the Arts Festival. I hadn't been allowed to. The only one I'd even seen outside of class was Josie, and she was the one who'd told Preston at the party that I'd done a great job on my monologue and had set him off.

"Are we clear on this?" Dad said.

"Yes, sir," I said.

Nothing could be clearer.

CHAPTER EIGHT

Until the next morning, I'd forgotten about the surfing thing. Mim hadn't.

She woke me up whispering my name, practically before the sun was all the way up. Copper glared at her the way I would have if I'd dared, and he wasn't even the one who was going to have to go out into the ocean and make a fool of himself. I wanted to crawl inside a conch shell.

But of course I got up and put on the one-piece and, at Mim's "suggestion," slopped ten tons of waterproof sunscreen onto my skin—even on the tops of my ears as she instructed—and slid into yet another long-sleeved shirt. I'd have to do laundry soon or I was going to run out of them. I didn't even try to use that as an excuse not to go.

Mim handed me a smoothie as we went out the door. She herself sipped tea in an insulated mug and didn't say much as we drove to the Surf Shack. At least there was that.

My luck ran out there. It was Shaun, not Goof, who greeted us, and although his brown eyes were still puffy from sleep—or lack of it—he appeared to be a morning person. If he remembered that I'd been pretty cold to him the day before, he didn't show it—unfortunately. Maybe it seemed as long ago to him as it did to me.

He had "my" surfboard set flat across the corner where the porch railings of the Shack came together. It looked nothing like it had the day before—all shiny and smooth. There was some kind of gunk clumped all over it, as if somebody had smeared it with cottage cheese.

"I waxed it for you," Shaun said. "But I left a couple places so you could get the feel of how to do it."

"Perfect," Mim said. "I'm going to go in and look at the sunglasses while you two finish up. Mine don't have enough UV protection."

Anxiety churned in my stomach. What happened to me not being alone with anybody except her or Dad? Why did that only apply when it was convenient for *them*?

"It's pretty easy," Shaun said. He had what looked like a bar of soap in his hand, and he was rubbing it into a clear spot on the board. "You just want to create traction so you won't slide all over. It's basically impossible to stand up if you don't." He pulled his hand away from it. "You want to try it?"

I did not, but I picked the bar up anyway and scraped it where he'd just been working.

"You can apply a little more pressure," he said.

Great. I couldn't even make a mess correctly.

"As soon as you start scraping off as much wax as you're putting on you can move to another place on the board."

I took a deep breath. Okay. As long as I had to …

"Like there?" I said, pointing to the front end of the board, which was still clear and shiny.

Shaun grinned the grin which was still all gleeful even at that hour of the morning. "Uh, no. You're never gonna be standing up there — and if you do by mistake …" He grinned again. "You're gonna go down anyway, no matter how much traction you have."

I must have looked stricken, because he immediately added, "Don't worry about that. You've got a good teacher. Really."

He put his hand on my arm — and I froze. When I stared at it, heart pounding, he pulled away.

"So, yeah," he said, "you're doing good — just rub it a little more and you'll have it. Windy'll probably tell you this, but don't leave this stuff in your car. As hot as it gets here, it'll melt all over your floorboards, and forget about getting it out. I wear, like, surf shorts when I'm out so I can just keep it in my pocket and put more on when I wear it off in spots. Only, don't wash your shorts with it in there. Major disaster. My mom had to buy a new washer when I did that. I'm still paying her back."

It didn't take a brain surgeon to figure out that he was talking without taking a breath to cover up the awkward moment when he touched my arm and I acted like he was burning me with acid. I felt like I ought to say *something*.

"Should I wear shorts?" I said.

Shaun glanced at my legs—and then took the bar of wax from me and went after a spot that was already globby with the stuff. A circle of red appeared on the cheek that wasn't turned away from me.

"Not in my opinion," he said.

"How's it going?" Mim said from the doorway. For the first time in my life I was glad to see her.

"You're good to go." Shaun lifted the board from the railing and set it upright. "You want me to carry it down for you?"

Mim gave him a look that actually made me want to laugh out loud. Shaun did.

"My bad," he said. "I hope you have some good rides."

Mim took the board from him and tucked it under her arm like it was an evening bag. That was when I noticed something that looked like a leash attached to it. I knew all *along* it was an instrument of torture.

"You probably won't actually have many 'good rides' today," she said as she walked down the alley toward the beach with me trotting along beside her. "Even learning the basics takes time—nobody does it all the first day. You're going to be training your body *and* your mind to do things they've never done before." She flashed me a smile. "It's exciting."

No. It's terrifying.

I wasn't even comforted by the fact that the beach was practically deserted. A couple of senior citizens strolled past and gave us "isn't-that-nice" nods. Other than that, it was just us and the gulls, swooping in to see if we had food.

I wouldn't have been any more frightened if we'd been in front of the boardwalk, the sand packed blanket to blanket with sunbathers. I'd gone beyond how I was going to look. I was way into how I was going to survive.

Mim stopped a little ways down the beach and laid the board flat on the ground.

"We're going to do a dry run here," she said.

"Mim?"

"Yes."

She waited, head tilted.

"Okay," I said, "so what about sharks?"

"What about them?"

"What if they're out there?"

"Did you worry about them being there yesterday?"

"No, ma'am."

She nodded. "The chances of getting attacked by a shark are less than you being electrocuted by your toaster. Good question, though, because there are definitely dangers."

Wonderful.

Although she was wearing the sleek black sunglasses she'd just bought at the Surf Shack, she shaded her eyes with her hand and looked out over the ocean. "The currents are our main concern, but I'll deal with that at first until you get the hang of it. Right now your biggest danger is getting clonked in the head by your surfboard, but I'll show you how to avoid that." She lowered her hand and smiled at me, teeth flashing in the sunlight. "Right now it's all on me. All you have to do is have fun. I will say this, though. If you hear any thunder before I do, let me know right away. We don't want to be on the beach when there's a storm."

Actually, maybe I did. Getting struck by lightning sounded like a better idea than going out there with a surfboard.

"That was a good question," Mim said again. "I want you to remember that the only stupid questions are the ones that don't get asked."

Why are we doing this? was my real question. It must have been a stupid one, because I didn't ask it.

Nor did I ask any others while Mim demonstrated, with the board on the sand, how I was going to lie on my belly, then get up on one knee—not two—and then stand all the way up. There was something about my feet being planted crosswise to their direction of travel—or was it parallel? Perpendicular? I was lost by then, tangled in the *I-can't-do-this!* knot in my head.

"You may forget all of that the first time you try it," Mim said. "And that's okay. It'll come to you."

I just nodded. I was close to tears. When she picked up the leash-looking thing, I nearly lost it.

"This is the cord," she said. "You're just going to cuff it around

73

your ankle—see, there's Velcro—and then you'll never be separated from your surfboard. That way you don't have to swim for it and it doesn't hit some other poor surfer in the noggin."

"What about *my* noggin?" I said.

Mim laughed. "*Excellent* question. When you fall off, which is going to happen a lot today, the cord's going to stretch out—" She showed me. "And it will yank the board right back to you. That means when you come up you have to immediately watch for it or it might hit you—probably on the end with the fins. The trick is to wait under water and let some slack develop in the cord before you come up."

The chances of me being able to do that were less than the chances of being electrocuted by the toaster.

"I want you to lie down on the board," she said. "On your tummy."

I thought about saying my hematoma still hurt, but I'd already told her yesterday it didn't. I stretched out.

"Now come up on one knee like I showed you."

"Which knee?"

"Whichever one comes naturally."

Naturally? Was she serious?

But I did as she said and rose onto my left knee.

"Now come to standing," she said.

I did.

"Good. So you're not a goofy foot."

You wanna bet?

Mim chuckled. "I suspect that's why they call that other boy 'Goof'—because he surfs with his right foot forward. That's called a goofy foot. So let's put this on your right ankle, which will be in the rear."

The real panic started then. I was attached to the surfboard. I was expected to be able to stand up on it while it was moving on top of a wave. I was going to fall off and it was going to bonk me in the head. And whatever it was we were supposed to accomplish was never going to happen.

But with my mouth going dry and my stomach turning itself inside out, I put the board under my arm like Mim showed me and walked with her to the water's edge. Keep it pointed out to sea, she told me.

Naturally, the first thing I did when a wave came toward us was turn sideways and get knocked down.

"Everybody does that at some point," Mim said.

I had a feeling she was lying.

I managed to get out to where the water was knee-deep without going down again, but it got harder after that. Mim showed me how to lay the board on top of the water and push it through the waves as they came at me. She made it look like she was floating a toy sailboat. I tried it and the thing smashed up against me. Down for the second time.

"Let's stop here," Mim said. "We don't want to get out past where the waves are breaking. We only want white water right now — soup."

It was definitely soupy. I felt like I was standing in a bowl of rushing foam being stirred by a giant spoon. And it was so loud Mim was having to talk above her normal tone. I was ready to scream.

"We're going to want to turn the board around to face the beach," she said. "That means for a second or two your board is going to be sideways to the oncoming surf."

I turned it.

"Duck!" Mim cried — just before a wave smacked into both me and the board.

It was the car accident all over again. My head took a square hit, and I went backward into the water. The board sailed over me, and I felt the fin scrape my leg.

I didn't want to come up, but Mim did that for me.

"You okay?" she said.

I couldn't speak yet so I nodded.

"I guess I'm going to have to talk faster." She looked behind us at an oncoming wave and grabbed the board with her hands on either side of the middle and swung it around until its nose faced the shoreline. The fins never touched the water. "You never want to allow a sideways board to get between you and an oncoming white-water wave. You sure you're okay?"

"I'm really bad at this," I said.

"No," she said. "You're just normal. How about if I handle the board and we just concentrate on getting you a ride?"

For lack of any other ideas, I nodded.

"Later you're going to learn to paddle," she said, still holding the board and watching the oncoming waves. "For now you're just going to jump—well, flop, actually. Go ahead and get on, on your belly."

Oh—my—gosh. I plopped myself on.

"Hold on with both hands, in the middle of the board. Scoot forward."

I did.

"Okay—don't try to stand up yet. Just ride in on your tummy. Here we go!"

She gave me a push and I was suddenly whizzing along at breakneck speed toward the shore. I felt like I was going to slide off the back so I scooted forward more. At the same breakneck speed, I dove straight downward. It was actually more as if I were thrown off headfirst. I hit bottom and came up gasping, just in time to see the board popping into the air. The cord tugged at my ankle, but I couldn't remember what to do. The thing came down inches from my head.

Oh—my—gosh.

"Your first wipeout," Mim said. "You pearled." She turned us both toward the waves, this time carrying the board herself. "That means you took a nosedive. Do you know why?"

Because I'm a spastic?

I shook my head.

"You were too far forward on the board. Try to stay in the middle."

I tried it again. This time I made sure I wasn't close to the front where that Shaun guy told me I'd never be. And this time, the nose stuck straight up in the air. The board stalled, me with it, and the wave went on without me.

"That's what happens when you get too far back," Mim said. "You want to be right in the middle."

Fine. The next time I was in the middle, but the board rolled sideways. I hung on for dear life and got dragged through the water with the surfboard on one edge. It felt like somebody was pointing a fire hose into my face.

"Once you start to fall, let go of the board," Mim said. "There's always another wave to try."

Unfortunately. We tried them all, and I made a different

76

mistake every time. Once, I realized I was at an angle and tried to wriggle myself straight. I went over sideways, forgot to let go, and rode several feet upside down.

Another time, I got on and didn't fall over but the board wasn't pointed directly at the beach. I tried to steer it and went sideways *and* pearled. That time I came up with the cord wrapped around my neck.

I got worse instead of better, until finally Mim said, "I think you're getting tired. That's enough for today. It's a good start, though."

I just stared at her.

"All right," she said, as if I'd just begged her for more. "One more try. Get your feet and your head aligned in the same direction as the centerline of the board and center yourself right over the middle. Try to get the nose just over the surface of the water. It's a lot to remember—but everybody figures it out eventually. Okay—let's catch this guy!"

I flopped onto the board like an exhausted flounder and hung onto both sides. All I could remember was "get the nose just over the surface of the water." Crying—out loud—"Please, please, don't let me make another nosedive!" I closed my eyes and waited for the wave to take me under.

But something else happened. The board shot along on top of the water with me on it. I opened my eyes to see the beach slamming toward me, and it freaked me out so bad I put my face down and the board went with it. But we were practically on shore by then and the board just stopped in the sand. I tumbled off the side.

I did it. I rode that stupid thing all the way in. A gurgle started up my throat.

"What was that supposed to be?" someone said.

I looked up. Two guys in baggy shorts and mirrored sunglasses were passing about six feet away. One of them, a redhead, glanced over his shoulder in my direction but they weren't actually talking to me.

Just *about* me.

"Everybody thinks they can surf," he said.

Not me, I wanted to scream at him. Not me.

CHAPTER NINE

I went to the car while Mim took the surfboard into the Surf Shack. I didn't want to have to report to Shaun that I hadn't had any good "rides," or even any mediocre ones. In fact, I didn't want to talk to anybody about anything. I just sat there in the steaming front seat wishing for pneumonia. Maybe appendicitis. I'd already mashed on my stomach a dozen times but it didn't hurt anymore. Even the place on my leg where the fins scraped me was nothing more than a mocking red line that said, "You really are a terminal klutz, you know that?"

All the way home, while I chafed at the sand that had gotten under my swimsuit into places I didn't even know existed, Mim assured me the hardest part was over. She said I'd ridden a wave to the beach and now I was only going to get more comfortable with the board. So, it was clear that the best I could hope for to get out of any more surfing was a rare disease, but even then Mim would probably say a morning almost drowning, and looking like an idiot doing it, would be good for it.

As soon as we got in the house she went to the kitchen to fix lunch, and I headed for my room, where I closed the door and locked it. I kicked my flip-flops into the closet and watched sand settle between the fibers in the carpet. As far as I was concerned, surfing wasn't good for anything except making me feel like even more of a loser than I already did. One more spastic "pearl," one more leash wrapped around my neck, and I might as well walk around with a large L written on my forehead in black Sharpie.

I showered and crawled into my bowl chair and pulled the hood nobody actually uses on a hoodie over my head. Something that didn't feel like a corduroy cushion pressed against my back. I reached behind me and pulled out the leather book.

I'd forgotten all about it, even after the few times when I'd

78

come across it and moved it. It really was a worn-out-looking thing. The cover was cracked and curled as if somebody had spent hours with it.

Maybe more than one somebody. Several people had scratched what had to be initials into the cover. One set—RL—looked like it had been etched professionally in the center. That must be the title, although to what, I didn't know.

Truth be told, I'd been afraid to look inside it again, afraid that maybe it didn't really say what I thought it said when I opened it at the hospital—and that I'd actually merely stolen it.

I *could* have been hallucinating that night, freaked as I was, although the memory of Preston following the police out, hating me over his shoulder, was all *too* real. I flipped back the leather cover. There it still was:

If you've found me, you need me. I was left for you for a reason. Read and discover what that is.

I ran my hand across the words. There was no doubt I needed *something*. It wasn't surfing. Maybe a convent, although I wasn't even Catholic. What I really wanted was to escape, and so far nothing, old or new, had provided the right route.

I read the words again. "I was left for you for a reason." Could that possibly mean what I wanted it to mean? I, Bryn Christopher, was actually supposed to have it, and not somebody else who'd accidentally missed it?

The biggest wave of desperation yet came over me, bigger than any the ocean had pushed at me. I had to believe that something was going to lift me out of the mess I'd made. I couldn't pass up the chance that this was it.

I turned the page.

Or at least, I tried to. The edges slid from my fingers and the pages turned themselves as if a breeze had just whispered through. I looked to see if the window was open, but I already knew the house was closed up like a bank vault to keep the air-conditioning in and the hair-melting humidity out. When the pages finally settled, I tried to flip back to page one, but they wouldn't move.

I yanked my hand back and stared down at the thing. It lay open in my lap like it was waiting for me to accept that it—

That it what? Had a mind of its own? I shivered and smacked it shut and waited.

It seemed to wait too.

There were only two possibilities: this was some kind of supernatural thing, or I was going crazy. I pulled the book open again and lay my hand flat on the page. The second I moved it away, the pages fluttered, cheery as little-girl giggles, to the same place they'd landed before. This time I had a familiar sensation—not familiar like it happened to me every day, but familiar like I'd just experienced it recently somewhere else. Like today.

Like maybe the ocean current, yanking me sideways as I tried to battle a smacking wall of white. I couldn't pull away from this any more than I could resist being moved down the beach by water I didn't even want to be in.

Once more I started to close the whole book, but I was too close not to see what it said:

You've finally come to where you need to start.

I shivered. It was just print on paper. Anybody could read it. This wasn't put there especially for me—even I knew that. Still, when I put my hand on the back of my neck to lift my wet hair off of it, my palm was clammy. The tide of the page pulled me back to it.

"Here's a story," I read, "A true one about Yeshua and his group of friends."

Now the name—"Yeshua"—I liked. It reminded me of the ones Emma and Isabel and I used to give each other. Names that were foreign and mysterious and swishy in the mouth. There was no one around to tell me I was a "strange child" now, so I read on.

This one day, they were walking on the beach—

Why was everyone so fixated on the beach? I would be fine with never seeing another wave for the rest of my life. If this story turned out to be about surfers, I was pitching it.

They decided to go by boat. It was a fairly calm afternoon, in fact so much so that Yeshua stretched out on the bow to enjoy the last strokes of the afternoon sun. A light breeze kissed his face and he drifted off.

Now that was the way to do the ocean, in my view. Mim should read this. I went into my imagination where the idea of a hunky Yeshua was already taking shape, despite my current vow to avoid all men. This one was imaginary, so it was okay to picture him with a bronze tan. Deep-dark hair—definitely

80

not blond. I was done with blonds. Smooth muscles on his back softening as he slipped into sleep.

But I could only think it. All I really saw was a blur, like he wouldn't fit into my design. Maybe I had let Preston take my fantasy mind away from me too. I went back to the page.

Who knows how much time had gone by when the sky went dark and a storm burst onto the scene, whipping the water into a frenzy and tossing the boat around like a toy. Seawater swamped the decks, and Yeshua's friends, eyes white and wild with fear, were sure they were going down. But Yeshua was still napping like a baby in a cradle through it all. If anything, the wind rocked him further into sleep, even as the boat was swept up into the curl of a wave that threatened to drive it straight to the bottom. They were going to pearl, and there was nothing they could do to stop it—

Wait. Did that say *pearl*? Was there no getting away from the surf speak?

One of Yeshua's friends managed to get to him as the boat tee-tered on the brink of disaster. Over the scream of the wind, the guy yelled, "Yeshua—wake up! We're going down!" Yeshua opened his eyes to a world gone mad. And yet he just sat up, and then stood up—

This was definitely a fantasy, a genre I knew well. Otherwise, there was no way he did that.

Oh, you haven't heard the most unbelievable part yet.

I jerked my hand from the page. Had the book just answered my thought? I tried to look back at the last paragraph, but I was washed down to the next one.

Yeshua stood up and looked at the wind as if he could see its face and said, "Silence." And then he turned to the wave that crested over them and ordered it to "Quiet down." The wind sucked itself back to a whisper. The waves fizzled like a spent tantrum. The sea was a sheet of glass.

My eyes flickered back to the top of the page, and this time the book let them go. I found the place that said it was a true story.

There is none truer, it said.

Okay, unless I was completely losing it, that sentence wasn't there the first time I read that part. My clammy palms had turned to ice, and yet now I didn't even try to close the book. I let it pull me back to the bottom.

Then Yeshua turned to his follower friends, and he said, "Why can't you trust me?" All they could do was look at each other, mouths gaping like open mailboxes, chins almost to their chests. Their eyes darted between disbelief and utter gratitude. When they could finally speak their shock, they said to each other, "Who is this anyway? He gives commands to the wind and the sea and they do what he says. Who is this?"

If you find out, please tell me, I thought. I think I want that.

I turned the page to read more. It said only,

That's enough for now. First do what he says.

"Do *what* that he says?" I said—out loud—because there was no denying now that this book was reading my mind and speaking right to me.

But it didn't answer. I went back through the story and read it again—normally—as if it had never pulled me around like a surfboard on a cord to begin with. I searched for anything Yeshua said that I could actually do, but all he said, besides "Silence," and "Quiet down," was "Why can't you trust me?"

I let the book fall shut on itself, let it slide off the edge of the chair and onto the carpet.

Trust a guy? I didn't think so. Especially one I didn't even know and was never likely to meet—even if it *was* nonfiction. I couldn't even trust the ones I *could* see.

I tapped the book with my bare toe. Too bad. I liked the story. It was the closest I had come to anything that felt spiritual in a long time. But maybe it was just as well. This supernatural thing, if that's what it was, wasn't the vision I'd once hoped for. This was way too real. And I was over real.

*

I did have one wisp of luck the next day: it was too stormy to surf. But even that was swept away when Dad came in from the clinic after work.

Mim and I were in the kitchen. A visit to the other Mexican restaurant that afternoon had convinced her there wasn't a decent burrito in the city of Virginia Beach, so we were making our own. I was chopping cooked chicken into small pieces and hoping for extreme lightning tomorrow—maybe an early hurricane—but I stopped doing both the moment I saw Dad's face. Either he'd just had to put down a baby Saint Bernard, or he had bad news for me. He was one long, thin line.

Mim obviously saw it too, because she stopped stirring the sauce she'd been muttering over and wiped her hands on a dish towel.

"Neal, what can I get you?"

"Nothing," Dad said. "I just talked to the DA's office. A preliminary hearing's been set for next Thursday."

"What's a preliminary hearing?" I said.

"We'll all go to court so the judge can determine whether there's enough evidence for our case to go to trial."

"Court?" I said.

Mim reached over and took the knife out of my hand, which was shaking just like the rest of me.

"We have to go to *court?*" I'd thought Regan was just trying to scare me when she'd told me that.

Dad pulled a stool up to the counter across from me, but he looked down at the chicken I'd been butchering. "That's how it's done, Brynnie. From what they told me, a person from their office—a witness coordinator, they called it—will sit down with you beforehand and tell you exactly what's going to happen. You'll probably have to tell her your story—"

"I have to tell it again?"

"Yes. Look, Brynnie, I know how hard this is for you—"

"No, you don't!"

He did look at me then, his pale eyes startling to a darker shade. "We're all trying to help you," he said. "I wish I could somehow make you see that."

And I wished he and everybody else would stop. I wished he would go back to being the father who nodded and smiled and made me wonder if he really heard anything anybody was saying because he was wrapped up in rabies and heartworms and feline leukemia.

"I don't want any help," I said. "I just want this to go away."

"That's not going to happen." Dad gripped his forehead. "I don't understand what you're afraid of, Bryn. Preston is the only one who has anything to worry about. I'm taking care of everything else—"

"You're taking care of it, and I'm the one who's going to—"

I stumbled on the rest and scraped my stool back so hard it tipped over into Mim's waiting hands.

"I'm not hungry," I said. "I'm going to my room."

"No," Dad said, "you're going to stay here and tell me what you think is going to happen to you."

I stared. Only by some miracle did my teeth not drop out. *Who are you?* I wanted to scream at him. *Has Preston twisted you into somebody else too?*

Even Mim was biting on her lower lip as she set the stool upright again. Dad was crimson-faced, and his eyes searched mine like he was looking for me just the way I was trying to find him. He wasn't going to have any luck. I wasn't in there anymore.

"Go on," he said. "We'll get back to this later."

I was almost to my door when I heard him say to Mim, "I'm really worried about her emotional state."

I didn't wait to hear how Mim answered. I already knew what emotional state I'd moved to.

I came down so hard on the bed, Copper clawed his way off and disappeared underneath. As I was considering joining him, my phone signaled a text message.

Don't even look at it, I warned myself—while I snatched it up from the table and stared at the screen.

CANCEL THE HEARING OR YOU WILL PAY.

LAST WARNING.

It was from a number I didn't recognize. Frantically, I checked my Recents for the call I'd gotten from Andrew and the text from Regan. It wasn't either one of theirs, or Preston's.

That raced right up my backbone. Who was I supposed to run from, then? How would I know to duck around a corner or hide behind something if I didn't even know who was after me?

I squeezed the phone in my palm and read the message again. It couldn't be from Regan, even from another number, because she never spelled things out when she texted. A lot of people texted Preston but he never lowered himself to text back, so Andrew didn't either. There were more of them now, then—more people to gang up on me over something I didn't even create.

"See, *Dad?*" I said between my teeth. "See what you're doing to me?"

The thought of taking the phone to him and shoving the message into his face ran into my head and then out again. Showing it to him would only make things worse. He would have the police tracking down the number and hauling in everybody Preston knew for questioning. But there would always be more of them, always somebody who wanted to get in good with Preston Almighty. Somebody else willing to take me down for him.

Thumbs trembling, I deleted the message.

*

I didn't sleep much over the weekend. My mind kept flipping back and forth between all the ways Whoever It Was could get to me, and the possibility that they were just trying to spook me. If that was the case, it was a done deal.

But I knew that wasn't it. Preston could see how terrified I already was when he'd warned me at Sonic. This wasn't just another you-better-watch-out. There was something menacing behind it, and it was making me jump up at every sound during the night to look out the window or check under the bed—as if someone could actually have snuck in with Dad acting like a trained Doberman.

The whole thing made surfing a little less frightening by comparison—though not any easier.

After an entire Monday morning of "proning it out" until I could make it to the beach on my stomach on the board every time without *wiping* out, Mim bragged to Shaun that I was ready to start learning how to stand up.

"Are you stoked?" he said to me when Mim had gone out back to hose off.

"Does that mean am I jazzed?" I said to my feet. Why did she keep leaving me alone with this kid? For somebody who watched me all the time, she sure wasn't picking up on the fact that all guys currently freaked me out.

Shaun leaned his elbows on the counter. "That's exactly what it means."

Then, no, I am definitely not stoked, I wanted to tell him. My arms feel like shoelaces. My legs are now made of Jell-O—I know it for a fact. And the only thing I've learned about surfing is that it's more about hanging on than hanging ten, not that I know what that even means.

"Semi-stoked?" he said.

"Sure," I said. "Why not?"

He tilted his head like he was about to say something that didn't involve a grin, but Mim came in and he just straightened up and shrugged and said, "Yeah. Why not?"

I felt like I'd just smacked him.

*

Tuesday I "graduated" to trying to ride in on my knees. It was like starting all over. I dumped it twice before I could get to the beach even holding onto the board with both hands. When I finally got that down, Mim said I was ready to take my hands off and go—so I'd get a taste of what it felt like to have to maintain balance with my arms and body with the bulk of me raised off the surfboard.

"Once you get good at riding in a kneeling position," Mim said as she held the board with me belly-down on it, "you'll find standing to be a lot easier if you just jump from this position. Okay—all the way in on your knees—hands off!"

Disaster. Once I was on my knees, I let go and skimmed along just ahead of the wave's crest—until I mentally flipped out at the whole idea of having nothing to hold on to. I tried to get my hands back down and had my worst wipeout yet. The board hit me in the shoulder and I had to sit on the beach until I could catch my breath.

Mim sat beside me, feet next to mine on the sand. I noticed in some random way that all four were shaped exactly alike, right down to the baby toes.

"Have I mentioned," she said, "that some people find balance more easily than others?"

Maybe she had, but I answered, "No, ma'am."

"Everybody does eventually. Those willing to take the risk find it faster."

"Do I have to take anymore risks today?" I said.

"Absolutely not." Mim stood up and brushed the sand from her hands. "The choice is always yours."

"Want to bet?" I muttered as she started to move away.

"Did you say something?" she said.

"No, ma'am," I said.

She shaded her eyes and looked down at me. "You can say anything you want to me, Bryn. I can't stop the waves that are coming at you, but I can help you find ways to keep from being knocked down by them."

Really. That didn't seem to be working so far. I poked at some grains of sand between my toes.

"Whenever you're ready," she said.

I didn't even go into the Surf Shack with her. And Wednesday morning I waxed my board out on the porch until the bar was down to a nub rather than go inside and get another one. I didn't have the energy to pretend to be even semi-stoked. Mim did go in, I assumed to do the stoking for both of us.

I was throwing away the tooth-sized piece of wax when a car spewed gravel as it came into the parking lot in front of the Shack. I didn't look up until somebody yelled, "Hey—Drama Queen."

Even as my face whipped toward the voice I knew I should be running away from it. But I was pulled to it like he had me on a tether—that redheaded boy in mirrored sunglasses who leaned out of the passenger-side window of a banged-up Volkswagen and pointed something at me. I gasped and stood there stricken, even after I realized it was a camera. Even after the car peeled out and screamed down the street. Even after I knew I'd seen that kid before—and that I would see him again.

I felt my face drain of all color as I stumbled into the Shack. I careened into Goof and knocked a stack of swim fins out of his hands, sending them spinning across the floor.

"Are you drunk again?" he said. "Just kidding."

"Goof, what's wrong with you, man?" Shaun came around the corner, and his grin dissolved like soda bubbles. "Windy," he said. "Uh—"

Mim joined him. As soon as she looked at me, standing there with my hands clinging to the back of my neck, she started toward me, her own hands out.

"Can we just not do this today?" I said.

"Are you all right?"

I shook my head. "I just really feel sick," I said.

And there was no pretending about it.

CHAPTER TEN

My eyes opened before dawn on Thursday, the morning of the preliminary hearing, and at first I couldn't figure out why. Copper was asleep in the crook of my knees. I didn't hear Mim moving around the house or Dad snoring in his bedroom. What time was it, anyway?

I rolled over and picked up my cell phone to check, and saw what had woken me up. I had another text message.

I shoved the phone under the covers, getting a growl out of Copper, and laid back down. But even with my eyes squeezed shut, visions of what it might say sprawled across my mind in blood-red letters. YOU'RE AS GOOD AS DEAD. NEXT TIME IT WON'T BE A CAMERA WE SHOOT AT YOU.

The shaking started, and I sat up. The actual message couldn't be as bad as what I was imagining, and what I was imagining was going to send me back into the bathroom where I'd spent most of the afternoon before throwing up.

I dug for the phone, this time driving Copper off the bed and into the chair. He curled up on top of the leather book and glowered at me.

"I'll read it and then we'll go back to sleep," I whispered to him.

When I brought up the message, I had to blink to make sure I wasn't still conjuring something up. HELP FOR ABUSED TEENS, it said, and gave a website.

Really?

I looked at Copper again. "You think it will tell me how to get out of this hearing?"

He turned his back on me completely.

I curled up under the covers again and shivered, phone still in hand. More visions—this time of what today was going to be like—crowded sleep from my brain. Between bouts of puking, I'd dreamed up everything from judges with long white wigs waggling their fingers at me to a dead ringer for Jack McCoy shouting in my face until I evaporated on the witness stand. They all marched before me again now, and I couldn't stand it. I threw off the comforter and went for my laptop. Copper yielded all of five inches for me to squeeze into the chair with it. I tossed the RL book onto the floor.

I carefully typed in the web address. Copper patted at the tiny whirling circle on the screen that told me it was loading. When it did, I pushed his paw away and stared in horror.

In the center of the site was a picture of me, standing on the front porch of the Surf Shack, wearing sunglasses and a long-sleeved yellow T over my swimsuit, tossing a piece of surfboard wax into a trash can. My board was in the picture too, as if I were posing for a surf camp ad. It could have been Mim's web-site—if the words below it hadn't said DOES THIS CHICK LOOK ABUSED TO YOU?

Beneath that was a subtitle: Drama Queen Throws Swim Star Under the Bus

I might as well have been reading RL for all the control I had over my eyes. They dug right into the blog that followed—a whole paragraph about how I had turned a minor fight that *I* had started with Preston into a Class C felony, how I'd lied to the police and cost his father a fortune in bail, how I was demanding that the case go to court where I was going to lie some more, until an innocent guy who could be the next Michael Phelps went to prison for the rest of his life while I pursued a career in surfing.

Maybe I would have laughed, if it hadn't been for the question at the bottom: "Does anyone have any ideas how we can get this—?"

I cringed at the word they used for me. By the time I read all twenty-two of the comments people had posted, I was in a tight ball in the chair. It was like being beaten up all over again.

"Egg her house."

"No, that's too good for her. Key her car."

"She's a loser—she doesn't even have a car."

"What's she got you could take away like she took Preston's whole future?"

"Take hers!"

"She doesn't have one of those either—and she definitely won't when we get through with her."

The suggestions got more heinous the farther I read. "Hack into her school records." "Out her on Facebook." "Poison her cat." After the last one, I staggered to the bathroom again and heaved until there was nothing left. Mim found me there on my knees.

"Here, Hon," she said. A warm washcloth curled around the back of my neck, and a glass of water found its way into my hand. "You might want to rinse."

I stayed on the floor and washed out my mouth and spit into the toilet. Mim sank onto the rug beside me and brushed my hair away from my face. She continued to stroke it.

"Stress can be worse than the flu," she said. "I wish it were as easy to treat."

"It's never going to be over," I said.

"You're going to put a big piece of it behind you today."

I didn't bother to argue with her. The sun wasn't even up and I was already exhausted.

"I stink," I said.

"Why don't I draw you a bath?" Mim crawled on all fours to the tub and turned on the faucet. "Let me see what I can find to help you relax. I'll be right back."

I stayed there on the floor, head buried in my knees, listening to the tub fill. But I could still hear my own questions crying desperately in my head. Who were all those people who hated me so much? How did they even know me? How could they write such—

Something beeped. My computer.

My head jerked up and I was on my feet before the next thought was even fully formed. I'd left my laptop open with the webpage still running. If Mim saw that—

But she was coming back in through my bedroom door holding a candle and a bag of pink salt. It was Copper who'd found the blog. He was sitting in the middle of the keyboard, blinking at the blank screen—and probably wondering how he'd made it disappear.

"I hope you weren't into anything important," Mim said.

"No," I said.

Just my doom.

*

The inside of the Virginia Beach Circuit Court at the Municipal Center was just like I'd always pictured an insane asylum. Mim, Dad, and I all had to go through a metal detector to get in and then show the contents of our pockets and purses to a huge officer who was obviously under orders never to smile. Ever.

There were hoards of people, most of whom I would have been scared to run into alone in a dark parking lot. A line of them with viciously shaved hair and tattoos in painful-looking places and piercings that turned their eyebrows into Slinkies shuffled through security and wrapped around the curved hallway and up the stairs we climbed. A lot of them were girls. The guys mostly had wet hair, like somebody had hosed them down for their court appearance, which seemed to have ticked them off even more than they probably were when they did whatever it was they were there for.

But I kept my eye on the ones who didn't look like they ought to be on death row. The girls with professional highlighting, and pedicures peeking out of Betsey Johnson sandals. The boys in Abercrombie shorts, jangling the keys to their Audis. If anybody was there to egg my house or key my dad's car or take away my future, it was one of them.

Mixed in with all us victims and perpetrators were people in suits carrying briefcases and Starbucks cups. One of them stepped out of the mob holding her coffee over her head and tilting her important chin toward the top of the steps where we were waiting as Dad had been told to on the phone.

"Bryn Christopher?" she said, chin now pointed at me.

I bit back the urge to tell her she had the wrong person and said, "Yes, ma'am."

She gave me a brisk nod and put out her hand for me to shake. "Vanessa Woodhouse, from the DA's office. I'm your witness coordinator."

While she introduced herself to Dad and Mim, I tried to focus on what she looked like so I wouldn't lose it and bolt. She was African American, with the shortest of short hair that snuggled her head like a black velvet cap, small pointy eyes behind black-framed rectangular glasses, and a wide mouth that spoke precisely, like she was exaggerating every word so we'd get it.

She glanced at her watch and then at the crowded upstairs hallway.

"All the benches are taken," she said. "This spot is as good as any."

She set her coffee cup on the stair ledge, whipped open a slim leather notebook, and poised a pen over it. "I have the police report," she said. "Your statement ..."

Her sharp eyes darted down the page, and I had the feeling she was seeing it for the first time. My mouth went beyond dry. I didn't want her to see it at all.

"All right, Bryn." She gave me a rehearsed-looking smile. "Our goal is to settle this thing out of court and save you a lot of hassle."

"I need to say something here." Dad's face was flushing from the throat up.

"Of course," Vanessa said. But she looked at her watch again.

"When you say 'settle it out of court'—I don't want to see this kid get off scot-free."

"Neither do we. We want him to take a plea—" She put up her hand before Dad could interrupt her. "A plea that includes some jail time, possibly a fine. 'Scot-free' isn't an option."

She smiled the same practiced smile at Dad. He looked like it was taking all he had not to push her down the steps. Fear pulled through my veins like hot wire.

"Now ... Bryn." Vanessa's eyes darted back to the paperwork, I suspected to be sure she'd gotten my name right. "Unfortunately, Mr. Oliver's willingness to take an offer is going to depend mostly on you. This is a he said/she said situation. We have the medical evidence that you were abused but nothing to prove he was the abuser—" Once again the palm went up for Dad. "Nothing beyond your testimony. What else can you tell me about your history of battering from this young man?"

My throat closed up. All my hot fear turned to ice and froze me where I stood. None of them seemed to see that. They all just waited.

Except for Mim, who slid her hand into mine and squeezed. That thawed me enough so I could say, "He was hitting me on and off for two months before the night of the accident."

"Okay. Can you give me specifics?"

"Specifics?"

"Details." She tapped the pen on the leather. "What I'm looking for is any incident someone else might have witnessed."

"Nobody else was ever around."

"Did you ever tell anyone what was happening? A girl-friend? A counselor?"

"No, ma'am."

She frowned at the page and looked at her watch for the third time. "All right, look, I'm going to take this to the prosecutor. Meanwhile, I want you to sit down—somewhere—and write down every instance of the abuse you can remember." She tore a piece of paper from her pad. "Then number them in order and rate them in severity on a scale of one to five—one being, like, an arm grab, five being assault with a weapon." She put the paper in my hand and shot her bullet eyes into mine. "Can you do that? It's the best chance we have."

And with a look that said it wasn't a very *good* chance, she slapped the portfolio shut and tapped her heels crisply down the hall, retrieving her coffee on the way.

Dad was already halfway after her, talking over his shoulder. "Windy, can you—"

"Absolutely," Mim said.

He took off in pursuit of Vanessa Woodhouse, and Mim cupped her hand around my elbow.

"Come on," she murmured into my ear. "If you don't sit down, you're going to fall down."

She'd obviously been scoping out the scene, because she steered me directly to a chair someone had left outside a door and carried it, and pretty much me, to a far corner no one had claimed.

"Sit," she said.

I did, while she produced a pen from her canvas bag, took the half-crumpled piece of paper from me, and squatted beside the chair.

"I got the impression from the Stress Princess that we don't have much time," Mim said. "I'd like to do some relaxation work with you first, but I guess we'd better get down to business."

Yet she put the pen aside and pressed her hand to my knee and closed her eyes. Her lips moved without sound. If I hadn't known my grandmother better, I'd have thought she was praying. It wasn't something I'd ever seen her do before.

"You all right?" she said when she looked up at me.

"No, ma'am," I said.

She nodded. "I think that's a good start. So, just tell me the story. And don't worry about order or 'rating.'" She threw a scowl behind her as if Vanessa Woodhouse was standing there to catch it. "We'll figure that out later."

"I don't think I can do this," I said.

"Nobody does. And then we just do it. When was the first time he touched you in anger?"

I closed my eyes, and there were Preston's hands coming at me.

"What do you see?" Mim whispered.

"Fear," I said.

"What does it look like?"

"Like a hand grabbing my arm and shoving me against a brick wall."

"Pull back and see if you can get a bigger picture."

I opened my eyes. The tears in hers matched the thickness in her voice. Crying was another thing I'd never seen my grandmother do.

I told her everything.

*

We'd just finished up when Dad came back with a guy who I thought at first glance was a college kid. He had a short, trim haircut the color of sand, and he was thin and wiry and moved quickly, as if to say, "I know where I'm going but I'm not sure about you." I'd seen guys like him on the beach, only they weren't wearing neckties and carrying file folders. He ought to be toting a shortboard.

"Will Quintera," he said to Mim and me before he even stopped walking. "I'm prosecuting the case."

Close up, from my chair, I could see sun-squint lines around his eyes, but he still looked like somebody Tara would go out with. Didn't you have to be, like, at least thirty to be an actual lawyer?

"How you holding up?" he said to me.

"I'm fine," I said.

He made a "wrong answer" face. "It would be better if you didn't say that on the stand. We want the judge to see you as vulnerable—strong enough to testify but not unaffected by what's happened to you."

"Testify?" I said.

"We offered Mr. Oliver a plea based on your interview with Vanessa and he basically laughed in our faces."

Hard as I tried not to, I could see that happening.

"Which means we'll have a hearing. This is just to determine whether there's enough evidence to go to trial, so I'll keep it brief and to the point." He looked at Mim. "Like I told your husband, we can basically get an indictment for a ham sandwich."

I stood up to tell him that Mim wasn't my mother, but he was driving on.

"The biggest thing is we don't want to give the defense anything to go with. All they have to do at trial is create reasonable doubt, and we want them to have to work at it." He hesitated, eyes on me.

"Okay," I said.

"Vanessa says you're not sure about the details."

Mim pressed the paper into my hand, and I stuck it out to him. Dad blew out air like he'd been holding his breath through the whole thing. Mr. Quintera gave him a waning look. They must have had some kind of "discussion" about this already.

Mr. Quintera then glanced over our notes and nodded. "I can work from this, but you'll still have to talk about it on the stand. I'll start with some pleasantries to get you to relax."

Good luck with that.

"Then I'll ask about your relationship with the defendant."

He raised his eyebrow at me.

"Okay," I said again.

"This is a rehearsal, Bryn," he said.

"Brynnie," Dad said, "try to—"

Mr. Quintera shook his head at Dad and looked back at me, arms folded over the file. "Can you recall for us the first time Mr. Oliver assaulted you?"

"Um—"

"Would you tell us exactly what happened?"

"I—"

"That's about how fast the questions are going to fly at you. Not necessarily from me, but from defense counsel."

"You mean *his* lawyer?" My heart tried to rip my chest open.

"She'll cross-examine you, but don't get too worked up about that. She isn't going to try to tear you apart like you see on TV."

That didn't help.

"She's just going to test your memory. See how credible you are. Don't worry about it. I'll object to anything that's out of line. Are we okay?"

Nothing about this was okay. Especially if—

"Do you have any questions?" Mr. Quintera's eyes swept over all of us.

"I do," I said. "Is Preston going to be there?"

He obviously didn't share Mim's philosophy about stupid questions. He all but said, "Du-uh."

"Yes," he said. "The accused has the right to face his accuser."

I couldn't help looking straight at my silently fuming father. I wasn't the one doing the accusing. Let Dad face Preston. Let him have his reputation smeared all over the Internet. Let me go home.

Mr. Quintera tapped the folder against his trouser leg and shrugged at Dad. "We're near the top of the queue but I can't tell you how long we'll have to wait. We just have to be ready."

Then forget it, I thought as we followed him toward the courtroom doors. Because I'm never going to be ready. Never.

CHAPTER ELEVEN

We didn't have to wait long *enough* as far as I was concerned. I didn't have a chance to either process or mentally escape, and Mim barely had time to start massaging my shoulders when we were called to the front by someone droning, "Docket number blah-blah-blah. People versus Preston Oliver."

Moving through a blur of near panic, I sat at a table in front next to Mr. Quintera with Dad and Mim behind us. A lady judge in a square hairstyle and half-glasses barely looked at any of us from her throne on high. In fact, nobody was paying much attention to anyone else until Mr. Quintera finally looked at me closely. For the first time he seemed to have a soul. His eyes were olive green. I stopped chewing the inside of my mouth off.

"How are you doing?" he said.

What was it he said I was supposed to be? Vulnerable and what else?

"You'll do great," he said.

I wasn't convinced of that, and I was sure he wasn't either.

"Mr. Oliver is charged with four counts of simple assault," the judge was saying, "and one count of aggravated assault." She looked over the top of her glasses. "Will all those who are here to testify please raise your right hands?"

Who else was there to testify? I looked back and saw Officer Day and the other policeman with the shaved head. I also saw Preston.

He sat at a table on the other side of the aisle, wearing a blue button-down shirt that I'd never seen on him before and a smirk that I *had* seen. A smirk that put him above everything around him. Including me.

I looked away before he caught me, and I put my hand to my mouth. I was going to throw up, right there in front of the judge.

"Bryn," Mr. Quintera whispered to me. "Raise your right hand."

I did. While we all swore to tell the truth, I felt sweat fill every one of my previously frozen pores. A trickle worked its way down the center of my chest, which I was already clutching with my left hand to keep from retching.

"You can put it down now," Mr. Quintera said. "And take some deep breaths. Here we go."

In another blur I found my way to the stand. At least it was enclosed so no one could see my legs convulsing. At least there was that.

And at least Mr. Quintera now looked a little less like I was the most clueless witness he'd ever had to question. He actually smiled as he asked me to say my name and how old I was and what school I went to. I answered in a voice frail as a cobweb, keeping my eyes away from Preston. They caught on a face on my side of the courtroom. A face that told me, "Nobody can do this, and then we just do it." If only Mim could be squeezing my hand—

"I'm just going to ask you a few questions, Bryn," Mr. Quintera said.

Although I never would have thought it, our "rehearsal" in the hall kept me from completely falling on my face as I stumbled through my answers. So did making the list with Mim. I closed my eyes and saw it, and then I spoke it in mumbles and stutters. I got through without puking or forgetting who Mr. Quintera was and who I was.

"That's all, your honor," Mr. Quintera said. To me he whispered, "You did great."

His eyes said I actually hadn't, but I didn't care. I only cared that I was done. I even started to get up, but the judge said, "You may cross-examine, Ms. Dorchester."

Who was Ms. Dor—

The part I'd forgotten crashed in on me as a petite woman with a precise brunette bun and stilt-like heels came toward me.

"Good morning, Ms. Christopher," she said. "How are you?" That must be the "pleasantry" Mr. Quintera talked about. It didn't sound pleasant at all. It sounded like she couldn't have cared less how I was.

"I'm fine," I said, and then moaned inside. That wasn't what I was supposed to say. I was messing this up already.

"Good to hear. I'm Kayla Dorchester, and I'm representing Mr. Oliver. I'd like to ask you a few questions, just to clarify some things."

She seemed to be waiting for me to say something, but she hadn't asked a question yet so I just stared at her. Right at her, so that I didn't have to look anyplace where Preston might be.

Yet even as I forced my eyes to stay on the lawyer's lipstick, my mind raced to everyone else who was probably out there, ready to "get me." Was that girl sitting with Preston's mother going to hack into my school records? What about that guy slumped in the back row? Was he planning to feed arsenic to Copper?

"Ms. Christopher?"

I jolted in the seat. The lawyer's eyebrows were arched and waiting.

"The date of the first time Mr. Oliver allegedly assaulted you?"

Mr. Quintera stood up, fingering his tie. "Objection. Asked and answered."

"I don't recall hearing an exact date." Ms. Dorchester gave me half of an expectant smile.

"I think it was April fourth," I said.

"You 'think'?"

"I'm pretty sure."

"That's all right. Details can be hard to recall exactly, can't they?"

"Yes, ma'am," I said.

Out of the corner of my eye, I saw Mr. Quintera burying his forehead in his hand.

"You've said Mr. Oliver — Preston — grabbed you, another time he shoved you —"

"Your honor," Mr. Quintera said, though I had no idea why.

Ms. Dorchester waved him off with her small hand and licked her already shiny lips. "But he didn't ever punch you in the face?"

"No, ma'am."

"Try to choke you."

"No, ma'am."

"Knock you unconscious?"

I didn't answer. She was moving to the other side, toward Preston, so that if I looked at her I had to look at him too. I kept my eyes locked straight ahead.

"Did he ever knock you unconscious?"

"No, ma'am," I said to the back wall.

"I'm going to ask you to speak up a little, Ms. Christopher," the judge said.

I nodded silently.

"Do you play any sports, Bryn?" Ms. Dorchester said. "May I call you Bryn?"

"That's two questions," Mr. Quintera said.

It was?

Ms. Dorchester gave a stagey sigh. "Do you play any sports?"

"No, ma'am."

"What extracurricular activities do you participate in?"

I didn't see what that had to do with anything, but I said, "I'm in theater."

"Ah. An actress." She paused as if that was significant somehow. "Have you been in any productions lately?"

"Yes, ma'am. I played Ponyboy in a scene from *The Outsiders* for our school arts festival."

"*The Outsiders*." She moved closer to me. "I loved that book in high school. What scene did you do?"

"The one where the Greasers and the Socs have their huge fight."

"So you beat each other up on stage?"

"It just looked like it. We choreographed our stage combat."

"Did you have to rehearse a lot for that?"

"Every day for a couple of weeks," I said.

"Got banged up, did you?"

I could almost hear the trap I'd stepped into snapping shut.

"Answer the question, Ms. Christopher," the judge said, once more peering over her glasses.

"We wore elbow pads—"

"It's a yes or no question," the lawyer said.

I didn't have a yes or no answer, but everyone waited—Mr. Quintera with his face smashed against his hand, Dad cringing as if he were watching me fall off a cliff. Only Mim nodded at me, but I had no idea what I was supposed to say.

"Let me put it another way." Ms. Dorchester stepped briskly back toward Preston. I looked at my lap. "Did you ever fall down during a rehearsal?"

"Yes," I said, "but—"

"Did you have physical contact with other actors?"

"Yes, but they—"

"Boys?"

"Ma'am?"

"Were the other actors boys?"

"Yes."

"Were some of them this tall?"

Before I could stop myself, I turned toward her. She stood next to Preston, her hand above his head. I glued my gaze to it, but I could still see him—face tilted curiously, arm slung across the back of the chair, cool eyes expecting that, as always, he'd get his way.

"I guess so," I said.

"You're not sure?" Before I could speak, she shook her head and smiled. "Those details can be so hard to remember, can't they? Try this: were any of the actors you performed stage combat with as big as Preston Oliver?"

I was so immobilized I couldn't even close my eyes. I could only stare at Preston while he stared back at me. Slowly, one side of his mouth came up and then the other. It was the smile he'd given me a hundred times. "I've got you," it said. "I've so got you."

Ms. Dorchester flicked impatient eyes to the judge. "Your honor—"

"I don't remember," I said.

She stopped, hand still in the air. I thought she was going to keep pushing me, but she just patted Preston's shoulder and said, "Nothing further, your honor."

The judge told me I could step down, but I was already out of my seat. Somewhere between there and the table, I heard her honor say she found probable cause to bind the case over to trial. At that point I said to Mr. Quintera, "I'm going to be sick."

Mim took me by the arm and in the last blur of the day got me to the restroom. From outside the stall, she said, "Just let it all go, Bryn."

If only I could.

*

I'd wished that I could be sick, and now I was. But it still wasn't the debilitating disease I'd longed for to get me out of surfing. I could come out of smallpox with a few scars and everybody's admiration without a whimper. But as I half-crawled to my bedroom chair from another bout with the dry heaves and pulled all my hair in front of my face, I was sure I would never come out this cave of shame, and if I did, nobody would want to come near me. I was toxic—I could feel it coursing through my soul.

I leaned forward to sink my face into my lap and my foot slid on the RL book I'd tossed on the floor that morning. The talking book.

I pushed out a moan from my middle. Why was it that the only "person" who understood what I was thinking was made of leather and paper?

Mr. Quintera didn't get it. He said he wished I'd told him about the stage combat so he could have coached me on how to handle that. He'd put his hands on his skinny little surfer hips and told me I was going to have to be more open with him.

Dad seemed to think I was losing my lunch every five minutes because Vanessa Woodhouse and Mr. Quintera were too hard on me. All the way home he'd just kept looking at me in his rearview mirror and asking me if he needed to pull over. I heard him ask Mim, under his breath, if he should take me to a doctor.

Mim herself was quiet. Just when I'd thought maybe she did know what I needed, she appeared to run out of ideas. Her praying and hand squeezing and hot bath hadn't kept me from blowing my whole testimony. Maybe she was giving up on me.

So who else did I have besides this book that read my mind and answered questions I didn't even ask?

With Copper watching disdainfully from the back of the chair, I put it in my lap, shook back my hair, and opened the cover. It did the same thing as before: flipped itself to a page and let it sigh down and stay there. I was watching myself—and I knew I wasn't making this happen, wasn't imagining that the words said:

So you're back. Good. I have another story for you.

I narrowed my eyes at it. I supposed it was going to tell me this one was true too.

They're all true. Truer than anything you think you believe right now.

That was safe, because the only thing I currently believed was that I was stupid.

Yeshua came back from Gerasenes, which was where he was going when they hit the storm at sea. You remember?

I found myself nodding.

Although he delivered a guy there from a swarm of demons, they weren't so happy with him in town, so he returned.

Why hadn't I gotten to hear *that* story?

It's not what you need at this point.

And like everyone else, you think you know what *I* need. Just so you know, they don't. My dad doesn't, or I wouldn't have just been humiliated in front of an entire courtroom. Preston never did, or my life would not now be the fifth circle of Hades.

I felt like I'd just thrown up again. I sat there, clammy and shaky and wet under the eyes. I didn't know what I needed either, so who was I to say which story to read? The page didn't have to pull me. I just went back to it.

When Yeshua got there, a crowd was waiting for him. That mass delivery of demons wasn't the first big feat he performed. People were coming to see him in droves. This particular day, a man named Jairus—

The book got quiet.

What? Why did it stop pulling me?

I just thought you'd like that name. Anyway, Jairus pushed his way to the front, and people let him because he was the president of the meeting place. Just think of him as anybody who seems to have it all together. Somebody who would totally lose his big-man-on-campus status if he had to reach out for help.

I could definitely think of someone like that.

Jairus fell down at Yeshua's feet and begged him to come to his house. Right there, in front of people who had never seen him so much as ask somebody what time it was, he was pleading, saying his twelve-year-old daughter was dying. She was his only child and he was desperate to save her. Yeshua said yes, he'd go with Jairus, which meant they both had to make their way through the mob of people, none of whom were budging because they wanted to get close to Yeshua and see this person who could apparently perform magic.

I had to admit, I would have been right there with them.

There was a woman in the crowd that day who had a different reason to be there. She wasn't just a groupie who wanted to witness some woo-woo-magic. She needed serious healing. She suffered from female issues—too much bleeding, probably something to do with her uterus or her ovaries—

Got it. I'd been known to watch the Discovery Health Channel.

She'd spent just about every penny she had on doctors—some of them quacks, some of them just clueless about what could be wrong with her—and she was still bleeding and in constant pain.

So, major cramps. I could relate. I could also picture her there, trying to avoid being hit in the stomach by elbows, while Yeshua moved out of her reach.

Exactly. She got that he was going to help a dying child. She didn't want to stop him. She just thought if she could touch him, she might be healed. The thing was, she didn't want anybody to know she was there, since she was considered "unclean" because of the bleeding. Even her own family couldn't touch her or they'd be "unclean" too. So, anyway, she managed to squeeze in behind Yeshua and just graze her finger-tips against his shirt. Just like that, her hemorrhaging ceased. Yeshua stopped moving through the crowd and said, "Who just touched me?" No one owned up to it. Pete, one of Yeshua's friends, said, "Y'know there are over a hundred people pressed in here. Of course somebody touched you. They all want to touch you."

I thought that too, but I was more interested in the poor woman. I could feel her palms starting to sweat.

Yeshua kept sweeping his gaze over the crowd, who were just blinking at each other. "Seriously," he said. "Someone touched me. I felt the power going out of me."

Huh. So that *was* what happened. He *did* have powers. You said this was true?

That's what I said. The woman must have realized that it was only a matter of moments before he'd know who did it, so she dropped to her knees in front of him—as people who believed in his power tended to do—and she poured out her whole story with a bevy of strangers looking on, hearing every word about her bleeding and her desperation and her sudden healing. She didn't seem to care that everybody heard all her private details. She was cured, and she now knew something the rest of them didn't know. At least not yet.

Know what, exactly?

The book ignored me.

Yeshua said, "You took a huge risk coming here and trusting me. Now you're not only healed, you're whole. Go. Have a full life."

I sat back and pushed the open book toward my knees. There it was again: the trust thing. After today, I trusted people even less than I did last time Yeshua said it.

But then I hadn't really come across anyone with mystical power either. *That* I might be able to put some faith in.

I shook my head, hard. What was he going to do? Smack down fake-smiled lawyers right in the courtroom? Reprogram my father's brain? Take me away to a place where I didn't feel like I should have a trash bag over my head? If I had that physical illness I longed for instead of this "disease" everybody seemed to think I had, *that* he might heal me from. If he was for real. And if he was, where *was* he? I was so confused—yet I slid the book back to me and let it pull me to the words.

While Yeshua was still talking to the woman, somebody from Jairus's house wove his way through the crowd and touched Jairus's shoulder. He said, "Your daughter has died. I'm sorry. There's no need to bother the Healer with it now."

That seemed a little cold to me, but he had a point. I felt bad for the little girl, but Yeshua couldn't be in two places at once. I might actually trust him if he could do that.

Yeshua overheard and he said, "Don't be upset. Just trust me—it's going to be okay." He went into Jairus's house where relatives and friends were already crying over the child. Losing an old person is one thing, but a twelve-year-old ... This was a tragedy of the first order. But again, Yeshua said, "Don't cry. She isn't gone. She's just asleep." Even in their grief, people laughed, probably bitterly. They'd felt for a pulse that wasn't there, heard the last breath rattle out of her, seen her eyes suddenly lose their life. But Yeshua just took her parents and three of his friends into her room and pressed her limp little hand between his and said, "Sweet baby girl, get up."

You're going to tell me she did, aren't you?

Oh, yeah. She sat up in bed and breathed and giggled and complained that she was hungry—all the things a lively pre-adolescent girl does. Yeshua told her parents to get her a snack, but of course they were so busy kissing her and hugging him, they barely heard him. He knew any minute they were going to fly out of the room and shout to everyone what just went down, and he had to warn them.

About what?

He didn't want them telling anybody at all. "Just let them believe she was only asleep," he said. "Don't say I brought her back from death."

I didn't get that.

Neither did they.

So are you going to explain it to me?

Yeshua will explain it to you.

"When?" I said—out loud—because I knew I was losing it, so what did it matter?

When you're ready.

"How will I know?"

Because you'll trust him.

"How can I? I don't even know him!"

Exactly.

"I don't even think he's real!"

Then there's your trouble, isn't it?, the book said.

And then it went silent. The words of the story I'd just read were still there, but without the book's answers to me. The page wouldn't turn. No tide pulled me in.

I squeezed it. I shook it. Nothing.

This was insane. I'd always believed in the power of the supernatural, and then I lost that. No more visions. No more sense that I was protected. Now I had a book talking to me, and I wanted to throw it across the room. This wasn't the other-world I thought was there. How could I trust it if it didn't reveal itself to me?

I didn't let the book drop over the edge of the chair this time. I shoved it. And then I got up and marched to my bathroom and stared at the face in the mirror I barely recognized as my own anymore.

"This is stupid," I said to that strange girl. "There aren't any mists of Avalon or vampire lovers or lords of rings. It's time to grow up."

Growing up must have meant you couldn't cry anymore, because I went the bed and lay there staring, dry-souled, at the ceiling.

CHAPTER TWELVE

My suspicion about Mim was confirmed when she woke me up early Friday morning to go surfing. She *had* run out of new ideas. She was falling back on the old ones.

Didn't some famous person say one time that insanity was doing the same thing the same way and expecting different results? Fine. So we were both nuts.

I did have to admit as we pulled up to the Surf Shack that as soon as I got palm-clammy-nervous about getting back on a surfboard, I forgot to get nauseously terrified about getting back on the witness stand. Since I could use a little forgetting, I marched into the Shack ahead of Mim and grabbed my board so I could wax it.

"Dude, who peed in your Fruit Loops?"

I glared around the board. Goof took a step back, hands up in surrender on either side of his bush of bleached-out hair.

"Just kidding," he said.

"No, you're not," I said. "I'm in a bad mood. Sue me."

He looked as surprised as I was. Where had *that* come from?

"I get it," he said. "PMS."

"Goof—shut up."

We both turned to look at Shaun. He was standing in the doorway in only a pair of board shorts, shortboard under his arm, droplets of water sparkling on his chest. A V-shaped chest tapered to a firm waist at the bottom and broadened to toned shoulders at the top. He wasn't weight-lifting-cut like Preston, but—

I swallowed down a bunch of bile and looked away, but not before I saw Shaun squint at Goof. "Who says that to a girl? Dude, you are remedial."

"What?" Goof said. "What'd I say?"

I only moved out onto the porch with my board so I wouldn't have to hear an instant replay of the conversation. I fumbled to get the surf wax out of my shorts pocket, and then froze at the thought of Redhead pulling in with his camera any minute, and then wished all guys would fall off the face of the earth so I would never be able to be stupid over one ever again—

"Hey."

I jumped and had to grab my surfboard so it wouldn't topple off the porch railing.

"Sorry about Goof," Shaun said. "He's a moron."

"Most guys are," I said.

I did *not* just say that, did I? The temperature of my cheeks told me I had. So did the grin that sprang to Shaun's face.

"A moron wouldn't have waxed your board for you," he said.

I stared down at my bumpy surfboard and then back up at him.

"Is that okay?" he said. "I didn't mean it like, 'oh, she's a girl, she can't do it like a guy' ..."

"No! It's ... thanks. Seriously." If I stammered that much onstage a director would replace me with Porky Pig. I looked at the bar of wax on the palm of my hand. "I guess I won't be needing this, then."

I went for my pocket but the bar dropped onto the porch floor. We both squatted down at once to get it, and our heads touched. When we looked at each other, we were close enough for me to see the centers of his Hershey's-Kiss eyes.

Eyes that suddenly turned cold and hard in my mind. Preston's eyes, making me think they saw something beautiful in me—and then slapping it away. Eyes that wouldn't let me pull back and run.

"Oh, sorry," said a voice from the doorway. "Why don't you guys go ahead and get a room?"

Shaun flipped his gaze back at Goof. I fled inside, nearly tipping Mim over on my way.

"New sunscreen," she said. She put a tube in my hand as I broke for the dressing room.

I barely got there before the real shakes started—the wracking ones that came from the inside out. I sank to the floor and squeezed the tube against my chest. Okay, okay—it was probably a case of, "I have to be nice to her because she's a customer with a grandmother who has a lot of money." That was all it was. So why was I huddled in the corner in a fetal position as if Preston himself were after me?

Because he was. And maybe I was never going to be able to trust anybody ever again.

The thought was so nauseating I almost went for the bathroom. But I was sick of being sick. Of boys making me hurl myself headfirst over a toilet. So instead I wriggled out of my shorts and pulled off my long-sleeved T to apply sunscreen to my arms—because Mim said thin cotton only had a sunblock factor of about 8. Even in a state of freaked-out-ed-ness I felt a flutter of surprise. Most of the bruises had faded, and the ones that were left blended with my freckles. I stuffed my shirt into my bag. Yeah, I was sick of being sick.

The minute I got to the door I regretted it. Mim was sitting on the porch steps and Shaun straddled the railing. There wasn't a grin anywhere within a city block.

"I'm sorry it didn't go better," Shaun said to her.

"Well, we learned a lot, I think," Mim said. "Please keep on—"

"Count on it."

I backed into the shadow of the doorway. Count on what? On him thinking of me as a "battered teen" like everybody else now did?

What I could count on was having that label for the rest of time. The easy target. The one you could probably get to do anything you wanted—or the girl who was too emo for anybody but a shrink. Clearly Shaun was "protecting" me from Goof only so I wouldn't go mental in the Surf Shack. Thank you, Mim, for spreading my new reputation.

"The waves aren't that good in here," Goof said from the counter. "You actually have to go down to the beach."

"Shut up," I said.

With a deep breath I stepped out onto the porch and picked up my board. With another breath I hauled it down the steps past Mim and looked back at her and Shaun.

"Are we going surfing or what?" I said.

I took off for the alley, board under my arm. Mim had to jog to catch up. Once she did, she kept quiet, though I knew she was looking at me. Of course she was. I was her project. That had to require a lot of concentration.

When we got to the beach and I kicked off my flip-flops with a vengeance, she removed her sunglasses and looked at me some more.

"What?" I said.

"I'm liking this anger," she said. "I'm liking it a lot. Let's go surfing."

Fine.

I pointed my board out to sea and walked into the water with it, sliding it over the waves that came at me, the waves I was totally sick of. At waist deep, I turned with the board and looked back like I actually knew what I was looking for.

Mim dove through a breaker and swam to my side. "Good job," she said. "Are you ready to—"

"Yes," I said. "Just tell me when."

Her eyebrow twitched, but she simply turned and studied the incoming swell.

"How about this one?"

"Fine," I said.

I flopped onto my belly on the board and gripped the sides at the middle. I could feel my toes dipping just off the back. In my mind I saw what the whole thing was supposed to look like: The nose of the board peeking just above the water. My arms straightening as I pushed onto one knee—no, skip that. Just me popping right up to a stand and firing straight for the beach. Then I'd be done. At least there would be one battle in my life that would be over. At least there would be that.

"Okay," Mim said. "It's your wave."

I nodded and let the roiling foam take me forward. It was one thing to envision it, but doing it was something else. I knew that even as my board steadied and I pushed up, even as I popped like a spring and found myself standing—left foot forward, right leg back, but facing sideways with my bare, free arms catching the air.

"Oh—my—gosh!" I cried out to the sun and the wind and the crystal drops that sprayed my face. "I'm doing it!"

I was still doing it when I reached the beach—surfing and squealing and shouting to anybody and nobody, "I did it!"

"Yeah, you did!"

Shaun was suddenly there, arm raised, high-fiving me.

"You were awesome," he said. "Seriously, that was a classic surfer's pose."

In spite of myself I smiled up at him with face muscles I hadn't used in weeks.

"I totally had no idea it was going to feel like that," I said.

"Well, yeah. Nobody can describe it. You just have to feel it."

"I did!"

He grabbed my hand again and pulled it up and shook it like I'd just boxed my way into the world heavyweight championship. I managed to get it away from him just as Mim, standing calf-deep in the water, clapped and then whistled through her teeth.

It was a magic moment. I decided to let it be that. There had been no magic for so long, I could at least let this one last until it blew away on its own.

"Who's that coaching you?"

I turned around. A girl about my size, maybe even smaller, was standing beside Shaun. He dropped my hand and took a step sideways so she could join us. A blotch of red appeared on each of his cheeks.

"Who is she?" the girl said. She looked up at Shaun, spilling her reddish hair back over her shoulders and catching the sun in it. She moved like light.

"It's my grandmother," I told her. I might as well. I was already losing cool points by the second.

She watched, hazel-eyed, as Mim emerged from the water. "She's a pro, right?"

"Oh, yeah," Shaun said, and proceeded to give her Mim's complete surfing resume—stuff even I didn't know.

I took that opportunity to size the girl up. Her eyes were huge and so was her smile *and* her teeth, which were so white they were almost blue. She looked like a girl in a milk commercial. Wholesome. Except that she had a body in her neon-yellow bikini that made Jennifer Aniston look like your middle-aged math teacher. It struck me that her figure was kind of like Mim's in that sixties surfing picture, only tinier. But her size didn't keep her from looking like she could seriously kick your tail if you crossed her.

Which was why I took several steps backward. I so did not need her thinking I was making a move on Shaun. Especially when she grabbed his arm and said, "Introduce me."

"This is Bryn—"

"No, moron—the coach."

She nodded toward Mim, who had almost reached us, and then she startled back to me.

"Not that I don't want to meet you too." She rolled her enormous eyes. "I'm such a geek. Is it Bryn?"

"Yeah," Shaun said. "Bryn, this is—"

"Fielding Hyatt," she said, only she was talking to Mim.

"Windy Paiana." Mim continued to look at her as she slung her arm around my shoulder and pulled me in. "You were superb, Bryn."

"Yes, she was," Fielding said. "And I've seen you teaching her so I know how far she's come." The big eyes came to me. "No offense—I mean you *were* amazing just now—"

"You've already blown it, Fielding," Shaun said, his grin back. "Move on."

She did, right to Mim. "I want you to coach me too. I'd pay you of course—that's not a problem."

For the first time, in my experience anyway, my grandmother didn't seem to know what to say. That obviously didn't bother Fielding.

"I already know how to surf. It wouldn't be basics."

"So what's your goal?" Mim said, but she immediately shook her head. "I don't want to compete with the local surf shops. They have instructors, and I don't like taking their business."

Mim looked at Shaun, and Fielding spurted out a laugh.

"I'm so not going to learn anything from Shaun. Have you actually seen him surf?"

She laughed again and leaned against Shaun, who gave an even bigger grin and said, "Nice."

113

Fielding pulled herself away from him, and her cute face sobered. "I'm serious, Grandma Windy. I would love to learn from you. I won't even take up that much more of your time." She flung a hand toward me. "You could work with both of us at once."

The corners of Mim's mouth twitched. "You really need to work on that shyness issue, Fielding."

"I know. It's a problem. So will you?"

Mim ran her hand across my shoulder. "How would you feel about that, Bryn?"

"Ma'am?" I said. I was still back on Fielding calling her "Grandma Windy."

"Would that work for you?"

"It would be a blast," Fielding said to me. "I just moved here and I don't know that many people—and it's like, here you are—somebody I can relate to."

"I tell you what," Mim said. "Let me talk it over with Bryn, and then maybe we can see if my coaching style matches your learning style—"

"It will. I totally know when somebody's miles better than me, and I totally listen." She leaned toward us, away from Shaun, and said in a loud whisper, "Not like guys."

"Like I didn't hear that," he said.

Fielding rolled her eyes at me. I found myself kind of liking her.

"You know what, Mim?" I said. "I'm fine with it. Go ahead and coach her."

"Yes!"

Fielding did an adorable little happy dance and then stuck her hand out to shake Mim's. "Thanks, Grandma Windy. Is it okay if I call you that?"

My grandmother looked at me.

"Call her Mim," I said.

"I love that. So—do you want to watch me right now—Mim? See what I can do?"

"No," Mim said in a voice that allowed no argument. "Bryn's time isn't up."

I started to say that was okay, but I really did want to try to get up again. Fielding shrugged happily and turned to Shaun.

"Go get your board and I'll show you how it's done."

"In your dreams," Shaun said. "I gotta get back to work."

He walked back up the beach, but Fielding didn't seem to notice he was gone. As Mim headed out to the water, Fielding looped her arms around mine.

"Thanks for doing this," she said. "I know I come on, like, strong, but I'm not going to be all competitive with you or anything."

I laughed out loud.

"I'm totally serious. Besides …" She wiggled her velvety eyebrows. "There's only one person I want to show up out there, and he isn't you."

"Is that why you want Mim to coach you?"

"That's part of it. And I can't pass up a chance to work with somebody like her. Do you have any idea how lucky you are?"

I nodded but I wasn't thinking about my luck. I was actually thinking about Shaun's. If Fielding worked as hard as Mim was going to make her, his surfing luck was about to run out.

Too bad I couldn't care less about that.

*

"I think I know what I did wrong on the sauce the other night," Mim said to me that evening. We were in the kitchen again, making another attempt at burritos. The woman was obsessed. If these turned out as bad as the last ones, I wasn't going to be able to blame my upset stomach totally on nerves.

"I looked it up online," she said. "The trick is to cut the canned sauce with another can of tomato sauce. So what did you think of Fielding?"

I was getting used to Mim's sudden changes of direction. Whichever way she went it was still straight ahead, and it was pointless not to go with her.

"I liked her okay," I said. "She's a little pushy, maybe."

"A little? The girl's a bulldozer."

I laughed and accidentally spit into the chicken.

"Don't worry about it," Mim said. "A little saliva can only improve on it. I was just like her at that age."

"At that age?" I said—and then went straight to a ten on the blushing scale. What was wrong with me today?

"Am I to infer from that you think I'm still that way?"

"No, ma'am!"

I looked up to find her eyes twinkling. "Then what *were* you implying?"

"You aren't like that now," I said slowly, into the pile of chicken bits. "But you were when, you know, we visited you in Hawaii. But, then, I was just a kid—"

"And I was obnoxious."

I started to disagree but she was shaking her head at me. She tapped the wooden spoon on the edge of the pan and set it on the counter so she could stick her hands in the pockets of her cargo pants.

"I don't know how anybody stood me, Bryn, to tell you the truth," she said. "I had an ego the size of the Atlantic. Make that the Pacific. And I flattened anybody who couldn't roll with me. I know I flattened you."

I fiddled with the knife.

"It's all right to say it, Bryn. You need to say it."

"Why?"

"Because you need to see that your feelings count. That not everybody you disagree with is going to attack you for it."

I looked up at her, because her voice was thick, the way it was the day at the courthouse. Those eyes, so filled with tears, weren't going to hurt me.

"Okay," I said. "I hated being at your house. You tried to turn me into something I wasn't."

"And there is nothing worse that a person who supposedly loves you can do to you, is there?"

I shook my head.

"You need to say it out loud."

"No, there isn't," I said. "But everybody ends up doing it."

She came to the stool next to mine and sat down. When I didn't look up, she took my face in her hands and lifted it to hers. "Who, Bryn? Who has tried to make you into someone else?"

"Preston," I said between my teeth. "His friends. Dad."

"Really."

"I think Dad wants me to be a fighter, like Tara would be if this were happening to her." I felt my own eyes fill. "But this would never happen to Tara."

"We don't know that. Nobody's immune to abuse." Mim dropped her hands to my knees. "What about me, Bryn? Do you think I'm still trying to change you?"

I tried to look away again, but I couldn't. "I'm never going to be a surfer like you."

Her eyes widened. "Do you think that's what I'm doing when we're out there?"

"Isn't it?"

"Oh, Bryn. I'm not trying to turn you into somebody else. I'm trying to help you set yourself free so you can be all that you are. You could get there oil painting or horseback riding or dancing your heart out, but the only thing I know how to teach you is surfing. It's what I do." I watched her swallow. "If you're not enjoying it—"

"I am now—after today. But—do you think it's working? Am I getting free?"

"You're the only one who knows that."

The door creaked open and Copper streaked from nowhere across the kitchen to meet Dad.

Dad ignored him. His eyes seemed hollow, the lines around them deep and hard.

"News?" Mim said.

He nodded. "Bad news."

My stomach oozed toward its knot.

"Will Quintera called. Preston turned down the plea again." Dad put his hands on the back of his neck. "We're definitely going to court. Now, Bryn—"

"Do we have to talk about it?" I said. "It is what it is, so what's the point?"

He blinked at me and then at Mim. She patted my legs and went back to the stove.

"I don't think this sauce is any improvement over my last attempt," she said. "Anybody up for a pizza?"

I didn't know what had just happened, but I was glad it had.

CHAPTER THIRTEEN

The weekend wouldn't have dragged like it was hauling a ball and chain behind it if Mim and I had gone surfing. How ironic was that? A week before, I would rather have consumed large quantities of her burritos than hit the waves again. But Saturday morning it depressed me as much that Mim *wouldn't* give me lessons when the beach was crowded as it had when she'd dragged me out of bed to do it every weekday.

All right, so I would still have more wipeouts than good rides, but at least when I was out there trying not to drown, I wouldn't be thinking about everything else that was trying to take me down. I could do something to improve my surfing. I couldn't do a thing about any of the rest of it.

And yeah, I was bitter that Shaun was being more than decent to me only because he felt sorry for me. But even though I couldn't trust him, at least it wasn't because I was afraid of him. Too bad he looked hot in a pair of board shorts.

And, okay, Fielding was — what did Mim call her? — a bulldozer, but she seemed to accept her own flaws, so she might accept mine too. I was afraid I was going to start watching *Wheel of Fortune* if I didn't spend some time around people my own age.

But the biggest reason, the one that broke me into sweats and had me drinking Pepto-Bismol right out of the bottle, was that getting out of the house might keep me from looking at the text messages that were constantly beeping on my cell phone. If I wasn't in the same room as my computer, I wouldn't be able to check the blog where people were planning the end of my future.

There were just too many people in the water on Saturdays

and Sundays, Mim said. And I wasn't ready to surf in the remote locations where the locals went. So there was nothing left to do but let the battery run down on my phone and lock the charger and my laptop in Tara's room, which didn't have a key to it. I was that desperate to pretend that nothing was going to happen—that Preston and his followers' threats were all just words on a screen.

I was awake before Mim on Monday morning, swimsuit on, marinating in sunscreen.

*

Only Goof was in the Surf Shack when we got there. His hair was all sticking out like a lion somebody had just awakened from a nap, and he looked at me as if I was the one who had done it. I picked up my board and headed for the door.

"You got me in trouble the other day," he said.

"That's my new career," I said.

"Shaun says I have to be nice to you."

I stopped, half in and half out of the doorway. "Who died and left him in charge of me?"

"That's what I'm saying."

"If you don't want to be nice to me, don't be nice to me."

"Yeah. Well, no." Goof's forehead twisted into a question mark. "What are we talking about?"

"We're talking about I don't want anybody pretending they like me when they don't."

"Who said I didn't like you? I actually think you're pretty hot."

"Shut up, Goof," I said.

He smiled a smile that matched his name.

I was still trying to figure out, as Mim and I worked our way out beyond the breakers, why I could talk to Goof like I actually had a backbone. I almost missed it when she said, "You're ready to paddle and catch your own waves."

"What does that mean?" I said.

"It means I'm not going to do all the work for you anymore." Her eyes sparkled within their sun ray of lines. "You're going to do some real surfing."

I was a little deflated that what I'd been working so hard at was fake surfing, but I nodded. She laughed.

"What?" I said.

"Bryn, you might as well say what you're thinking, because it's written all over your face anyway. You thought you *were* surfing—and you were. My bad."

My bad? She'd been spending way too much time with Shaun.

"You're just going to feel like you're more in control of it now, that's all." Mim drew her mouth into a line. "And I definitely think you're ready for that."

I had a feeling we weren't just talking about surfing. It dawned on me at that moment that maybe we never had been.

She explained that I needed to learn to sit up on the board while I was waiting for the waves so I could see them coming. As she started to give me the steps—get on my belly, then grab the sides and push my torso away from the board and scoot my butt forward a little—I expected to dump myself the way I'd always done when I was moving on to the next thing. But I managed to get the board dead level with the water and me sitting on top of it with my legs over the sides.

"Impressive," Mim said. "Most people go over at least three times before they get the hang of it. The only thing tippier than a canoe is a surfboard."

"I don't get how I'm supposed to see the waves coming when I'm faced away from them," I said.

"You aren't. You have to turn toward them to watch and then get changed to the opposite direction when you see a wave you want. And you have to do it fast or the wave will pass you by." She wiggled her eyebrows. "I'm going to teach you to pivot."

I wasn't so impressive learning how to do that. I was supposed to shimmy back until the nose of the board rose out of the water. Naturally, I toppled all the way over backward. Once I got that I shouldn't move too far to the rear, it took me about ten tries to learn how to pull with one hand, let go with the other, and then yank on the board. The nose was supposed to instantly pivot around. Evidently, nobody told the board that.

"This thing didn't get the memo," I said after my ninth attempt.

"You're in charge," Mim said. "Show it what to do."

I did. The board pivoted. But I forgot to re-level it and went over the side. I came up laughing.

On the eleventh try I did it. I wasn't done, of course. Mim told me to get prone, because we were going to paddle shoreward to where the waves were breaking. When we got there, finally, there was a lull before the next set of them started to stack up on their way in. Mim told me to face them, sitting on the board.

"What do you think of this one?" she said.

"It's big!" I said.

"Do you think it's yours?"

"I don't know!"

"You don't want one that's going to break on top of you."

It actually looked pretty safe. I looked at Mim, who nodded. I pivoted the board and got prone.

"Okay—paddle!" Mim cried. "Paddle like a mad dog and stop when the wave hits you!"

It was going to hit me? I couldn't *not* paddle, arms pumping on either side of the board like the rest of that pack of mad dogs was after me. When did she say I was supposed to stop?

Ridiculous question. The wave jolted me hard from behind and I went from zero to sixty before I could gasp for the next breath.

"Stand up!" I could hear Mim shouting behind me.

Oh, yeah. Stand up.

Still hurtling toward the beach, I pushed myself up and jumped to my feet. For five exhilarating seconds I was surfing—until I slid sideways and ate a mouthful of seawater. Still, I couldn't remember ever feeling that way before. Like the ocean and I were friends and she was letting me ride her. I did my thing and she did hers, and we rocked.

"Don't you need a rest?" Mim said when I paddled back to her.

"I'm just getting started," I said.

I wanted to paddle way out just past where the white water started breaking so I wouldn't get clobbered waiting for a nice one. So we did. I sat on the board while Mim showed me how to get a sense of what the waves looked like just before they broke and how long it took for a wave to first rise up, then tumble over. We counted how long that was and then how long it took me to get to my feet.

"I have to stand up faster," I said.

"And you can," she said.

I sized the waves up after that. Some I tried to catch too soon and exactly nothing happened. They lifted me and left for the beach without me. One I rushed and caught too close to breaking. It crashed on me while I was still lying on the board paddling and pushed my face to the deck.

"I know what I did wrong!" I said to Mim before I was even done spitting and choking. "You don't have to tell me."

"I wasn't planning on it," she said. "You're on a learning curve."

As she herself would say, *You think?*

I got to my feet on the rest of the waves I tried. On one I went down in the mother of all pearls. On another I just made it to standing when the force of the breaking wave knocked me sideways. I finally figured out that the best way to get a good ride was to paddle like I was ticked off at something and get way out ahead of the wave before it broke.

So as I hauled my arms through the water, both at the same time as Mim suggested, I thought of Kayla Dorchester, attorney-at-law, trying to catch me in a trap. Of Regan, pulling out her friendship like a rug. Of Andrew, setting me up for Preston. Of Preston himself, smirking across the courtroom aisle as if he had already won. I rode the Preston wave the best. All the way to the beach.

Fielding and Shaun met me there.

Shaun had on a Surf Shack tank shirt with his shorts — drat — but Fielding was in a lavender one-piece and carried a gleaming white shortboard under her arm. Her huge hazel eyes were talking as excitedly as she was.

"Okay, Mim *is* an awesome teacher. I mean, look how much you improved in, like, an hour."

"You were watching the whole time?" I said.

I was looking at her, but the question was for Shaun. I wanted him to say no. He didn't actually say anything. He smiled, but it didn't make it all the way to his chocolate eyes. Ugh — men.

"Yes, I was watching," Fielding said. "And I'm not messing with you or anything—you're a fast learner. We totally need to go surfing together, like, just for fun."

I started to say that I wasn't ready for that, but she darted off to meet Mim before my grandmother could even get out of the water. She was babbling something about Mim being as good a teacher as Dorian Paskowitz—whoever that was.

"She doesn't have to butter Mim up," I said to Shaun— because it felt awkward not to say *something*. "She's already decided to coach her."

"You don't mind?" Shaun said.

I really looked at him for the first time. I'd been right—he wasn't his usual grinny self today.

"No," I said. "Do you?"

I had no idea why I'd said it. I was already shaking my head as Shaun shook his.

"She's not going to take lessons from any instructor around here," he said. "Not that any of us would want to take her on." The grin did kind of appear then. "She's high maintenance."

That sounded like the voice of experience. So they *were* going out. I suddenly felt a little guilty that, in a way, I was helping Fielding show him up. Weird dating situation. Of course, the only dating situation I'd ever been in wasn't about showing somebody up. It was about shutting somebody down.

"Did you just slip off to the Caymans or what?" Shaun was grinning all the way at me, and then he pointed to the surf. "Looks like Fielding's going to show Windy what she's got."

Mim was standing on the shore, hand shading her eyes, as Fielding paddled out. It was a good thing she had no intention of competing with me, because the way she looked, taking the waves like a duck—I knew it was nothing like the way *I* looked when I was panting and paddling to get out there. Laughter bubbled up my throat.

"What?" Shaun said.

He tugged at my hand and pulled me to sit on the sand beside him. My laughter froze. So would Fielding's when she found me next to her boyfriend. I scooted away, aware that it looked like I thought he had cooties. I was such a mess.

He didn't seem to notice, great pretender that he was. This guy really was too sweet to be for real. All of them probably were—

"There she goes," he said.

Fielding was already astride the crest of a wave, riding it as if she had tamed it. Tiny as she appeared, with her whipping red-gold hair the biggest thing about her, she had harnessed an energy that still scared the spit out of me. The wave zippered, slick and sparkling, breaking one piece at a time, and she sliced down its angle as if she were skating on glass. I wasn't sure I'd ever seen a person do anything more beautiful.

I glanced at Shaun to see if he thought so too.

He was grinning the same way he grinned at everything. "She's such a little show-off," he said.

It didn't sound even a tiny bit insulting. Yes, definitely too sweet to be true.

I watched Fielding whistle down the wave as if she were willing it to keep whistling along with her. She stayed on its face not like she wanted to outrace it, but like she was one with it. It was all I could do not to clap.

"You could totally do that," Shaun said.

"Me?" I said. "Seriously? No."

"Why not? You've gone from kook to catching your own waves in—what—a week?"

"Eleven days."

"But who's counting, right?" Shaun eyes were shiny again, like they were looking for the next fun thing. Like maybe I was it.

I moved an inch farther away.

Fortunately, at that moment, Fielding hit the beach chattering to Mim. I wasn't sure what to do with Shaun's shining eyes, except to get away from them before Fielding saw us. I didn't want any more people hating me.

"I'm going back in," I said, and escaped into the ocean with my surfboard in front of me.

*

By the time we got home and I had retreated to my room with a Mim-made raspberry smoothie, my brain was in a braid.

One strand was Shaun, being all sweet because I was the

124

wounded victim. And me wishing there were guys you could actually trust. And if there were, that they looked fabulous in surfing shorts.

The second strand was Fielding, going after Mim's approval but acting like she wanted me as her friend too. I longed for a girl connection, but why did it have to be with the girl whose boyfriend was practically hitting on me in the name of—whatever it was he told Mim she could count on? It was a recipe for disaster. I'd had enough disaster.

The third strand? That was the one that said "Do you really think you can have normal friendships and everyday, stupid teenage angst when an entire pack of powerful people is planning to attack you? Do you actually believe surfing and a love triangle are going to distract you from people stalking you and threatening to take you down?"

It might all be locked behind Tara's door, but I could still see it in my head. The minute I hit the chair, smoothie in hand, the waves and the surfboards and the sitting side-by-side on the beach all washed out to sea and left me alone with my fear again.

Except that I wasn't alone. I could feel the presence of something in the room. At first I thought it was Copper, but a quick search revealed that he wasn't under the bed or behind the curtain or curled up inside the wastepaper basket. Then I thought somebody might be hiding in the closet or the shower, waiting to spring out on me. I even broke into a sweat across my upper lip as I tiptoed around and flung open doors to find nothing but clothes and shampoo bottles. It wasn't until I returned to my chair that I realized it was the RL book.

Even as I reached for it I could feel its pull on me. In spite of all my vows to give up my fantasies, I took it into my hands and sensed—what? That it wanted to talk to me? Again?

It had before, there was no denying that. It had spoken to me after the hearing. And since then, hadn't things changed maybe a little?

"Am I being stupid?" I said out loud. I wished Copper were there so I could pretend I was talking to him and not this lifeless book that seemed to have some kind of power over me. Except that it didn't. No, it didn't.

I opened it, determined to read what I wanted to read. The pages didn't chatter over each other and pick a place for me. No words tugged at my eyes. So far, so sane. I ran my finger down the lines and stopped at what looked like the beginning of a story. Okay, no question and answer. Just what was actually there.

Yeshua went up to a mountaintop, I read, in my best academic-sounding mind, *and he took three of his follower-friends with him—Pete, of course, and Jimmy and Jon, the Zebedee brothers.*

I still dug the names.

Yeshua was praying, and his friends fell asleep. Could have been the fatigue from climbing the hill, late party the night before, whatever—but they stretched out in the sun for a nap and almost missed it.

Missed what? I was still trying to picture a mysterious Yeshua stopping to pray during a hike. Where were the guys like *that*? I'd promised myself I wasn't going to ask any questions out loud, but they popped into my head. The story went on as if I hadn't interrupted it.

They almost missed his face taking on a glow like God was shining directly on him. His clothes shimmered with a light almost too bright to bear. And suddenly there were two men there talking to him—men who shone even more vividly and exquisitely than he did.

And they were ... ?

Elijah and Moses.

Baby-in-the-bulrushes Moses?

It was one of the few stories I remembered from my total of about thirty minutes in Sunday school. That and something about ten commandments.

It was an awesome thing, the three of them together. When the other guys woke up—Pete, etc.—they couldn't wrap their minds around it. It probably wasn't even so much seeing Moses and Elijah, who, by the way, was a famous prophet. They were more blown away by the sight of their Yeshua, transfigured.

I could actually feel my nostrils flaring as I glared at the book. All this time, I hadn't caught on to who Yeshua was. Somebody who'd actually paid attention in church probably would've picked up on it from the first page, but me, Little Miss

Dream-in-the-Pew, I was clueless until that very minute that the hunky Yeshua—was Jesus.

The hope drained out of me like bathwater, and I sat there shivering, naked in an empty tub.

Yeshua was Jesus. Duh. Healing the sick. Bringing little girls back from the dead. Even I should've known that. But, oh, no, I got sucked into believing maybe there was some *person* with power who I could trust.

I actually shook my head. Nuh-uh—I couldn't trust Jesus. Not the Jesus who had come to me at Young Life and then never shown up again. Where was he when I was being beaten up? When I was being harassed by my so-called friends and humiliated by adults who basically called me a liar?

I looked down at the page. Once again I'd been gullible. Once again it was my own little fairy-tale mind that made me think there was something more than just the mess I could see in front of me. Even after I told myself I was going to grow up and get over it, I'd been pulled back into my own fantasies.

But no more. I slapped RL closed and held the covers together. It didn't try to open itself.

Of course it didn't, because all of it had been me, making something happen because I wanted it to be true.

What about now?

I stared at the battered front cover. I didn't see "What about now?" etched into the leather with the other stuff. I hadn't even been looking at the thing when I heard it—in my head—in a voice mine but not mine. A voice whose silence closed in on me until I had to whisper, "What do you mean, what about now?" *You wanted a vision. I've given you more than one right here.*

I hurled myself out of the chair and paced across my room. I had the book pressed to my chest, but I couldn't tell whether I was holding it or it was holding me. Neither one of us was letting go.

"Just tell me this," I whispered. "Am I losing it? Is it because of all the stress?"

There was no answer. Just a gentle pulling from the book, another current tugging me back to the chair and into its pages. I was shaking so hard I could hardly do it. And yet the minute

I sank into the seat and the cover fell open, I stopped. And I breathed. And I let my eyes go to the words.

You have ears to hear. You wouldn't know my voice if you weren't meant to. Listen.

It was all right there on the page, and yet it was as if it whispered in my mind as well. I was afraid if I didn't hold on to it, if I didn't cling to every word, I would be lost.

"Okay," I said. "But I'm scared."

Of course you are. So were the disciples. So is everyone who truly hears it, because it's hard.

Thanks for that.

Another story?

I sucked in a breath, and then I nodded.

Yeshua—that was Jesus' name in Aramaic—started off on his final journey to Jerusalem with his followers. There was something about the group that attracted people even if they weren't familiar with all the things he'd done. When people see a good thing, they want to get in on it. One guy said, "I want to go with you, wherever you go." Yeshua didn't soft-pedal his answer. He said, "You ready to rough it? Because we're not staying in five-star hotels, you know." Sometimes HE would ask someone they met to follow him. Most of the time he got replies like, "Sure, but let me go take care of my father's funeral." Yeshua would say, "You know what? You need to be thinking about life, not death. We don't have a minute to waste—we've got to let people know that the time to live, really live, is now." Another guy said he'd go with, as long as he could take care of business at home first, maybe pay a few bills, lock the place up, stop the newspaper delivery. Yeshua said, "You can't put this off until it's convenient, and you can't look back. God's putting his kingdom together now. Forget what you think you have to do from the past, and be part of what's ahead."

I hesitated, thumbnail between my teeth as I sawed away. That sounded sort of like what I'd wanted to do at first: forget all the stuff that was happening to me and go to a higher place. Was that what it was talking about? If you were a Christian you could do that? I thought back to Young Life—to Andrew and Regan and Preston. None of them were doing it, that was for sure. The inside of my mouth went bitter, but the book pulled me back to itself.

Not everyone got it, but a lot of people did follow, and they learned, and they grew, and they were healed. But just so you know, the disciples didn't have any more mountaintop experiences for a while. It was hard core. The good news is that's what they learned the most from.

I stopped sawing at my fingernail and slapped my hands onto the open book in frustration. Hadn't I had enough "hard core" already? Hadn't I already figured out what there was to be learned from it?

It was painful to even swallow. What exactly had I figured out that made any sense? To stay away from guys for the rest of my life no matter how nice they seemed to be? To trust absolutely no one—not parents, doctors, lawyers, so-called friends? That left me so cold I shuddered. I'd thought today was kind of a turning point, but maybe it wasn't. My mind was churning white water and I couldn't get away from it.

And then the book grabbed me like a riptide and swept me back to it. There was nothing to hold onto to keep from drowning in my own confusion but the words themselves.

No one "figured it out." They just followed. And they knew.

"You're telling me to follow Jesus. Really." I didn't give it a chance to answer. "How am I supposed to do that? Tell me and I'll do it—I swear I will!"

I've given you the first steps.

There was nothing more. I couldn't turn the page ahead. Almost frantically I dug back through the story for everything Yeshua—Jesus—had said.

You ready to rough it? ... Think about life, not death ... Don't put this off until it's convenient ... You can't look back ... Forget what you think you have to do from the past and be part of what's ahead.

It wasn't a lot to go on as far as I was concerned. But what else did I have?

I let the book sigh shut and tucked it carefully into the cushion of my chair, where I held its spine for a long moment.

"I hope you're right," I whispered. "I seriously hope you're right."

CHAPTER FOURTEEN

Dad came in that night while Mim and I were loading baked potatoes and told us the trial date had been set for July 5. Twelve days away. I tried not to think about the number of blog posts that were probably coming in that very moment behind Tara's closed door, and focused instead on why Dad always had to bring us nauseating news when we were about to eat supper. He was a walking diet program.

"Are you going to be all right with this?" Dad said.

"I don't know," I said.

That evidently wasn't the answer he expected or the one he wanted, because he sagged on the stool he'd sat on across from me and gave me a faded look. He seemed older by the day.

"What I mean is, what can we do to help you get ready?" He put his hand up. "Besides drop the charges."

"Then you can't help," I said. "Has anybody seen Copper?"

"Brynnie—"

"Seriously, Dad, this is like the most awful thing I've ever had to do, and you can't make it any different unless—" I glanced at Mim, who was spooning salsa onto Dad's potato but watching me. What was it she had said—something about a sea change? "I have to be, like, transformed into a totally different person for this to be 'okay,' and nobody can do that *for* me, so let's just not talk about it, okay?"

Mim turned away with the salsa bowl, but I caught the small smile in her eyes.

"Windy," Dad said. "What do you think?"

"I'm not sure that what I think makes a whole lot of difference," she said with her back to him.

"It does to me."

If I'd actually been eating instead of just poking at the sour cream, I would have choked. Dad must really be desperate if he was actually asking Mim for her opinion.

"All right then." She turned around. "Bryn's right. You can't change the waves that are coming at her — they've already been set in motion. All we can do is help her choose which ones she should go with and which ones she needs to let pass on by. The goal is for her not to let any of them knock her down and wipe her out."

She looked at me, eyebrows up, like she was waiting for me to tell him the rest. I just wasn't sure what the rest was. All I could think of was *Think about life, not death.* Wasn't that what the book said? Did it actually make sense?

"Have we given you enough help, though, Brynnie?" Dad said. "I don't feel like I have. I feel like you and I have just fought every step of the way."

"So let's not fight anymore," I said. "I mean it — let's just talk about something else. Has anybody seen Copper?"

Mim gave me a long look before she glanced back at the counter. "He hasn't come in for his dinner."

A pang of fear went through me. "I'm going to go look for him," I said.

Dad caught at my wrist as I passed him on my way to the back door. His hand felt thin. Come to think of it, he must have lost ten pounds in the last two weeks. The eyes that searched mine were sunken into their sockets.

"Brynnie," he said.

"We're okay, Dad," I said. "Really."

I wasn't pretending. The desire to scream that he was a horrible father for torturing me this way just wasn't there anymore.

The air was thick-hot when I stepped out onto the back porch. Even that close to the ocean, five thirty in the afternoon could be like a sauna in Virginia Beach. Which was why it scared me that Copper would be outside. Not only was it his suppertime, something he wasn't one to miss, but he was usually stretched out over an air-conditioning vent the minute the temperature hit eighty degrees. We were way beyond that.

"Copper?" I called to him in my kitty voice — the one that sounded like a little old lady. "Kitty-kitty-Copper..."

I peered under the porch and behind the garbage cans in the gravel beside the garage and under the wheels of Dad's Tahoe in the driveway. Those were his favorite spots from which to observe the world and reach out and grab unsuspecting legs, but there wasn't a trace of his orange fur.

I crossed the front yard and looked down the sidewalk, although I didn't expect to see him. Copper knew that he had a good thing going as the son of a veterinarian. He never left the yard. At least not of his own free will.

A chill shuddered through me in spite of the breath-sucking heat. The threats — they were real?

I strode back toward the front porch. There was no way. If somebody who wasn't me or Dad had tried to pick Copper up, they would have left a blood trail. He'd scratch a stranger's eye out if they got within claw's reach.

"Kitty-kitty-Copper?" I called again.

I was answered with a low growl from somewhere.

"Copper?"

This time the growl was louder and more indignant. It was definitely him — and he either had a bunny cornered or he couldn't get out of wherever he was stuck.

Wobbly with relief, I called him again and followed his angry reply to the azalea bushes that bordered the front of the house. They were tall and thick and nested in deep piles of pine needles, and I had to crawl on my belly like a reptile to even see him. A pair of yellow eyes, narrowed nearly to slits, glinted at me. The message was clearly, "What took you so long?"

"Come on, kitty," I coaxed him. "Let's get you in the house."

He didn't budge. The growl went deeper, as if he were suffering the worst of indignities.

"What's wrong?" I said. I pushed some low branches aside, not easy with my mother's fertilizer-fed bushes, and scooted in so I could see his whole body. He didn't appear to be hurt, but when I put my hands cautiously around his hind legs and pulled him toward me, I could only move him about two inches. He was caught on something.

"What in the world have you gotten into?" I said.

He gave me an "It wasn't my fault" yowl, and in the next second I saw that he was telling me the truth. Both hind legs were tied like a calf's to the trunk of the azalea bush with a black cord. A surfboard leash? From the looks of the pine needles in front of him, he had obviously tried to claw his way out. And from the looks of his left thigh, he'd even resorted to chewing on himself.

"Poor baby!" I said. "Oh my gosh."

It took some doing to get him untied, and I had to endure his panicked raking at my neck to get him out under the bushes. Only then did I see the envelope duct taped to the cord. On the front, in red Sharpie, was the five-letter word they'd called me on the blog. Under that it said "Drama Queen Christopher" in parentheses. It dug into me more sharply than Copper's claws.

I stuck the envelope into my shorts pocket and hugged the still-squirming cat against my chest. I forced myself not to look over my shoulder for some lurking Audi or Mustang and hurried straight around the house. But I stopped at the back door.

If I went in there now, Dad and Mim were going to know something was wrong. Like Mim said, whatever I was thinking was usually written across my face. And if I told them about this, I'd have to admit that I'd been getting threats I *hadn't* told them about—and Dad would want to go to the police—and we would be fighting again. That was one wave I'd already let pass by.

Find out what it says first, I told myself. *Maybe it's just another you-better-watch-out warning.*

I opened the door, dropped Copper inside, and headed for the gazebo in the backyard. It was shielded from the house by a line of dogwood trees. If I did become momentarily hysterical, Mim and Dad wouldn't see me.

Huh, I thought, as I took the two steps up and perched on the curved bench out of the scorching sun. At least I wasn't convinced I was going to lose it completely the minute I opened the envelope and stared at the computer type.

And then I almost did. "Dear"—five-letter word again—it said. "Are you the stupidest bimbo on the planet? You're actually going ahead with this trial? Can you say 'perjury'? They put people in jail for telling lies on the witness stand," five-letter word yet again.

I turned the paper over on my lap and squeezed my eyes shut. Every time I read that word, it was like being punched in the stomach one more time. I wanted to tear the thing into small pieces and toss them over the fence.

But the note burned against my bare knees, as if it contained something I'd better read. Not because I was a masochist. Because I had to know what wave was coming at me next.

I turned it over again, wiped the sweat beads from under my nose, and read the remaining lines. "You obviously haven't believed any of our warnings, or you would have dropped the false charges by now. We're through threatening. We WILL take you down. Maybe your cat won't be so lucky next time. Maybe your family won't either. But there is no maybe about you. Whatever you think is going to happen to Preston, is going to happen to YOU. Believe it."

I crushed the paper into a ball in my fist and sucked in hot air and the mocking scent of honeysuckle. What *did* I think was going to happen to Preston? That even if the judge sentenced him to jail his father would get him out of it somehow? Yes. That everybody was going to believe he was a coward and a brute and an abuser and never speak to him again? No. Nobody was going to believe that, because he was Preston Oliver. He would have his way no matter what happened in that courtroom.

I felt my hand fall open. As I looked down at its smashed contents, a strange kind of relief came over me. They couldn't make me suffer any more than I already had. They already believed I was a drama queen and a liar and that five-letter word. What more could they do to me?

So it was already behind me. Was that what the RL book meant? That I could forget what I thought I had to do from the past and be part of what was ahead? Was that it?

So what was ahead? Was it just the trial—or was my life more than that? I couldn't see much farther ahead than Mr. Quintera and Ms. Dorchester and the judge with the square haircut. But still I straightened out the paper and tore it and tore it until it was confetti—the envelope too. Before I went into the house, I dumped it all in one of the garbage cans. And then I forced myself not to look back.

For the next four days, it did seem like I'd left my fear of Preston and Company in the garbage cans. I surfed with Mim and Fielding every morning, and even though Fielding handled her shortboard like a pair of ballet slippers and shot through menacing curled waves as if she was using their energy on her own terms and never seemed to even take a tumble, much less wipe out totally, I really didn't feel like a complete kook next to her.

In the first place, Fielding wouldn't have that. As driven as she was to show up Shaun, she was all about encouraging me, sharing her sunscreen and board wax, asking me for tips on where to shop and how to do her hair, and quizzing me on whether Goof was actually a moron or just a jerk who liked messing with everybody's head.

There was plenty of time to discuss those topics, because she went to lunch with Mim and me every day, and twice came home with us afterward to watch movies and paint toenails. I thought Dad was going to cry when he put it together that I actually had a friend over. If he had, there *would* have been a fight, because I had chosen not to tell Fielding about the trial and I was pretty sure Shaun hadn't. I was trying to look ahead, way out in front of that.

Besides, I was making surfing progress of my own. I learned to take a real surfer's stance—mostly by practicing on the ground behind the Surf Shack first, with Goof hanging out the back door making oh-so-witty remarks and me telling him to shut up. By Wednesday I could jump to it in a heartbeat at the exact second I caught the wave. By Thursday I could control the board instead of feeling like it was taking *me* for a ride. It felt like a piano sounds when someone runs their hand all the way down the keys.

I started learning how to angle, which meant I had to figure out where to turn to keep surfing instead of always going straight and running out of the slick, smooth part of the wave. While Fielding was having her one-on-one time with Mim, I sat on the beach and studied the surf. That wave was a closeout, not good for angling, nothing to gain. That one peeled off nicely—oops, no, it closed out. That was where Shaun found me, mumbling to myself, at almost noon on Thursday.

He sank into the sand beside me and parked his forearms lazily on his propped-up knees. He was wearing his sunglasses but I could still see the brown eyes shining behind them. I felt myself quivering, but I didn't scoot away. At least not physically.

"She's working on her backside," I said, and then, of course, blushed all the way down the front of my swimsuit. "You know, like in trim—with her back to the wave—"

"Who?" Shaun said.

"Fielding."

Any other guy would have said he'd been trying to work on Fielding's backside for quite some time, but Shaun shrugged.

"I actually came down to talk to you," he said.

"Oh," I said, using all my most-impressive vocabulary.

"You want to go surfing Saturday?"

That left me with absolutely no vocabulary whatsoever. I recovered before my chin could drop to my chest.

"What about Fielding?" I said.

I thought his shoulders sagged. "I guess she could come," he said. "But I was thinking just you and me."

"I don't understand," I said.

He knitted his eyebrows like he didn't either. "Like a date—you know, do some surfing, have some food, hang out."

"I thought you were going out with Fielding."

I had never seen anybody look that relieved. His face fell into its grin, and he leaned his head back and laughed so loud he scared off a seagull, which takes some doing.

"Fielding and me—no," he said. "I told you, she's high maintenance—and way too competitive."

"I got that part," I said. It was tempting to tell him why she was out there with Mim, but since I'd put my foot in my mouth up to the ankle already, I kept quiet.

"So, yeah, I just thought we could spend Saturday together. I have it off since I have to work the whole Fourth of July weekend. You up for that—or did I just make a total fool of myself?"

All I could do was stare at him, until the grin slid from his face. "I did," he said.

"No ..." I shifted my stare to my toes. Now that I knew he and Fielding weren't together, he looked better than ever in those board shorts. Not to mention the grin. The basic lack of macho-ness. The tinge of respect. The niceness —

That was it. The niceness.

I looked up at him. "You don't have to do this," I said.

"Do what?"

"Ask me out."

"Why would I 'have to'?"

"Because you feel bad for me because of what's going on and you want to fix me." I tried to smile, although I was sure I looked like a rotting jack-o'-lantern. "Don't feel bad — there's a lot of that going around."

"I have no idea what you're talking about, Bryn."

My heart took a dive that surprised me — since I thought it had already dipped as far as it could go. Why couldn't even the good ones tell you the truth?

"What?" Shaun said.

"I heard you and Mim talking the other day — that Friday after the hearing. She asked would you keep doing what you were doing for me, and you said you would."

"What hearing?" he said, and then he put a sandy hand up. "Wait. All your grandmother ever asked me to do was pray for you. I asked her if you were okay one day, and she said you were just going through a tough time. I said I'd pray."

"Pray."

"Yeah. She told me that Friday that something hadn't gone the way y'all wanted it to, and I said I'd keep praying."

I gazed out over the ocean where Mim and Fielding were bobbing in the water, hair soaked and slicked back, blurring in the tears that came to my eyes for no reason and every reason.

"It's none of my business what you're going through unless you want to tell me," Shaun said. "But I'm not 'nice' to you because I feel sorry for you." He tilted his head. "What's the other reason?"

"I'm sorry?" I said.

"That's not the only reason you said no." He picked up a piece of shell and poked it into the sand between his feet. "I'm not your type."

It would have been so much easier if I had just agreed with that. He would have gotten up and walked away and been hurt for seven seconds, or at least until the next girl noticed he gave new meaning to the word "hot," and I could have crawled back under my covers and been done with it. But I just couldn't say it, because that wasn't the reason. Yesterday, or maybe the day before, I could have said, "Look, *no* guy is my type, okay?" But something had changed—and now I was more confused than ever. That was why I blurted out:

"I don't think my father will let me."

At least that was true. Let me out of his and Mim's sight with the trial this close—and with a guy? If I even asked him he'd probably lock me in my room until July 5.

"He's pretty strict, huh?" Shaun said.

His shoulders were slumped again. I was starting to believe he really did want to go out with me. And for some reason, anger at Preston surged up.

Because he was taking yet another thing away from me.

"You know what?" I said. "Let me ask my dad. We might have to have Mim in the background or something—which would be stupid, I know, and you'd probably rather take somebody that doesn't have to be chaperoned, but—"

"Hey."

I looked up at Shaun. It was hard not to with his hand lifting my chin toward him.

"I don't care," he said. "You can bring your whole family if you have to. I just want to be with you."

It was hours before I realized that Shaun had touched me and I hadn't played dead like a possum. It was a small shimmer of hope.

*

"Absolutely not," Dad said. He dropped the bag of fish tacos on the counter and shoved it aside with the heel of his hand. "Out there on the beach on a Saturday—what's going to keep

138

the Oliver kid or his lackeys from harassing you? Or worse. No—and that's the end of it, Brynnie."

"I liked you better when you let Mom do all the yelling," I said.

"Well, your mother isn't here to do it. Although she and your sister are coming home for the trial. Let's celebrate that instead of fighting over this."

He reached for the taco bag.

"I'm not fighting," I said. "I just asked a question. What if Mim came?"

"What?"

"What if Mim came and surfed with us? I asked Shaun and he said that was fine."

"That may be 'fine' with him—"

"Dad, Mim is with me every day at the beach. I don't see what the difference is."

"He's a nice boy, Neal."

We both looked at Mim, who was setting a stack of paper plates on the counter.

"Nice has nothing to do with it," Dad said. "Who's going to protect Bryn if those kids gang up on her?"

She grunted. "Shaun has a better chance of doing it than I do!"

Dad hesitated, and I held my breath. But he shook his head and dug into the bag. "Going out with a guy is what got you into this mess in the first place, Brynnie."

Ire went right up my backbone—and I realized something that hadn't come to me until that moment. "No, Dad," I said through my teeth. "Going out with *that* guy got me into the mess. *This* guy is different."

"And you know this how?"

"Because I'm not as stupid as I used to be."

His mouth was already open with an answer, but I watched it stick on his lips. What was he going to say? *"Yes, you are still stupid"*?

"I'm not, Dad. I haven't been sitting around waiting to do the same dumb thing all over again. I've learned things."

"Like what?"

"Like what waves to take and—"

"Enough with the surfing talk!" Dad actually shot an accusing glance at Mim. "Just because you can 'catch a wave' doesn't mean you know how to handle a boy."

I looked, helplessly, at Mim. She was folding the wrapper of a now-naked fish taco, but her eyes were on me. They said, "This one's yours."

I turned my gaze back to my father, who was squeezing hot sauce onto his plate like he was wringing someone's neck. Was he right? Was I ready for this? Did I even know anything about Shaun?

My hands clutched the edges of the stool so I wouldn't sag. I didn't know Shaun at all. I hadn't spent that much time with him. I hadn't spent much time with anybody except myself—

Myself.

I spread my hands out on the counter and leaned in so that Dad had to look at me. "I've learned what I did wrong," I said.

"What you did?"

"I let it go on after the first time. That's what I did wrong. But I don't think every guy in America is like Preston." My shoulders came up to my earlobes. "I'm sick of feeling like they're all out to get me. Some of them might actually be like you."

Dad swallowed. His eyes watered, and he looked at Mim.

"You'll go with them, Windy?"

"No, I will not," Mim said. "I think that would be an insult to two responsible kids."

I wanted to tell her I would be happy to be insulted, but Dad closed his red-rimmed eyes and nodded.

"All right," he said. "But you will be home before dark and you'll call me every hour on your cell phone."

I stopped in mid nod. "My cell phone is locked in Tara's room."

"Why on earth?"

I felt a smile come to my face. "Because I know which waves are too much for me."

CHAPTER FIFTEEN

Fielding spent the night on Friday so she could help me get ready Saturday morning. We stayed up late talking, and I discovered that she'd done some theater too and that she liked cats—Copper decided he'd rather sit in her lap than mine, the beast—and that she, too, had felt lost and lonely and out of it when she first moved to Virginia Beach. We also spent a lot of time talking about Shaun.

"I totally knew he liked you the first time we watched you surf," she said. "I practically had to wipe the drool off his chin."

"No, you did not!"

"He's definitely a hottie."

I was suddenly uncertain, and I bobbed my straw up and down in the root-beer float Mim had made.

"What?" she said. "You have that look on your face."

"What look?"

"That look like, 'oh my gosh, I just did something horrible.'" Fielding snorted, as only a girl as cute as she was could do without resembling Miss Piggy. "Like you could even think of something horrible to do. So—what?"

"I just want to make sure," I said. "You don't like Shaun, do you? I mean, as a boyfriend?"

"Uh, no, he's definitely not my type. I mean, he's the real deal, but he's way too nice."

It was my turn to snort. "I don't think they can be 'too nice.' I did 'not nice' and it was evil."

"No kidding?"

Fielding rolled to her stomach on my bed and looked way too interested. Quickly I said, "It makes sense now. I didn't see why you'd want to show up Shaun if you were going out with him."

She shook her head. "Shaun's not the one I'm trying to show up. Trust me—this guy thinks he is all that on a surfboard and I figure the only way to handle him is to humble him a little."

"So I guess this guy is not 'nice,'" I said.

"He is on the inside or I wouldn't be dating him. Besides, he likes the challenge. He'd try to walk all over a girl like you—no offense."

I just shrugged. "I don't date guys who want to walk on me. I'd rather have one who doesn't even think that way."

"Then you've picked the right one." She squeezed my hand. "Tomorrow is going to rock for you."

*

It definitely rocked that Shaun picked me up in his army-green Jeep with the top down and looked Dad straight in the eye when he shook his hand and hugged Mim. We actually got out of the driveway without being reminded to be home before dark and to call in on the hour. Dad had gotten my cell phone out of Tara's room, but he said that calling just once or twice would be fine. Mim had reminded him that it was hard to make a phone call from a surfboard. I was loving her more all the time.

Shaun had classic rock going on the car stereo, but we talked over it as we cruised past all the spots that were going to be clogged with umbrellas and sandcastles by noon and drove south of the beach to a place Shaun said the locals went to surf. I stopped him before we climbed out of the Jeep.

"Do you really think I'm ready to go out there with real surfers?" I said.

"What are you, a virtual surfer?" he said.

"I just never surfed *with* anybody before, except Fielding."

"Here's the deal." Shaun turned to me and put an arm on the back of my seat. In spite of my little speech to Dad, I still tensed up. "Don't take off on a wave in front of anybody angling in your direction."

"Okay."

"If you're paddling out, the guy on the wave has the right of way. That basically means you have to get out of his way, not the other way around."

"Got it."

"The big-time surfers don't come here, but if anybody gives us attitude, we'll go someplace else. Okay?"

I smiled at him. He grinned back.

That went on all morning. The breeze was blowing off the shore into the shiny faces of blue-green waves. Their spray arched like diamonds off their tops when they broke and I was riding just ahead. I smiled at Shaun when we squealed ourselves onto the beach. He grinned back.

I charged down the line of a peel-out wave and looked up and saw a gull flapping beside me, enjoying the ride with me. I finally got the hang of the backside turn and Shaun cheered me on. He took a ride that had everything in it a wave could do—and he surfed it as if he and his board were in love with each other. I watched in pure awe—and kind of envied the board.

Through it all we smiled and grinned and laughed. There were other surfers out there, but I gave up every wave to them until one guy said, "Go ahead. This one's yours." Most of the time, though, it seemed like it was just Shaun and me, and I liked it. I liked it more than I thought I would.

"Mim told me I had to feed you or I'd hear about it from her," Shaun said at one point.

The sun was directly over our heads by then, and I realized we'd been surfing for two hours without stopping. My stomach realized it too and growled at me like Copper.

"I know," I said. "She packed us a lunch. But just so you know, it's probably all healthy stuff. Carrot sticks, guaranteed."

Shaun wiggled his eyebrows, which sparkled with sea drops. "I took care of the unhealthy stuff."

We spread out a blanket he pulled from the back of his Jeep and I unpacked the cooler Mim had put together. She surprised us. Amid the crab salad sandwiches on kaiser rolls—which Shaun moaned ecstatically over—and the inevitable carrot sticks, she'd sent chocolate chip cookies from our fave bakery, which I moaned over. There was also a note in there for me. *Hope you're having an awesome time*, it said.

I realized that I was.

Shaun handed me a Kit Kat bar, already unwrapped, and wiggled his eyebrows. "I won't tell Windy if you won't."

"She'd have to torture me," I said. I took an oversized bite and chewed happily.

"That's another thing I like about you," Shaun said.

Bring on the blushing.

"You're not, like, all worried about every mouthful you take, like it's going to go straight to your thighs. I hate it when girls ask if they look fat."

"Uh-huh," I said, and popped the rest of the candy bar into my mouth.

"I don't know—you're just different." He dropped back onto his elbows.

I couldn't help myself. "How?" I said, mouth full.

"You don't drag your baggage into everything. Mim told me you were going through a tough thing and I'm down with that—I've been there. But you deal with it." He tilted his head at me. "You're mature for fifteen."

By now, I was wishing I'd helped myself and not asked. Okay, so I hadn't brought my baggage down to the beach with me, but it was still packed and waiting for me at home. He had no idea what was in there. And I wanted to keep it that way. Part of me crawled back under the covers.

I called home like a good daughter and was reapplying sunscreen like a good granddaughter when Shaun gave a grunt that didn't sound happy.

"What?" I said.

He was still stretched out next to me on the blanket, propped up by his elbows, and he pointed down the beach with his chin. "I've seen these guys down here before. Talk about a 'tude."

I didn't like the shadow that passed over his face. It passed over me too, so I didn't look where he was still slanting his chin.

"Do we need to move someplace else?" I said.

"Maybe not. It doesn't look like they're here to surf. That's a good thing."

"Why?"

I offered him a cookie but he shook his head. He was still watching whoever it was from behind his sunglasses.

"They're okay surfers," he said. "But they jump line out there in the lineup—get in front of the really good locals, take their waves—I mean, everybody messes that up sometime, but these guys do it on purpose and act like Daddy owns the beach." His face relaxed. "They're not staying. Cool. I'd have to get all up in somebody's dental work if they said anything to you."

"Me?" I said.

"They hit on any girl that looks like you do in a swimsuit." He grinned at me, the best grin yet, the one that melted me inside said swimsuit. "Not that anybody looks like you do in a swimsuit."

Too bad I had on so much SPF 40, or I could have blamed the blushing on a sunburn. In the interest of saving myself from stammering like an idiot, I turned to look where Shaun was watching the 'tude surfers' departure.

And then I froze. The guys striding off the beach like Daddy owned it were a guy with red hair and mirrored sunglasses—and Andrew—and Preston.

There was no mistaking the sun-bleached blond heads on those two, or the swimmer's shoulders, or the Billabong board shorts. Even that might have been my imagination torturing me if it hadn't been for the arrogance that surrounded them like a swarm of flies—or Preston turning his head and boring his cold silver-blue eyes right into me.

I jerked my own head away, so hard I heard my neck crunch. But I wasn't fast enough. I knew before I could even pull my eyes from his hatred that he'd seen me. And that it hadn't been an accident.

"Bryn?" Shaun said. "You okay?"

"Huh?" I said. It was all I could get out. My heart was pumping in my throat.

"What's wrong? Did one of those guys do something?"

"What? No." Oh my gosh, yes, one of them did something. Again. And again. And again.

Shaun put his hand behind my head and pulled my face close to his, but I jerked myself away. Mim was right—and so was Fielding. I was sure it was all scribbled across my face, and I didn't want him to see that it said, I HAVE BAGGAGE AND THERE IT GOES UP THE DUNES!

But then, he didn't have to see it on my face. My body

screamed it as I crabbed away from him on the blanket and staggered to my feet and snatched up my board.

"I'm fine," I said, just the way Mr. Quintera told me not to. "Let's go surfing."

I hit the water before he did, but I couldn't concentrate, and it showed. I tried to catch waves that wanted to eat me up and did. I accidentally got in front of somebody who already had a wave and got called a kook by a twenty-something with eyes almost as intimidating as Preston's. When I got to the beach, Shaun was frowning at the sky.

"There's a storm coming," he said. "We should go."

I was sure the gathering clouds weren't going to dump on the beach for at least another hour, but I nodded. We hadn't smiled or grinned since Preston left the beach. I might never smile again.

All the way home I fought back the tears and the urge to tell Shaun everything. It was hard to let him think I didn't like him ... but I couldn't stand to watch him stop liking me when he found out I wasn't that girl he wanted to be with. That I had a ton of baggage I didn't deal with. Besides, he was like a wall in the other seat. My guess was he wouldn't have responded even if I'd poured out the whole stupid story. I'd basically shoved him away—and like every other guy on the planet, he wasn't going to forgive that.

"Thanks," I said when he pulled into the driveway. "It was a great day."

"It *was*," he said. "Look, Bryn, did I do something wrong?"

I was surprised, but I shook my head, harder than I had to. "No," I said. "Seriously—it's not you."

"Then what is it?"

"I can't," I said.

And before I could turn into even more of a drama queen right before his eyes, I bolted from the Jeep and ran—all the way into the house and into my room. My door closed on Mim calling from the kitchen, "How was it?"

It was the best day of my life, I screamed inside my head, into my pillow. *And the worst. The absolute worst.*

I scrambled for the RL book, which Copper vacated as I snatched it up. Choking on my own sobs, I flapped through the pages, and they let me. When I found where I'd stopped, I held the book out in front of me and read out loud.

"You can't look back ... Forget what you think you have to do from the past and be part of what's ahead."

I swiped viciously at my tears. "You said if I followed, I would know. You said if I trusted you I could move forward." I shook the book until the words jumbled. "Nobody will *let* me move forward, don't you see that?"

It didn't answer. I gave it one more cruel shake and flung it across the room, and curled into a sobbing ball on the bed. That was where Mim found me.

She let me cry for no longer than a minute before she wrestled me to a sitting position and held onto my shoulders. Her face was one big knot of concern.

"Bryn," she said, "breathe. Come on."

I tried, but my own inhales rattled my body. She kept saying it and I kept doing it until I could take in air without feeling like I was going to die. She propped pillows behind me and pushed me back into them. In another minute she had a glass of water in my hand.

"Well," she said as I drank on command. "I'm glad to see that finally."

"What?" I said. "Me having a nervous breakdown?"

"No, you getting some of that bottled-up emotion out of there. It was either that or depression. This is a lot healthier."

"It doesn't feel healthy."

"It never does. What brought it on?"

I didn't even consider not telling her. It all came out as she sat there pushing water on me and nodding and making understanding noises in her throat. When I was done, I felt like a piece of overcooked pasta. I handed her the glass and snuggled down farther on the pillows, and she covered me up with a throw.

She wasn't going to let me sleep, however, which was what I really wanted to do. Forever. At least until I was forty.

"Do you really think Shaun is going to think less of you because of this thing with Preston?" she said.

"I know he is."

"Huh."

"What 'huh'?"

"I don't think you're giving Shaun enough credit. Or yourself."

"What does that mean?" I said.

She set the glass on the table. "You were right when you told your father that you aren't as stupid now as you were when you were going out with Preston. Not that you ever were."

"I was."

She erased that with her hand and a scowl. "If you tell Shaun your story, it isn't going to come out like you're some clueless little masochist who *lets* guys whale on you. You're going to tell it like the young woman you are now—braver and wiser and stronger."

"I don't want to tell it at all. I just want to move on." I flung my hand in the direction of RL, which lay splashed against the baseboard. "Even Jesus says to move forward."

"Yes, he does."

I stared.

"But, Bryn, if you don't start talking about it to the people that matter, no amount of surfing or new girlfriends or new boyfriends is going to heal you. It's still going to be in there, festering, until you get on a witness stand and have to tell it to strangers who not only don't love you, they want to prove you wrong." She cupped my face in her hands. "Jesus moves you forward by moving you *through*."

I closed my eyes to stop my head from reeling. "I didn't even know you were a Christian," I said.

"I wanted to wait for the right time to bring it up. I think this is it." She pulled her hands away and settled herself into the pillows beside me. "When your grandfather Paiana died, I tried to start a surfing school for women in Hawaii. They weren't having it."

"Who?"

"The natives, basically. I was a Howlie—a nonnative—and I could live there if I wanted, but I wasn't worthy to teach what they consider to be their sport. I still tried it—because my ego was bruised, not because I wanted to help women learn to surf—and fell flat on my face in every way possible. I actually had to move away from the islands and go back to California. That's where a woman with terminal cancer introduced me to Christ. I don't think I would have accepted him if I hadn't been so far down." She tilted her head at me. "If I still thought I was in control."

I wriggled around to look at her straight. "Did it change everything?"

"Not like that," she said, snapping her fingers. "I had to study the Word—the Bible—be around authentic Christians, not the ones baptized in vinegar."

I snorted a laugh.

"And I had to learn how to worship. It all taught me who Jesus actually was—not some ethereal figure in white, herding sheep and carrying babies on his hip. He's very real to me—very gritty. And forgiving—heaven knows, I'm thankful for the grace. But he doesn't let me use that as a free pass. I'm always working on things with him. I have my cross to bear just like everybody else." She pressed her forehead to mine. "I'd love for God to make me softer, more like you."

I pulled away. "Don't do that," I said. "Don't do it. Then you wouldn't be the Mim I love."

I started crying again, but this time the tears were loose and free. I didn't feel like they were killing me.

"I just don't get what Jesus wants me to do," I said into her chest.

"I think he wants you to depend on him to pull you through this."

"Then why isn't he doing it?"

"Isn't he?" Mim straightened me up to look at her. "Tell me why you like Shaun so much."

I didn't want to talk about Shaun, and yet I did. She nodded me on like she knew that.

"I want to believe he's honest. I didn't think so at first—I thought he was just being nice to me because you told him what I was going through." I waved off her frown. "We got that worked out. Anyway, I tried to think of him as just like Preston and Andrew and every other jerk—but I really do think he's real."

"Talk about that."

"I don't know—with Preston it was more like a fairy tale that never got to the happily ever after, because he looked like a prince and pretended to be a prince, but he was the evil wizard or something."

"I see that. Go on."

"I didn't even like him for very long. I just didn't want to fail at being his girlfriend. I didn't want to give up the dream, even though it was never going to come true." I blinked at her. "I really was stupid."

"Don't go there with me," she said. "What about Shaun?"

"I don't have a dream with Shaun. It just is what it is. He's really funny and cute—he really is cute."

"Adorable."

"And he's always telling Goof to shut up when he says stupid things to me, instead of laughing with him like most guys would. He said he prays. 'Course, Preston said that too, but only because he knew it would impress me." I blinked hard. "And I guess I like who I am when I'm with Shaun—and now I've—"

"Before you go there—who are you when you're with him?"

"Not, like, afraid I'm going to say something wrong every minute. I feel kind of pretty around him. Not like I have to look like ever other girl he looks at." I felt a shadow pass over me.

"What?" Mim said.

"But am I really that person? Can I be with this thing that's happened always hanging over my head?"

"Yes," she said, with old-Mim, don't-argue-with-me firmness. "But only if you don't try to pretend it didn't happen. Why don't we pray about this—see what Jesus has to say about it?"

"Okay," I said. I was suddenly self-conscious.

Mim pulled me into a hug. "Oh, Bryn, I love that tell-the-world face of yours. We don't have to be 'good' at praying. We just have to do it."

And she did it, as if she were talking to a person who had all the answers and was going to give them to us—in time—and with love. Sometime after the amen, I fell asleep in her arms.

CHAPTER SIXTEEN

I woke up the next morning, Sunday, to the ringing of the land-line from someplace that seemed far away. It turned out it was me who was far away. Mim was there in a moment handing me the phone.

"It's Fielding," she said. "She sounds like she's about to pop."

She was. I had to hold the phone away from my ear to protect my hearing health.

"Okay," she said, instead of hello. "You know the guy I told you about, Mr. Not-Nice?"

"Uh-huh." I watched Mim go out the door and wished she'd stay and take this while I at least went to the bathroom. Speaking of being about to pop . . .

"Okay, so, he's going to meet me on the beach at Seventeenth Street today, and I am going to knock his board shorts off. Well, not literally. You know what I mean."

"Uh-huh," I said again. I swung my legs out of the bed. "Good luck. We'll be thinking about you."

"I want you to do more than that," Fielding said. "I want you to come. I need the moral support."

"You're gonna rock," I said, sidling my way into the bathroom.

"I know, but I'd feel better if you and Mim were there. I'm serious."

"Really?"

"Yes. I've got, like, the worst case of nerves ever."

"Okay," I said, "let me ask Mim. But first can I go to the bathroom?"

"Oh—yeah. Take a whole bath if you want. We're not meeting until eleven o' clock, which is—an hour from now. And Bryn?"

"Yeah?" I said.

"You are the best. I want to hear all about your date with Shaun—we'll go to lunch after or something."

"Whatever," I said. "You just need to stay focused."

When I hung up she was still chattering.

*

Mim and I got to the beach at ten to eleven. Fielding was already there, big surprise, with her hair curled and up in a ponytail and her lip gloss shining in the sun. I didn't ask her why she was wearing makeup to surf. I knew why. I'd done the same thing the day before. I hoped it worked out better for her.

"So where is this Mr. Wonderful?" Mim said. She had an expression halfway between amusement and disapproval hiding under her visor and sunglasses.

"He's always late." Fielding jiggled around like she was the one who had to go to the bathroom. "I can't look like I'm anxious to see him."

"Well, if you're going to play that game, you should go out in the water and get warmed up," Mim said. "Surf in this condition, you'll drown."

Fielding closed her eyes and jangled her hands at her sides. "You're right. I can't believe I'm such a basket case about this. It's just a guy, right?"

"Yes," Mim and I said together.

"Okay, I'm going in." Fielding adjusted her swimsuit and leashed her board to her ankle and adjusted the suit again and finally headed for the surf.

"I don't give this relationship a week," Mim said as she unfolded her beach chair.

I sat in the sand beside her and shaded my eyes with my hand to look up the beach. I didn't see anybody hot enough to warrant Fielding having a meltdown.

"He must be here." Mim nodded toward Fielding, who was waving coyly at somebody from a prone position on her surfboard. "I hope the boy's impressed or we're going to have to give her therapy."

I laughed and looked where Fielding was waving. For the second time in less than twenty-four hours, I froze where I sat, right down to my bone marrow.

"Oh no," I said. "Oh, Mim, no."

She lowered her sunglasses at me. "What is it?"

"It's Preston. She's waving at Preston."

Mim twisted to look, and the grim pull of her lips told me I wasn't imagining it this time either. Preston strolled down the beach, watching Fielding like he owned her. I could smell the smirk from five yards, and for the first time in many days, I thought I was going to throw up.

"I can't be here, Mim," I said.

"No, you can't. Let's go."

"You can't leave Fielding. I'll just—"

"Go up to the Surf Shack and wait for me there."

"Tell Fielding I—"

"Just go," Mim said. "And don't run. The way he's looking at her, he isn't going to notice you if you just stay calm."

Stay calm? That wasn't happening, but I did manage to get behind where Preston stopped with his board without him making eye contact with me. After that I broke into a run, and didn't stop until I got to the Surf Shack. I hadn't planned what I was going to do when I saw Shaun. It would have been pointless anyway. All rational thought circled the drain and disappeared when he stepped out the door and met me on the porch.

"Okay, what the *heck?*" he said.

"He's here—on the beach," I said, breathing like a freight train.

"Who?"

"The guy from yesterday."

"Bryn—what's going on?"

"I know him, Shaun," I said. "And I have to tell you—I want to tell you—"

For a second he looked like he had a set of covers of his own he'd like to dive under. Then he glanced over his shoulder toward the inside of the shop. "Okay—but let's not do it here. Goof's got the counter." He took my arm, and this time I didn't pull away. I let him lead me down the steps and along the stone path that led to Al's Crab Shack next door.

"You want to sit here?" he said, motioning to a concrete table and bench with big hunks out of both. "I'll go get us some drinks—they won't let us stay without ordering. Don't go away, okay?"

I nodded and watched him disappear into the bowels of Al's and let the whole thing crash in on me. *Preston* was the guy Fielding was working so hard to impress? Was he dating her because he knew she was my friend? Was that possible? How would he know that?

Probably the same way he knew I was going surfing with Shaun on Saturday. And where we were going. Even now I shivered and looked over both shoulders. Was he actually stalking me? Was somebody watching me fall apart right this very minute?

"You okay?"

I jumped and knocked my knee on the concrete table. Shaun set a Coke in front of me and straddled my bench.

"You can tell me anything, Bryn," he said again. "Something's freaking you out, and that's freaking *me* out. Talk to me."

His eyes begged me, like if I didn't share my pain with him, he wouldn't be exactly whole. I could hear Mim's voice in my head: *You're going to tell it like the young woman you are now—braver and wiser and stronger.*

That's what I did. I started from the beginning and told him every detail of the fairy tale turning into the nightmare. Once I began, I couldn't stop, but I still watched for signs that he thought I was high maintenance. That I had too much baggage. That I wasn't dealing with it. And yet—I wouldn't have stopped even then, because I had to know if he saw me as who I was now, not who I was then.

"So when I saw him yesterday, I did freak," I said.

"Why didn't you tell me? I thought you just decided I was roadkill or something."

"No! I thought you'd think I had too much baggage."

"Baggage."

"You said you didn't like girls with baggage."

Shaun pulled his hand through his spiky hair. "I said I didn't like it when girls dragged their baggage into everything. You're not—you don't—what the heck, Bryn, nobody would even know you *had* any issues if you didn't tell them." He moved himself closer to me. "Everybody's got issues. You have a couple hours? I'll tell you mine."

"I have a lot of hours," I said. I wanted to hear it all, but I sat up straight on the bench. "He's down there with Fielding."

"Who—Preston?"

"Yes. He's the guy she's trying to show up so she can humble him or some stupid thing. She can't humble him, Shaun. She's gonna get hurt."

"We should go down there." He got halfway up, but I shook my head.

"I can't," I said. "I've got a restraining order against him."

"That's *his* problem."

"Mim's down there."

Shaun sank back to the bench. "Then he does have a problem."

"Maybe it's okay," I said without believing it. "Fielding's different from me—she probably won't let him get away with what I let him do."

"You wouldn't do it now."

I looked into the tone of his voice. It was husky. It wasn't grinning.

Mim joined us about five minutes later, and I could tell by her walk that she was ready to take somebody out. I hoped she already had.

"What's in here?" she said, picking up my glass.

"I'm sorry—it's Coke."

"Great." She took a swig and sat down across from us. "So help me, if that boy wasn't already going down, I'd take him there myself after what I just saw."

She took in a sudden breath and looked from me to Shaun, but I nodded at her. "It's okay. I told him."

"Excellent."

"So what happened?" Shaun said. "Do you want your own drink, by the way?"

Mim emptied my glass and shook her head. "What I want is a cattle prod. First of all, Fielding surfed like a professional. She ought to be out there competing instead of chasing after—whatever—she put on a performance that had old men standing up

155

and cheering, and that—creature—after he wiped out and she never missed a move, he acted like he was doing her a tremendous favor by working her into his schedule. Actually, it was worse than that." Mim took off her visor and flung it onto the table. "He pretended to be bored by the whole thing, but he was ticked—royally. I could see it in his muscles. She outsurfed him and he knew it and he's not having it."

"I guess it didn't humble him," I said.

"Fielding was expecting that result?"

"Uh-huh."

Mim sniffed. "She's not as bright as I thought she was."

"Mim," I said, "did Preston see you?"

She shook her head. "As soon as he was focused on her I moved away from shore, and I got out of sight as soon as she came out of the water. She forgot I was even there, I'm sure."

My stomach was twisting into a square knot. "We shouldn't have left her."

"She's all right for now. I waited until they both took off, separately."

"So maybe they broke up," I said.

Mim licked her lips like she'd just tasted poison. "You don't kiss like that if you've just broken up. You okay, Bryn?"

"No." I dropped my face into my hands. "I'm scared for her. I don't know what to do."

"I think we should go home and sort it out."

"I have to get back to work," Shaun said. He touched my arm. "Do you swear you'll call me if you need me?"

"Uh-huh," I said. It was all I could do not to whip out my cell phone and punch in his number right then. Maybe there was real hope after all.

*

"Do you want to talk this through?" Mim said on the way home.

"I need to do something first," I told her.

When we got there, I went straight to my room and picked RL up from where I'd thrown it. I didn't even wait for it to wash me to wherever it wanted me to be. I just dropped into the chair with it and got in its leather face.

156

"All right—I get it. You weren't kidding. Hard core all the way." I gripped its sides tighter. "I trust you, already. Please—show me what to do."

I could have sworn the thing sighed in my hands. Just when I thought it had freaked me out all it could, it did something new to make my palms sweat. And I'd once thought I wanted "mysticism."

My room seemed airless all of a sudden, as if everything was holding its breath and waiting in reverence. Everything but me. I loosened my grip on RL and folded my hands on it. What was that thing in one of the Shakespeare plays about the king shooting the messenger that brought the news he didn't want to hear? It wasn't the book's fault I was in yet another impossible situation. It was just telling me what Yeshua said.

What Jesus said.

I pulled my hands up from the book and joined the rest of the room that was holding its breath. I'd been yelling at Jesus. Telling him what I did and did not want. Maybe it was amazing I hadn't been electrocuted by a toaster or something.

"I'm sorry," I whispered. "I just need help. I'm desperate."

Barely touching the leather, I opened the cover and watched the pages flutter into place. My eyes were pulled to a line dead center.

I have another story for you. Hear it. Don't fight it.

"Okay," I said.

By the way, you aren't the only one who ever argued with Yeshua. The religion professors were constantly heckling him, trying to trap him into a debate. Most of what he said didn't jive with what they were teaching—and with what made everybody else think they were smart guys—so they took any opportunity to make him look bad.

I wasn't trying to make him look bad. I was just trying to understand.

Then listen. This one day, Yeshua was out teaching and one of the smart religious types stood up and said, "So, Teacher, what do I have to do to get eternal life?" It was a trick question. The guy didn't really care anything about eternal life.

Neither did I at the moment. I was having enough trouble with the one I was living right now.

157

He and Yeshua went back and forth about the Law of God say-
ing you needed to love God with everything you had and love your
neighbor the way you do yourself. The smart guy said, "Okay, so,
define neighbor." As usual, Yeshua didn't give him a definition out of
the dictionary. He told a story—and this is it.

For a second I could relate to the religious guy. A simple
answer would've been a nice touch about then. But I had to go
with this. What else did I have?

A man was traveling from Jerusalem to Jericho, a pretty bad
stretch of road, high crime rate. Anybody would be crazy to go it
alone, and, big surprise, he was attacked by a gang who stripped
him, beat the living snot out of him, and made off with everything
he had, including his clothes. They left him lying in the road, naked
and half dead."

I stirred a little. We were talking "hard core."

Fortunately, a priest came along, the perfect person to take this
poor guy to a hospital and help him get through the trauma. But
when he saw the guy bleeding in the gutter, he crossed to the other
side of the road and kept going.

A priest?

It gets worse. The guy was losing ground fast. He was dehydrated,
practically unconscious, and his eyes were swollen shut. Who knows if
he even realized a second man approached on the road and saw him?
If he did, insult was added to injury when this dude, a Levite priest,
who was even higher in the church, also avoided him.

Fingers snapped somewhere in my brain. I knew this story.

A Samaritan happened to be traveling the Jerusalem-to-Jericho
route that day as well.

Okay, so this was the Good Samaritan. I didn't even learn
that one back in Sunday kindergarten. Everybody just kind of
knew it.

Which meant I could fast-forward to *why* I needed this
story right now. Fielding wasn't bleeding in a gutter—

Not yet.

I didn't even have to be pulled back to the page.

The Samaritan washed off the caked blood from the guy's nose
and mouth and bandaged up his wounds the best he could with a
first-aid kit and then loaded him onto his donkey and took him to the

closest safe place, which was basically a bed-and-breakfast. He got a room there for the guy—whose name he still didn't know—and got him settled in, and then spent the night making sure he didn't have any more serious injuries. Nobody else showed up to take over—no friends or relatives of the traveler, no local doctor. He was in transit so there really wasn't anybody to step in. In the morning, the Samaritan left money with the bed-and-breakfast owner and asked him to take care of the guy until he was on his feet. He even said if there were any additional expenses to just add them to his bill.

Right. Like I said, I knew this story.

There's more. Yeshua said to the religion professor, "So you tell me, which of the three people traveling on the road that day was a neighbor to the injured man?"

That was so obvious.

It was to the professor too. He said (probably with his eyes rolling), "Of course it was the one who stopped to take care of him." Yeshua said, "You go and do the same thing."

The book was quiet. I was allowed to sink back into the chair, which I did, not feeling a whole lot clearer than I was when I first sat down. I knew the story—I knew the moral—I knew I was supposed to warn Fielding about Preston because it was the right thing and nobody else was going to do it.

I leaned my head back and closed my eyes. Faces narrowing down to points jockeyed for position in front of me. Regan, Andrew, Ms. Dorchester. Preston himself. Threats jeered in my ears and flashed their cruel lights in my eyes, from people I didn't even know.

"Don't you see?" I whispered. "Nobody's going to believe I'm trying to help Fielding. They're going to think I'm just trying to make things worse for Preston because I'm a tramp and a witch and every other heinous thing they've decided I am."

Do you know what a Samaritan was?

That voice again. Mine but not mine. A thought but not one I'd ever have on my own. Almost in tears by then, I said, "A person from Samaria?"

I waited for an answer. All I heard was a soft silence. It was so tender I couldn't yell, "What are you *talking* about?!" All I could do was listen to the echo in my head. *Do you know what a Samaritan was? You go and do the same thing.*

159

CHAPTER SEVENTEEN

Mim was in the sunroom typing on her laptop and sipping a Vitamin water, probably to counteract the toxic Coke she knocked back at Al's Crab place. Surrounded by sunlight, she glowed like some kind of wise angel. I almost hated to disturb the peace that seemed to come from her inside out.

But she looked up at me and patted the chair next to hers. "You better ask that question before you self-destruct," she said.

"I might anyway." I sat cross-legged in the curved-cane swivel chair and held on to my feet. "What's a Samaritan? I know it's a person from Samaria and one of them saved the man in the Bible story. I just read it." I swatted back the hanks of hair I hadn't even bothered to brush when we got home. "I need to know what the big deal is with him being a Samaritan and not just some really nice guy like Shaun."

Mim studied my face as if she didn't know which thread to pull out of all that first. She closed her laptop and leaned her chair back.

"First of all, you need to realize that the guy lying in the gutter was a Jew, and that the people Jesus was talking to were too. A Samaritan was definitely not—at least not their kind of Jewish. The Jews basically hated the Samaritans and vice versa."

"So, it was like a racial thing?"

"No. It was more a difference in the way they interpreted Scripture. The Jews thought the way the Samaritans practiced was a desecration of the temple, and the Samaritans thought the temple was a sham. It was a mess. Anyway, the hatred had grown over the centuries, and Jews avoided all contact with them. They'd go out of their way not to go through Samaria on their pilgrimages to Jerusalem. It was like they were a disease."

She must have seen me fidgeting in the seat, because she stopped. "This is probably more than you wanted to know." She put her fist to her mouth for a moment. "Okay, here's the thing. I think when Jesus started describing a Samaritan coming toward this man beaten up in the street, they were probably all geared up for yet another reason to hate the whole Samaritan crowd. There was no other way the story could go but for the Samaritan thug to kick the man when he was down or harvest his organs or some other atrocity."

"But it didn't go that way."

"Right. And what makes it an even better story is that they knew the man who was hurt, being a Jew, wouldn't want some low-life, unclean person touching him. It would make *him* unclean."

"Like he cared about that when he was dying in the road!"

"True—but he might care about it later. When you know all that, you realize that the Samaritan was taking two huge risks by helping the Jew." She cocked an eyebrow like she was waiting for me to tell her what they were.

"The Jews might beat *him* up if he touched their guy," I said. "Not that any of *them* helped him."

"Yeah."

"And—" I said, "I guess the hurt guy might use his last, like, ounce of strength to tell the Samaritan to get off him. Or he'd sue him or something when he got well."

"Bingo." She picked up her water bottle and took a sip. The fact that she wasn't pushing it on me meant she was giving me a chance to come to some conclusion.

I only found one. "Fielding's in the gutter," I said, "or she might get there."

Mim nodded.

"If I help her, they could turn on me even more." I swallowed. "Or she might."

"There is that possibility."

"But I still have to do it."

"You don't 'have' to." Mim shrugged and watched me over her water bottle. "Nobody would blame you if you didn't."

"Except Jesus."

161

She looked at me as if she'd never seen me before. "How can I help?" she said.

I shrugged, and then I said, "Could you pray?"

*

After Mim assured me that Dad would be occupied in the clinic for a while — he was doing an emergency cesarean on a Boston terrier — I took my cell phone out to the gazebo. It wasn't as oppressively hot as usual because there was another storm blowing in, and I didn't want to talk about Preston inside. It wasn't just that I was afraid Dad would deliver those puppies too fast and overhear me. It just seemed like too poisonous a topic to be talking about in my home. Preston had infected every other part of my life, but he wasn't getting his toxins into my house ever again.

Fielding answered on the first ring. "Bryn-Bryn! What happened to you guys?"

"We had to leave — but Mim says you were fabulous."

She laughed like a bubble machine. "I kind of think I was. My guy was impressed — he tried not to show it, but he was."

"Preston," I said.

"Pres — oh, yeah. He told me to call him Ollie, but how — "

"Because his last name's Oliver."

"Yes! Do you know him?"

"Yeah."

The bubble machine stopped bubbling. "Why does it sound like you have that look on your face?"

"Because I do. I have to tell you something, Fielding."

Her pause was thick. "I'm not going to like it, am I?"

"You're going to hate it."

I took in a breath and pulled my knees into my chest and told her, just the way I did Shaun. When I got to the end, I wished I had done it in person, because I needed to see the look on *her* face. She didn't say a word through the whole thing.

"I'm only telling you because I don't want you to end up like I have," I said. "Fielding?"

"Yeah. Sorry. I'm just trying to — I can't believe we're talking about the same person."

"I know. But we are."

She left us in another silence so long I thought maybe she'd hung up, but she finally said, "Okay, well, I guess I better make a phone call."

"Text him," I said.

"Huh?"

"If you try to break up with him, he'll say he's going to kill himself."

"What?"

"That's what he did to me."

"I've only been dating the guy for like ten days! Look — I'm going to call him and I'll call you back."

"Okay," I said. My mind was already off calculating. She'd been dating Preston for ten days. That was about how long it was since I'd met her ...

"Fielding — wait," I said. "How did you two get together?"

"At a party. It was weird — this guy I met on the beach that I didn't even like that much invited me, and I went because I wanted to meet some people." Her voice was starting to shake. "Preston was there and we just clicked. It's been great ever since — which is why I can't — "

"Who was the other guy? Does he have blond hair?"

"You mean the guy that introduced us? No. It's red. I never liked redheaded guys that much. It was never happening with us so I didn't feel bad when I went with Preston instead of him."

I grabbed on to the edge of the gazebo bench. Don't tell her — don't. She's going to break it off with Preston anyway. Don't hurt her any more.

"I have to call him," she said.

I closed my eyes. "I'll be praying for you."

"Oh," she said. "Well — thanks."

*

Fielding didn't call me back that day. I did a lot of pacing and re-reading parts of RL I'd already read and watching the rain pelt the windows like the sky was throwing a tantrum. Mim said it was a lot for Fielding to take in, that she might be processing. Then we just looked at each other because we knew Fielding wasn't much of a processor.

Monday we didn't go surfing because there was what everyone called a "nor'easter" coming in—a storm out of the, duh, northeast, which even I knew was the worst kind.

"The waves are great," Shaun told me on the phone, "but you'd have be insane to try to ride them. Some people actually are. I miss you."

I rode on *that* for the rest of the day. But thoughts of Fielding wouldn't leave me alone. The more I paced and chewed on the whole thing, the surer I was that her meeting Preston wasn't an accident. Whoever that redheaded kid was, he must be Preston's spy—which made the hair on the back of my neck stand up every time I even considered it. Did he see her hanging out with me and tell Preston?

But why would Preston want to date her just because she was my friend? Wouldn't he figure I'd tell her?

Probably not. He probably still thought I was a wimp. After all, I hadn't even told anyone when he was abusing *me*. And I hadn't shown that much improvement on the witness stand at the hearing, so what else was he going to think?

The whole thing was driving me nuts—the not talking to Fielding, the not seeing Shaun, the not surfing, the endless blowing rain. When we couldn't hit the beach again Tuesday, I was ready to shimmy up the fireplace.

And then Fielding called.

"Hey," she said—in a shaky little voice that didn't even sound like her. "I'm sorry I didn't call back—it's just been ..."

"Fielding?" I said. "Are you crying?"

"I never cry—I hate this."

"What happened?"

"Listen—can you meet me—at the movies?"

"The movies?" I took to pacing a path in my bedroom rug again. "We can't really talk at the movies."

"It's a matinee on a Tuesday. Nobody will be there. It's the best place *to* talk." She gave a juicy sniff. "I just want to make sure nobody hears us."

"You could come here."

"I said nobody. Not even Mim."

"She'll leave us alone—"

"Can't you just come to the Regal?"

Her voice was about to snap, I could tell. I knew that kind of desperation.

"Okay," I said. "I'll have Mim drop me off. What time?"

"Two thirty. And I'll make sure you get home."

"I really hate this for you, Fielding," I said.

I heard a sob shudder through her again. "You don't even know the half of it," she said.

*

She was right about nobody going to the movies on a Tuesday afternoon. Even with the rain, it obviously wasn't many people's idea of a good time. There might have been five people in the lobby, and there was absolutely nobody in the theater as Fielding and I fumbled our way into the inky dark. The movie had already started. I didn't even know what it was and I didn't bother to look as I groped behind Fielding and into a seat almost in the back row.

Next to me, Fielding jiggled her legs back and forth. I'd already checked out the hair clipped up in a haphazard bun and her clothes thrown on like an unmade bed. She was a wreck. I knew about that too.

"Do you want to talk about it?" I whispered.

"Yeah, I want to talk about it," she said, definitely not in a whisper. "You need some serious help, Bryn."

"I what?" I said.

She spread out her fingers and talked at them. "See, I don't think you're just a witch who likes to ruin people's lives. I really do like you and I thought you had it together." She finally looked at me, eyes swimming in the dark. "But, you know what? You've got, like, emotional problems."

I tried to stand up, but she tugged me down by my sleeve and held on. Her face was close to mine and I could see the confusion in it.

"I told Preston everything you said. And he almost cried. He doesn't understand why you're telling everybody all these lies."

"They aren't lies," I said.

"Okay, call them 'exaggerations.'" She let go of my sleeve to make quotation marks with her fingers, and I tried to get up

165

again. She grabbed me harder this time, brought her face closer. My heart raced.

"And what about all the parts that you conveniently left out when you told me? Like you messing around with the theater guys. You being abused by your father. You accusing Preston of being the one who hit you because he was about to break up with you for not having sex with him."

Somewhere in the middle of that, my heart stopped beating. It was hard to breathe in a space so empty of the truth. I had to get out of it.

"You know what?" I said. "If you believe all of that, then I can't help you."

I wrenched my hand away from her and jumped out of the seat. This time I was grabbed from behind by the shoulders. And it wasn't by Fielding. Strong, masculine hands pinned me to the back of it.

Fielding whipped around to look behind us. "What are you doing?" she said.

A muscular arm slammed into my chest and held me there until I could barely breathe. But I could bite. I sank my teeth into it until its owner swore and pulled away. I struggled once more to get up, while Fielding kept crying, "Stop it — you said you just wanted to talk to her!"

Someone else's savage hands dug into my upper arms and yanked me backward. My tailbone hit the arm of the seat and I fell headlong into Fielding's lap. She wriggled out from under me, and my head smacked into the other armrest. I was left staring up into a mass of blond hair.

"Are you dumber than a box of rocks?" Andrew said.

Spittle from his mouth sprayed into my face. When I pulled my arm up to wipe it off, he snapped onto my wrist and twisted my arm below the seat. I kicked both feet, but someone else clamped onto my ankles. Someone with red hair.

"Get — off — me!" I screamed at them.

"Stop it, you guys!" Fielding's voice had dropped to a terrified whisper. "I didn't bring her here for you to do to this!"

"Preston's waiting for you out front," Andrew said to her.

"You're hurting her!"

I was still writhing and managed to get my legs free from the red-haired kid who wasn't quite so tough without his stupid sunglasses. But Andrew was swimmer strong, and he pinned me down again.

"I'm not gonna hurt her. As soon as she stops freaking out I'm just gonna deliver a message from Preston."

Fielding was sobbing by now. "I'm sorry about this, Bryn. I didn't know they were going to—"

"Get her out of here," Andrew said to the other kid, who climbed over the seat and clamped on to the back of Fielding's neck and steered her down the aisle. Something he hissed to her made her stop yelling and let him usher her out the door.

As I watched her go, it occurred to me that this group always followed the same script. All I could do was cling to the hope that Fielding would come up with some different lines than the ones I'd memorized.

Andrew hoisted himself over the seat too and sat next to me with his arm around my shoulder. He pulled me into him like we were making out in the dark and pinned my hands into my lap with his other hand.

"One thing and I'll let you go," he whispered hoarsely into my ear.

His hot breath turned my stomach, but I stopped struggling. Andrew wasn't enjoying this the way Preston did. It wasn't delicious to him. It came to me like a slap in the face that he was as desperate to stay off of Preston's hate list as any of us.

"*What?*" I said into his throat. His Adam's apple was bobbing like it hurt.

"You've gone way too far and we aren't turning back now. Not unless you drop the charges within two hours. If you don't, tonight's the night."

He sounded like he was reciting from a script, and not very well.

"The night for what?" I said.

He obviously didn't know the next line. He just let go of me and got up. I guessed he was trying to look menacing as he stood over me, but that wasn't working either.

"I'm gonna go. You wait until I'm out and then count to fifty before you leave."

I wanted to laugh, but I knew that would only prolong this and I really wanted him away from me. His nervous sweat was nauseating.

Once he was out of sight, my desire to even smile was snatched away by full-out fear. The entire time they were attacking me, no one from the theater had come to see what was going on. Andrew and that other kid could've ...

I shoved that aside and stumbled down the aisle and out into the hall. They could've done just about anything to me in there, and they didn't. But what they did do was enough to keep me running down the hall and into the lobby where at least there were people behind the refreshment counter and numbed guys hanging out to take tickets from people who weren't there. None of them even looked at me as I sank onto a bench and wrapped my arms around myself and tried not to let the questions scream right out of my mouth.

What was going to happen tonight? Was that just a bluff? They'd been threatening me for weeks—should I believe they were actually going to do something to me now?

My throat tightened until I could hardly breathe. They already had. They'd taken away my only friend. Preston had dated her on purpose, knowing I'd tell her, knowing he'd be able to make her believe him and not me and I would lose her too, just like I'd lost everything else. Who was going to be next—Shaun? I closed my eyes and saw Preston's smirk—the look that said, "I've got you. I've so got you."

Only this time he didn't have me. Not anymore. Not ever again.

I stood up and charged for the glass doors. Rain was coming down in sheets, but I plunged out into it, and with my head down and my arms hugging my body, I stalked—across the parking lot, down the sidewalk, all the way home. I shook myself off at the back door and slammed it behind me before I marched into my room, feet squishing in my sandals.

Copper vacated the chair like someone had just shot at him. I flung myself into it, clothes clinging to me, and hugged the book. It wouldn't do any good to open it—I wouldn't be able to see the words yet.

Which was probably why I heard them instead.

Don't let them bully you into silence.

I shoved back a shank of hair that had stuck to a wet place on my face and stayed there like a leaf on a rainy windshield. "Okay," I said out loud—emphasis on the loud. "I'm ready—but, please, you have to tell me exactly what to do. Please."

I let the book drop to my lap and opened it. The pages turned, like waves marching to shore, and flattened themselves open. There was no doubt about the spot where I was supposed to start reading.

Yeshua was sitting at dinner with a bunch of those smart-guy types I was telling you about—the ones who were always waiting to trap him. They were serious by this time. This wasn't just about making him look bad. They were aggressively seeking a way to get rid of him, because HE was making THEM look bad.

Something in me started to calm. I wasn't sure, but I thought I felt the book nodding at me.

They poked at him one time too many, and Yeshua went off on them. Not necessarily a smart move in the opinion of his friend-followers who felt like he was walking right into a trap. "You're a bunch of lousy hypocrites!" he told the smart guys—the powerful guys. "You pretend to care about people. You've got all these rules for how they're supposed to act, but you always find a way to get around your own rules when they don't work for you and what you want."

I envisioned Preston and Andrew and Regan and the red-haired kid staring at him with forks poised at their gaping lips. "You talkin' to *us*?" their eyes said.

"You have to be in control of everything. Have the best table in the cafeteria. Decide what's cool and what's not. Make sure everybody's watching what you do so they can be like you."

I was beyond nodding.

"People think you're all that," Yeshua went on, "but they don't see what's behind the muscles and the cars and the makeup. They don't know you're already half dead inside." One of the big shots got all huffy and said, *"Do you realize you're totally dissing us?"*

You think?

"Oh, I haven't even started yet," Yeshua said. "You make it impossible for people to live up to your 'standards,' and when they

don't, you treat them like last week's garbage, and then you stand there and watch them suffer. The whole time, you talk about all the things you're doing for your 'community.' Your pictures are all over the place. You get all the awards."

That did it. Jesus had been reading my yearbook.

"But here's the deal: you've basically made a joke out of all that social consciousness and recognition, all those medals and certificates. It's about popularity—and there's a price for that. From now on, the people who shadow you, wanting to be in the in-crowd—they're going to follow you right off a cliff, and that's going to be on your head."

Fielding.

Yeshua couldn't stand being with them anymore and so he left the table. They were livid—their heads were ready to explode. At exactly that point, the planning got extremely serious. Yeshua was going down.

I went cold. So things were going to get worse.

Yeshua's follower-friends were in the same spot as you are now. But Yeshua didn't just warn them about that—he told them what to do.

So he's telling me too.

It wasn't a question. It was suddenly something I knew. I pushed the last of the rain from the pockets under my eyes and read on, like I'd never read before.

Yeshua said to them, "Don't let these clueless people rub off on you. You have to stay real. Wearing a phony mask is working for them right now, but it's going to slip eventually. Don't let that happen to you. You've got to be true to what I'm telling you is right. Don't let them bully you into silence."

Wait. I flattened my hand on the page. So was I still right where I started?

Somehow I didn't think so. I couldn't think so.

"I'm speaking to you as your best friend," Yeshua said. "If they threaten you, don't back down. They can't take away who you are. And they can't separate you from me. Be awestruck by what I say, not by what THEY say. Look, if I take care of the seagulls and the hermit crabs, which I obviously do or they wouldn't be there on the beach day after day, then I'm sure going to take care of you, who are, frankly, worth more than a crab salad."

So what do I do?

"Stand up for me, and I'll stand up for you. That means represent the way I show you, not the way THEY show you. But if you pretend you don't know me—act like we've never had these conversations—I'm not going to be there for you."

I swallowed hard. I never acted like I didn't know him. I just made up who I wanted him to be—

"I'm not holding any of those old mistakes against you. But now you know, and I expect you to be true to me."

But what do I say?

"Don't worry about that. When the time comes, I'll give you exactly the words to say through my spirit."

There was quiet, and in it I realized the book itself had stopped talking a page ago. It was just Jesus and me. No story. No disciples. Just us.

I left the chair, and my bare feet hardly hit the floor as I flew to the kitchen, calling Mim's name. She burst out of the laundry room, face going white.

"Bryn—what in the *world!*"

"There's been a sea change, Mim," I said.

I peeled off the last soaking panel of hair from my cheek and reached for the towel she was already handing me.

"Okay," she said—slowly. "You want to tell me about it?"

"I want you and me to pray for the trial. I want Preston—and all of them—to know they can't take away who I am—who anybody is."

"Well, amen, Bryn," Mim said. She put her hands on my soggy shoulders and smiled from one classy hoop earring to the other. "Amen."

CHAPTER EIGHTEEN

When Dad came in from the clinic, I told him what happened at the movie theater. I guessed it was my turn to deliver bad news at suppertime. He lost all appetite, as well as all color in his face, and went straight to the phone to call the DA.

There was nothing Mr. Quintera could do, of course. Since Preston hadn't been there, it had no legal bearing on the case. We could press charges against Andrew and whoever that red-headed kid was, but it would be simple assault, a misdemeanor, and once again I'd be in the position of having to prove it, especially since Andrew didn't leave any marks. It was a no-brainer that Fielding wasn't going to admit she'd been a part of it. In fact, when Dad called her house to talk to her dad—father to father—a girl he said sounded like a young adult told him Fielding had gone out of town for the Fourth of July holiday. Her cell phone went straight to voice mail. We didn't leave a message.

Dad also told the DA about the threat—that tonight was supposedly "the night." Mr. Quintera said unless we had something more to go on, there wasn't much he could do about that either. But we all saw a police car cruise up our street when we were finally having a belated supper in the sunroom at about eight o'clock.

Still, I was jittery when I went to bed. I made sure Copper was tucked in beside me, and I could hear Dad checking all the dead bolts for about the tenth time. When I woke up later, I heard him in the hall, muttering about us not having any flash-light batteries. I looked at my clock but it was off. The storm must have taken out the electricity. I burrowed back down under the covers and prayed sleepily that Dad would go back to bed.

He must have, because when I was awakened sometime later by the squeal of tires, I was the only one who went to the front window in the living room. The rain had stopped, but the glass was filmed with condensation and the streetlights were out. All I could see were retreating taillights as the vehicle careened around the corner. It could have been a truck—it growled like one. Whatever it was, it was in a hurry to get away. I could hear it winding up all the way to the main road.

What was it they were getting away from?

I tiptoed into the hallway, but there was no sound from either Mim or Dad. I felt my way back to the living room and listened at the front door. The world outside was silent in the aftermath of the storm. Working soundlessly, I undid the dead bolt and eased the door open just enough to slide out sideways. I wasn't sure what I was looking for as I crept barefoot down the slick steps and across the grass. The bottoms of my sleep pants were immediately soaked, but I kept going until I could stand back and look at the house.

No eggs had been thrown. No windows broken. Dad's tires hadn't been slashed. That was all I could think of that somebody could have done—unless they'd thrown a bomb that hadn't gone off yet.

Don't be stupid, I told myself. Even they wouldn't—

Something mechanical groaned loudly, and the streetlights suddenly blazed in my face. I slapped my hand to my mouth, but it was too late. I'd already squealed like a dog with his tail caught in the door.

It took me a full thirty seconds to realize it was just the electricity coming back on. Still shivering, even in the close, sticky air, I headed toward the back of the house. Something off—something that shouldn't have been there—caught my side vision. I stopped and squinted over at dad's clinic next door.

The lights on his sign didn't reveal the red letters that proclaimed it to be North Beach Animal Clinic. The whole sign was black and shiny and wet, and it ran down into the grass like a sickening abstract painting. I ran to it, but even before I turned to look at the front of the building I knew they hadn't stopped at the sign.

The hate was scrawled from one end of my father's clinic to the other. DR. CHRISTOPHER IS A CHILD ABUSER, it jeered in black spray paint. I put my hands over my ears, squeezed my eyes shut, screamed back at it, "Liars! *Liars!!*" But it was still there when Dad got to me and I looked again. I went limp in his arms.

*

As the remaining small hours of the morning crawled by, I found myself remembering that other night, when this had all started, how it had gone past me in a blur. This one was sharp and clear and brutally real.

Two police officers came and snapped pictures of the clinic and took my statement and wrote down Andrew's name and Preston's and Regan's. I held nothing back. Dad sat next to me, face color fluctuating between beet red and death white as I told them about the text messages and the blog and handed over my cell phone and my laptop. By the time I got to the movie theater attack, Mim was serving them coffee. I just kept talking—about Andrew and Preston stalking me at the beach, the other kid taking my picture at the Surf Shack and somebody then posting it with the blog, and somebody tying Copper and the threatening letter to the azalea bush with a surfboard cord. I let it all pour out as the words came into my head. The police were gone before I realized where my lines had come from.

When the time comes, I'll give you exactly the words to say through my spirit.

When Dad came back to the sunroom after showing them out, I pulled myself out of the blanket Mim had wrapped me in.

"I'm sorry, Dad," I said. "I should have told you all of that before. I just thought somehow it would go away."

He ran his hand over the thin spot at the top of his head and sighed from a place I guessed only he knew was there. I felt so bad for him I started to cry. He was beside me before I got the first tear out.

"It's not your fault, Brynnie," he said into my once-again damp hair. "I'll call somebody first thing, and they'll come out and sandblast it off—"

"No one's going to believe you're a child abuser, are they?" I sobbed.

"Of course not," Mim said.

It was actually the first thing I'd heard her say all night. She sounded like she was going to take out an ad in *The Virginian-Pilot*. I choked back the next sob and sat up.

"They won't believe it after I get on the witness stand, Dad," I said. "I swear they won't."

"I'll call Quintera," he said. "Maybe Preston will take a deal now."

"No," I said.

They both went still.

"I want to get up there and tell what happened. I have to do it. They've come after me and my friend and my cat—but they're not gonna do this to my family. They're not."

Dad caught the fist I was banging on my knee and put it to his lips.

"No, they're not, Brynnie. No, they're not."

It was the first thing we'd agreed on in weeks.

*

The four days between then and the trial were the longest of my life—longer than December first to Christmas when I was a kid.

The police came to question me again. Everybody had an alibi for the time of the vandalism on the clinic—Preston, Regan, Andrew, and Kane West, the mysterious red-haired kid. Solid alibis, the officers told us—parents in Preston and Andrew's cases, an entire sleepover in Regan's. Kane was working the all-night window at Wendy's. I couldn't think of anyone else, and nobody I knew had a truck. What I did know was that the people I'd labeled as suspects now hated me more than ever.

I had to go see Mr. Quintera to prep for my testimony. He lectured me about not giving him all this information before. I asked him, politely with plenty of "sirs," what difference it would have made, since it wasn't making much now. He just stared at me like I'd had a face transplant. Still, when I told him I was totally ready to testify, he didn't look all that convinced.

"I admire your courage," he said. "But just remember that Kayla Dorchester is going to—"

"I'm ready for her too," I told him.

He advised Dad to keep me at home over the weekend, which he said he knew was a drag since it was Fourth of July. That didn't bother me that much. I knew Shaun was working all weekend, and he was the only person I wanted to see. I slept a lot and read more RL and watched movies with Mim and tried not to have a meltdown every time I heard the sandblasters working on the clinic. Dad swore the graffiti wasn't the reason business was nearly nonexistent at the moment, that it was typical for a holiday weekend. That didn't keep me from vowing yet again to let it all come out on the witness stand. All of it.

But by Sunday night, I was pacing again and chewing Pepto-Bismol tablets. Ready or not, it was still nerve-racking to think about Ms. Dorchester and her stilettos. And Preston and his arrogant smirk.

Mom called from Mexico City while I was in the shower. She told Dad to assure me that she and Tara would be there first thing in the morning. They would get a cab from the airport to the courthouse. That was reassuring, but at the same time I felt like I was going to see two people who didn't know me anymore. I was getting a little wobbly thinking that they might be able to erode my courage with one, "What were you thinking?", one "Lesson learned, right?"—when Mim tapped on my bedroom door.

"Someone's here to see you," she said.

Her voice didn't sound like she was announcing more cops, and I knew Mom and Tara hadn't left Mexico yet. Could it be Fielding?

Heart throbbing, I redid my ponytail on the way to the living room and tried not to turn to jelly. I didn't have to. It was Shaun.

Okay, I did turn to jelly—the sweet kind. The kind that made me smile out loud and forget tomorrow.

"Why don't you two talk in the sunroom?" Mim said. "Anybody thirsty?"

Neither one of us exactly answered her.

"I think I'll turn in early then," she whispered, and disappeared.

The second she was gone, Shaun had his arms around me, lifting me off the ground. We both talked at the same time and pulled back enough to grin at each other. He hugged me one more time before he put me down.

"Come on," I said and led him by the hand to the sunroom.

The Sunday paper had been folded and left on the table, which meant Dad had gone to bed too. Their trust—his and Mim's—wrapped itself around me like the blanket she was always rolling me up in like a burrito when there was a crisis. I loved them both so much right then, my eyes filled with tears.

"You okay?" Shaun said.

"I am now."

I folded myself up into my corner of the couch and he sat facing me so he could hold both of my hands. His chocolaty eyes had so much in them, I could tell he didn't know where to start. So I went ahead with the whole movies thing, but I didn't get very far.

"I talked to Fielding," he said. His gaze shifted to my hands.

"Seriously?" I said. "When?"

"Monday. She came to the Shack all messed up."

"Did Preston hit her?" I said, but I knew before it even came out of my mouth that he couldn't have or she wouldn't have accused me of lying the very next day.

"I asked her that," Shaun said.

He was still looking at my hands, which made them sweat. What was going on here?

"I thought she came to me for support, you know, since we were getting to be friends before any of this went down. But she said she was there to warn me."

I pulled my hands away. "You mean about me."

"Yeah."

He took my hands back and finally looked at me. He'd been avoiding my eyes because he was about to cry.

"It made me sick to hear her call you a liar and say all that garbage about your dad. I basically told her she was stupid to believe Preston over you—and she came right back telling me I was an idiot to trust you." He squeezed my hands. "When she got to the part about how you would eventually try to take me down too, because you had emotional problems, I told her she better leave."

"You threw her out?" I said.

"Not physically, but I said either she should go or I was going to. She went emo at that point, and Goof came and cussed me out for making her cry."

"Goof?" My voice was going up into that pitch only poodles can hear.

"Yeah, go figure. He even took her over to Al's to get her calmed down."

"Preston better not find out about that," I said. "He'll be in there trying to punch Goof in the face."

Shaun shook his head. "He'll have to find him someplace else. Goof got fired."

"Seriously?" I didn't think my eyes could open any wider or my voice go any higher.

"Somebody got in the shop last night and stole a bunch of stuff and painted graffiti on the walls. There was no sign of a break-in, which meant Goof didn't lock up when he closed. He swears he did, but the owner kicked him out anyway. He's been cool about letting us run the shop, but Goof screwed that up." Shaun gave an eyebrow shrug and kissed my hands. "He was getting annoying anyway—picking at you—"

"Graffiti?" I said.

"Huh?"

"They painted graffiti on the walls?"

"Yeah."

"In black spray paint?"

"Some black, but it looked like that ran out so they finished in red." Shaun cocked his head at me. "You think it was the same people?"

"What did they write?"

"It was hard to read—there isn't that much wall space in there so they sprayed over boards and stuff. The best we could figure out it was 'queens can't surf.' Like they were saying Goof and I were gay, I guess."

"Did it say 'drama queen'?"

My voice had now dropped to a level *nobody* could hear. Shaun leaned into me, his grin fading, his eyebrows crunched together.

"Preston and his friends keep saying I'm being a drama queen," I said.

Shaun shook his head harder than he had to and held my face with his hands. "There's no way."

"Why?"

"Because there just isn't."

"Yeah, there is, Shaun." I curled my fingers around his wrists. "Preston is trying to take everything away from me, one piece at a time. You don't know him—"

"I know he's not going to take me away, because I'm not going anywhere. I'm going to be at the trial tomorrow."

"No," I said.

He pulled away a little, but this time I was doing the holding on.

"I'm serious." I gave our woven-together hands a shake. "I want all of that to be separate. Besides, the less you have to do with it the better."

Shaun searched my face with his Hershey's-Kiss eyes, and I knew he was seeing what I wasn't saying.

"You think if he gets off, he's going to come after me next," he said.

"I think he already has."

He shook his head again. "Let him bring it. After tomorrow it's going to be over."

"I hope so—"

He put his finger to my lips in that soft way he had, that way that didn't say "shut up."

"I know so," he said. "You're going to get up there and tell it until everybody in the courtroom's ready to lynch the dude." He grinned the grin I loved. "'Cause you're the strongest, bravest woman I know."

*

Even with all of that holding me up, I didn't feel that strong and brave at five the next morning when I woke up in a sweat that soaked the cami I was sleeping in. But I didn't pace and reach for the antacid. I went to the chair and picked up my leather book.

I sat with one leg slung over the side as I ran my fingers across the letters "RL" on the front cover. I hadn't exactly treated it with a whole lot of reverence. Jesus either, actually. But through all the arguing and crying and throwing temper tantrums that would have given a two-year-old a run for her money, I'd actually come to respect it. Him. And his word.

I brought my leg in and wriggled to a sitting position. Mim called the Bible the Word. Was that basically what this was? The Bible?

It was Jesus talking to me, that was all I knew. All I needed to know at the moment. And right now, I needed for him to talk to me more about what was going to happen today.

"Please show me," I whispered.

Like it ever did anything else. The pages shuffled themselves quietly into place. It only took a little edging to get me to the story I was meant to read.

Yeshua was having a serious conversation with his follower-friends. They were getting close to Jerusalem where the big test was going to happen, and he wanted them to be ready.

I knew the feeling.

He said to them, "Basically, I've come here to start a fire, you know? A fire that's going to change everything. I wish we didn't have to go through it, but there it is. I hope you didn't think I came to make everything easy for you—"

Frankly, no, I'd never thought that. Okay, maybe I had back when I had my first Young Life vision of Jesus, but since then, no, I pretty much felt like I'd been walking through fire the whole time.

"It's going to be like this," Yeshua said. "Say there are five people in your situation—"

I counted on my fingers. Dad. Preston. Fielding. Regan. Andrew.

"—you can bet it's going to be three against two and two against three. It could be father against daughter. Boyfriend against girlfriend. Friends against friends."

For once he was being perfectly clear.

Then he turned to the whole crowd, not just his friend-followers, and he said, "When you see that the wind's coming in from the northeast, you know that's going to mean some pretty rough seas. It could make for good surfing, but you're going to get yourself killed if you try it."

What?

I blinked, but then I let it go. There was a time when that would have been grounds for breaking out in hives. Maybe I *had* made some progress.

"Yes," Yeshua went on, "you know how to predict a shift in weather that's going to happen LATER, so don't be trying to tell me you can't tell that there's a whole sea change going on here NOW."

I grinned until I was sure I looked like Shaun.

"It doesn't take a rocket scientist to understand this," Yeshua said. "It's just about what's right—things you already know in your heart. It's the same way you know that if you've got a fight going with somebody, it's better to settle it between the two of you than drag it into court where you have no control over how it's going to come out."

My heart sank right down to my ankles. Was I doomed, then?

"I didn't get to decide this, Jesus," I said. I looked down at the page, but there was nothing more. When I tried to turn it, of course it wouldn't move.

"I don't get it," I said. "It isn't my fault this went all the way to a trial."

I'm not talking about you.

I closed my eyes and drank in the no-sound voice that hadn't failed me yet. I wilted into the chair.

You're not?

Who am I talking to? Read it again.

I sat up straight and let the book drag my eyes to the part where Yeshua turned to the crowd. Who was in that group? Not me—I was a disciple. Who knew the surf report but couldn't see a sea change?

The crowd gathered in my mind, as sharp as any fantasy I'd ever conjured up—only real, harshly real. The whole student body was there. And the lawyers. Preston's parents. Regan and

Andrew were in the second row. And there, front and center, was Preston. His hair was wet. He was wearing Billabongs and an arrogant smile. His shortboard was tucked under his arm.

"It doesn't take a rocket scientist to understand this," Yeshua said again.

To Preston.

"It's just about what's right—things you already know in your heart. It's the same way you know that if you've got a fight going with somebody, it's better to settle it between the two of you than drag it into court where you have no control over how it's going to come out."

The page let me turn it this time. There was more.

"The judge could turn you over to the officer," Yeshua said. *"And the officer could throw you right in the slammer. There's a chance you could do some serious time—and have to pay a fine to boot. Think it through. Know what I'm about and you'll make a better choice—in everything."*

Preston isn't going to do that, is he?

I didn't get an answer. But something struck me that had never really hit me before. No matter how the trial turned out, I wasn't going to go to jail. Even if the judge didn't believe me, he'd just let Preston go. I would *look* like the loser, but I knew I wasn't. If the judge did believe me, Preston could go to jail or have to pay a lot of money. He had a lot more to lose than I did.

I could almost feel sorry for him. Win or lose, he didn't have this Jesus. Without his way, Preston was always going to have to fight to get *his* way no matter what it took. It was actually kind of sad.

Those were the first kind thoughts I'd had about him in a very long time. I had no doubt that the book sighed in my hands.

CHAPTER NINETEEN

The courtroom seemed different to me that morning than it had two and a half weeks before. In spite of the clouds that had been in front of the sun since dawn, the light seemed brighter, the wood shinier, and the clerks smilier. As I took my place next to Mr. Quintera, I had less of a feeling that the knots in the paneling were staring at me like accusing eyes.

But I still didn't want to see *Preston's* eyes. Not because I was afraid of them, but because I wasn't sure I could look into them without telling him how pathetic he was. So when I turned to see if Mom and Tara had arrived, I was careful to keep my gaze on my side of the aisle.

There was still no sign of them inside the heavy wooden doors. Just the guard who stood there as if he were watching a golf match on TV. I was thinking how disturbing it was to see someone that bored while all around him people were having the very worst days of their lives, when Dad slid in and hurried down to join Mim on the bench behind me.

"Your mom and Tara are stuck in Atlanta because of the storms," he said. "They may not be able to get a flight out today."

He ran his hand along my arm like he expected me to cry. I kind of wished I would, so he wouldn't see that I was secretly relieved.

"It's okay," I said, and patted his bony hand.

"I'm sorry for you, though. I know Mom helps you."

Mim's eyebrows went up, and she looked at Dad. "I think she's done just fine without her, actually. I think we all have."

"All rise," someone droned. The trial had begun.

Mr. Quintera touched my elbow when we sat down again.

He was in a navy blue suit today and a red tie, and he looked a couple of years older than thirty.

"You can relax for a while," he murmured to me. "We have to select a jury first."

"A while" didn't even begin to describe it. If I hadn't been keyed up, I probably would have gone into a coma as he and Ms. Dorchester asked twenty people the same questions and accepted some and dismissed others for reasons I couldn't even begin to figure out. It did give me time to study Ms. Dorchester's shoes—she was in pumps instead of stilettos, like she was ready to get down to serious business—and Mr. Quintera's mood—he acted confident but intense—and the judge's body language. She looked as mind-numbed as I felt.

They didn't settle on twelve jurors and an alternate until after ten thirty, and then there was a brief recess.

"They don't drag it out this long on *Law and Order*," I said to Mr. Quintera.

He almost smiled. "It'll go faster after this. Hang in there." He started to turn back to his long yellow pad, but he stopped and nodded at me. "You're doing great," he said.

This time he looked like he kind of meant it.

What he didn't really mean was that things were going to go faster. There was something he called preliminary motions to deal with that I didn't understand a word of, and then the emergency room doctor, Dr. Wooten, had to be certified as an expert. What, didn't anybody believe he was a real doctor? Ms. Dorchester finally agreed that he would do, and we got on with their opening statements.

Mr. Quintera's was quick and made it sound like in a matter of minutes Preston was going to be hauled off to jail. The people in the jury did a lot of nodding, and a couple of the women glared at Preston. I was finally able to unclench my hands from the deadlock they had on each other.

Ms. Dorchester's statement hooked them back together again. She said she was going to show that there were other possible reasons for my injuries, none of which were incurred in my relationship with the no-previous-violations Preston Oliver. "Why would he ruin his promising future that way?" she asked them. "And yet"—she pointed to me—"why would a wholesome-looking young woman lie?" With a tap on the jury box, she said she intended to show that I had every reason to.

I twitched in my chair, and Mr. Quintera leaned in until his lips almost touched my ear.

"Don't sweat it," he said. "You're just watching a performance."

I felt better when Mr. Quintera called our first witness to the stand—Officer Day—who testified to everything I'd said that night as if he'd memorized it from the tape. I started to breathe—until Ms. Dorchester asked him what he saw when he found Preston and me at the scene of the accident.

"He had his arm around her, like he was comforting her," he said.

"That's all," she said, before he even had the last syllable out.

My lungs stopped working again.

It was like that with every witness Mr. Quintera presented before and after the lunch I couldn't eat. I'd think we had it made after he questioned them, and then Ms. Dorchester would ask one thing and I'd be certain I was the one who was going to jail.

Dr. Wooten described my injuries so vividly the jury looked like it was going be unanimously sick. The blown-up photos didn't hurt either, although they brought back pain that once again took my breath away.

Then Ms. Dorchester started in.

"What was your first thought when you saw the extent of the bruises on Ms. Christopher, Doctor?" she said. She was tilting her head like she was really sorry she had to put him through this.

"That they weren't caused by the accident," he said, "and that someone had been abusing her over a period of time."

"When you questioned Ms. Christopher about them, did she immediately accuse the defendant?"

Dr. Wooten gave a half-smile. "She said they were from playing football."

Ms. Dorchester whirled to the jury, and I was sure she was going to say, "Do you *believe* this?"

"Football?" she said instead.

"She was trying to make light of it, I think."

"Why would she do that?"

185

"I got the feeling she was trying to protect someone."

"Objection," Mr. Quintera said from a half-standing-up position. I didn't know why he was objecting. Protecting someone was exactly what I was doing.

"Yes," Dr. Wooten was saying in answer to a question I missed. "Unfortunately, I've had a lot of experience with abused patients, so I do feel qualified to tell when someone is lying to protect someone they care about."

"Yeah," I muttered. "Me."

Mr. Quintera looked at me twice, and then scribbled something on his pad.

"Did you ask her again who had done it?"

Dr. Wooten licked his lips.

"Doctor?"

"I just told her that her father could get help for his temper. She corrected me and said—"

"That's all. Thank you, Doctor," Ms. Dorchester said, and swivel-hipped her way back to her table.

Mr. Quintera stood up. "One more question, Doctor Wooten. What did Ms. Christopher say when you suggested her father had abused her?"

His face brightened. "She said her father would never do that. She said it was her boyfriend."

Mr. Quintera sat down with a small sigh and patted my hand. But when I looked at the jury, most of them were looking at Dad, like they wanted to ask some questions of their own.

Next came Josie Lentz, from my Drama I class. I had hesitated to give Mr. Quintera her name when he asked me who saw Preston drag me out of the party. Everybody else I'd involved in this had ended up the worse for it, and of all the people I'd met in the theater department at Tidewater Prep, she was the one who had given me the most hope that we might actually become friends. I abandoned that hope as she took the oath.

But when she sat down and faced Mr. Quintera, I knew immediately that she wasn't minding this that much. Josie loved an audience, and her finely chiseled Asian face was ready to take it on.

After the usual "pleasantries"—which I'd now heard so many times I probably could have gotten up there and done them myself—Mr. Quintera had her tell what she'd witnessed at the party.

"I was talking to Bryn and Preston," she said, "and I was telling him how fabulous her final monologue was in Drama I. It was one of the best in the class, and you'd think he'd be proud, right?"

"I take it he wasn't."

"Not even close from what I could tell." Josie cut her eyes over to Preston. "He got up from the couch where they were sitting—I was sitting on the coffee table in front of them—and he yanked Bryn up by her arm and—literally—dragged her through this bunch of people behind us." Josie turned to the jury. "*Dragged* her."

"Did you go after them?"

"I started to but this girl stopped me. Regan Yates."

I could feel my eyes bulging. I hadn't heard this before.

"Why did she stop you?"

"Partly because she's a queen bee and thinks she can tell people what to do. Especially people who aren't in her crowd—like me. I don't usually go to those parties, but my date wanted to."

"Uh-huh." Mr. Quintera scratched his chin, though I'd have bet it didn't really itch. More theater went on in here than on any stage I'd ever been on. "You said it was partly that."

"Oh, right. And partly she stopped me because she said whatever went down between Preston and Bryn was none of my business. I said 'Didn't you see him drag her out of here by the arm?'" Josie gave a dramatic pause. "She said that happened all the time."

"Thank you," Mr. Quintera said.

I was ready to get up and hug her.

"Ms. Lentz," Ms. Dorchester was saying as she approached the stand. "Or may I call you Josie?"

"You may call me Ms. Lentz," Josie said.

A couple of the jury members tittered.

"All right, Ms. Lentz. You say Ms. Christopher is a fabulous actress. Can you define 'fabulous' for us, in theatrical terms?"

"Yes, I can. She gets inside the character and becomes her, so you forget you're even watching the real Bryn Christopher."

Beside me, Mr. Quintera sucked in air.

"How well do you know 'the real Bryn Christopher'?"

"We've worked on several scenes together in class—"

"What about outside of class?"

"That party was the first time I've ever really seen her outside of class, but—"

"Thank you, Ms. Lentz," Ms. Dorchester said. "I'm through with this witness, your honor."

Mr. Quintera stood up while Josie was still glaring at Ms. Dorchester's back.

"Ms. Lentz, in your opinion as a person with theatrical experience, was Bryn acting the night you saw Preston take her out of the party?"

"No way," Josie said. "Even she isn't that good."

Our final witness before me was Mr. Chadwick, my drama teacher. I was surprised he even remembered me. My brief life with him seemed like it had belonged to someone else long ago. But he smiled at me when he took the stand, and I remembered his bunny teeth and his fuzzy moustache and the way he wrinkled his nose when he smiled. His curly hair was damp, like he'd tried to tame it to look more serious for the court.

Mr. Quintera got right to the fact that I had been involved in a scene that required stage combat, and Mr. Chadwick went into so much detail about the kind of training I'd had and the amount of protective equipment I'd worn and the scant number of times he'd seen me fall when I wasn't supposed to that the judge finally told Mr. Quintera to move on to another question.

Once again, he showed the blown-up photos, and Mr. Chadwick gave a gasp Shakespeare would have loved. I hoped nobody in the jury thought he was acting, because I was pretty sure he wasn't.

"In your opinion, Mr. Chadwick," Mr. Quintera said, "could Ms. Christopher have sustained those injuries rehearsing for and performing the scene from *The Outsiders?*"

"Absolutely not!" Mr. Chadwick said. His voice shook. "I would never allow anything like that to happen to one of my students. They're like my own kids."

He gave me a long, watery look that told me I was in that group. I thanked him with my eyes.

Ms. Dorchester popped up and tapped her squared-off white fingernails against each other. "Just one question, Mr. Chadwick. Did you supervise every rehearsal the students had for the scene?"

He opened his mouth like was going to say yes, but slowly he shook his head.

"Is that a no?"

"It's an I'm-not-sure."

"Not sure?" she said.

That was her favorite answer. At least, she'd loved it when I'd said it.

"The group was very motivated," he said. "They talked about rehearsing during lunch—I'm not *sure* that they did."

"Would they lie to you?"

"No!" he said. "I just didn't personally see them."

"And without you there, they might not have followed all the safety rules?"

"I'm sure they did—"

"How can you be sure, Mr. Chadwick?" she said with a smug smile that made me want to smack her. "After all, you didn't personally *see* them."

For a second, Mr. Chadwick looked like a tire somebody was letting the air out of. But he pulled himself up in the chair with the confidence he always told us to show and said, "No, but I personally *know* them."

She was already on her way back to her seat. "That's all, your honor," she said over her shoulder.

"She's reaching," Mr. Quintera whispered to me.

But I was watching Mr. Chadwick as he stepped down and moved toward the aisle.

"I hope you're going to audition in the fall," he said—out loud—as he passed me.

"Yes, sir," I said.

"I hate to interrupt anything, Mr. Quintera," the judge said drily, "but please call your next witness."

I started to blush, but Mr. Quintera smiled at me, for real. "She only gets sarcastic when she likes you," he whispered, before he stood up and said, "Your honor, I call Bryn Christopher to the stand."

CHAPTER TWENTY

I t was here. The moment I'd dreaded for so long. The same moment I'd prayed would come so I could say the words I'd been given. The moment I could show Preston Oliver that he couldn't take away who I was. Or anyone else.

Mr. Quintera took a deep breath after I swore to tell the truth and gave me an even deeper look. This time he didn't seem as if he were about to tiptoe across a bed of tacks.

"Bryn," he said, "will you give the jury in your own words a history of your relationship with Preston Oliver?"

"Yes, sir," I said.

He smiled at the jury as if to say, "Do you see how well-mannered this girl is?" and then backed away to watch me.

I faced the twelve people in the box, just the way Mr. Quintera had instructed me to do in our preparations — between the lectures about how I had to tell him everything — and I told *them* everything. "Don't dramatize it," he'd told me. "Just keep it simple and honest." He hadn't really needed to teach me that. I just used the words that came to me, the words that formed pictures in my mind as I told them about Preston sweeping me off my feet and then growing more controlling and more jealous. I described every punch and push, every threat. I included his vow that he was going to commit suicide if I broke up with him, and his forcing me to give up theater.

Mr. Quintera interrupted me there. "Why didn't you just break up with him, Bryn?" he said.

"Because I was afraid of him," I said.

"Is that why you told the ER doctor your injuries came from football?"

"Yes, sir," I said.

I remembered why I was there, who these words were really for, and I turned to look at Preston. He startled a little—stopped tapping his class ring on the table and fumbled with the tie that looked ridiculously out of character. Even as he recovered and pasted on his smirk, I went on.

"He convinced me that he had power over me. I couldn't see then that he's nothing more than a coward who has to push girls around to make him feel like he has control."

"I object!" Ms. Dorchester said.

"To what?" Mr. Quintera said.

"Overruled," the judge said.

Mr. Quintera cued me to go on with what happened the night of the accident and the afternoon at Sonic. I told that to the jury, and started in on the threatening text messages and the blog, but the judge sustained Ms. Dorchester's objection that time and told the jury to disregard my last statement. From their faces, I didn't think they did. One guy seemed like he wanted to pick Preston up by his daddy's necktie.

"What other possible reason could you have for accusing Preston Oliver of abuse besides the fact that it's the truth?"

"None," I said.

"You're not trying to get back at him for something—maybe he looked at another girl?"

"No."

"You said he made you give up the theater, which you obviously love. You're not accusing him as payback for that?"

"No. The night of the accident, I was going to break up with him. It was the first time I ever tried to get away from him when he hit me. I was going to ask my parents to let me change schools so I would never have to see him again."

"But you weren't going to turn him in?"

I took a deep breath and looked back at Preston. He had his head twisted away, like he wanted us all to think he was over the whole thing. But I saw the muscles twitching in his jaw. I knew that twitch. I knew it meant any minute he was going to go off.

"No. Even when my father first said I should press charges, I didn't want to, because I didn't think anybody would believe me." I turned back to the jury. "But now I know better. And I don't want him to hurt anybody else."

Mr. Quintera thanked me and sat down. From the other side of the aisle, I heard slow clapping from one person. Ms. Dorchester came toward me still smacking her hands sloppily together.

"That was quite the performance, Bryn," she said.

"Objection!" Mr. Quintera said.

"I'm just admiring Ms. Christopher's work—"

"Ask a question, Ms. Dorchester," the judge said. She glowered over her half-glasses. I was relieved to see no sarcasm in her eyes.

"Let me see." The attorney tapped her nails again like she was trying to decide where to start. "Since we've already established what a well-trained actor you are, I suppose there's no point in going over your stage combat experience again."

"Your honor!" Mr. Quintera shouted.

"Last warning, Ms. Dorchester."

It didn't seem to bother Ms. Dorchester a bit.

"All right, Bryn, let's talk about your relationship with your father."

"Objection—relevance."

"Your witness brought it up," she said. I expected a neener-neener-neener to follow.

"I'll allow it, but tread carefully," the judge said. Tread carefully? This lady walked wherever she wanted to, and she didn't care who she tromped on along the way. I let myself close my eyes for a second so I could gather myself up. Jesus was still there.

"You live alone with your father, don't you?" she said.

"No, ma'am," I said.

Mr. Quintera had told me that, unlike with him, I should give her a yes or no answer whenever I could and then shut up.

"I stand corrected," she said. "Your mother also lives with you."

"Yes, ma'am."

"But she's currently out of the country, is that correct?"

"Yes, ma'am."

"How long has she been away?"

"About five weeks."

"That's a long time to be alone with your father, isn't it?"

"I don't think it is," I said.

"Is your mother in the courtroom today?"

"No, ma'am."

"Is there someone else staying at your house right now?"

That wasn't a question I expected, but I said, "Yes, ma'am."

"And who is that?"

"My grandmother," I said.

"Your mother's mother or your father's mother?"

"Your honor, I do not see the relevance of this line of questioning," Mr. Quintera said.

The three of them argued about that while I sorted through my head. Mr. Quintera had said Ms. Dorchester wouldn't ask me a question she didn't already know the answer to. Preston didn't know Mim was staying with us—unless Regan told him. Or Fielding.

Who cared—it couldn't possibly make any difference. I steered my thoughts away from that. I couldn't think about Fielding right now. Or maybe I should. She was one of the people I was trying to protect from Preston.

"Whose mother is she?" Ms. Dorchester said. Her voice was a little snippy, as if she were getting tired of me.

"My mother's."

"When did she join your household?"

"She came for a visit about a month ago."

"A long visit without her daughter even there. Why?"

Without realizing I was doing it at first, I turned my head to look at Mim. She was sitting straight up in her seat, hands folded, fingers steepled under her nose. Her eyes were bright. And proud.

"She came to help me through all this," I said. "Because it's really been hard."

Mr. Quintera gave me a tiny nod.

"Didn't she actually come to protect you from your father?" Ms. Dorchester said.

I jumped like a spooked cat. "Excuse me?" I said.

"Didn't your maternal grandmother come to protect you from your father's abuse?"

"No, ma'am!"

"Then she hasn't protected you? Has the abuse continued?"

"It never started in the first place! My father has never hit me!"

Ms. Dorchester put up her commanding little manicured hand and shook her head, as if I was now so hysterical there was no point in pursuing this further. "I think I've made my point," her eyes said to the jury.

I looked at Mr. Quintera, but he was scribbling on his pad. Behind him, Mim pressed her palms together and placed them at her lips. *Pray. Pray, and the words will be there.*

I opened my fists and spread my now-sweaty hands out on my skirt. I could feel the dampness through the cotton. But it was okay. It was okay.

"Can I tell you what I think, Bryn?" Ms. Dorchester said. She started to go on like that wasn't really a question, but I shook my head.

"No offense, ma'am," I said. "But I don't really care what you think."

She jerked her head toward the judge. "This borders on contempt, your honor."

"You asked for it, Ms. Dorchester," she said. "Quite frankly, I'm not interested in what you think either. I'm interested in you asking a question that is going to move this trial forward."

Ms. Dorchester murmured, "Yes, your honor," but her eyes looked pretty hostile to me.

"I know you've said that you planned to break up with Preston that night of the accident, but isn't it true that he was breaking up with you? Wasn't that why he took you out to his friend's car, so you could talk in private?"

"I don't *know* if that was what he had planned. He didn't say —"

"You never had sex with him, did you?"

"No, ma'am —"

"Wasn't that the reason he was ending your relationship—because you wouldn't 'put out'?"

194

"Objection!"

"That's enough, Ms. Dorchester," the judge said wearily.

"You see, Bryn," the attorney said, as if nobody had interrupted her, "what we have here is your word against Preston Oliver's. Tell me why the jury should believe you and not him. Give them one reason."

"Because I'm telling the truth."

"My client says he is too, and I believe him." She shrugged. "What else do you have for us?"

I started to say I had nothing. That they were either going to believe me or they weren't. But once again my eyes went to Mim without any planning on my part, and then I remembered something.

"My grandmother always says I might as well always tell the truth," I said, "because it's always written all over my face anyway."

Ms. Dorchester rolled her eyes as if I'd just given her the lamest possible answer. But after she said she had nothing further, the way she dropped her pad on the table said maybe it wasn't so lame after all.

Mr. Quintera said the prosecution rested and the judge gave us another ten-minute recess, during which Mim gave me a shoulder massage and made me drink water and Dad went out to call Mom again. Mr. Quintera gave me a longer approving nod this time.

"You did great, Bryn," he said. "I mean it. And now you can relax—and I mean that too. The defense is going to try every trick in the book to make Preston look like the golden boy and get the jury to think you're out to get him. I want you to let it all roll right off your back. Okay?"

I said I would, but something niggled at me. Just as the bailiff was about to tell us to "all rise" again, I whispered to Mr. Quintera, "Preston's about to lose it. I can tell."

"Duly noted," he said.

It wasn't that hard getting through all Ms. Dorchester's witnesses who said Preston was the all-American hero. "Character witnesses," Mr. Quintera called them. Claire, Preston's girlfriend before me, said Preston had never laid a hand on her, that he was a big ol' teddy bear. His swim coach extolled his virtues as an athlete and team member and said he was shocked—*shocked*—by my accusation and devastated that this whole "misunderstanding" had kept Preston from going to the swim camp that would have guaranteed his place on the Olympic team. I didn't really blame them—they weren't actually lying. They just didn't know any better. The people who did—Andrew and Regan and Kane—were conspicuously absent from the witness list. They weren't even in the courtroom to support Preston.

Mr. Quintera didn't cross-examine any of them except Claire, who he got to admit that she'd broken up with Preston because he was too moody about his Olympic failure and sometimes punched walls because he was frustrated. Even though she swore he'd never taken any of it out on her, everybody on that side of the aisle glared at her when she was leaving the courtroom. I wanted to tell her she'd dodged a bullet once and she ought to keep going. Maybe I would call her later.

Finally Ms. Dorchester announced that she was calling the defendant, Preston Oliver, to the stand. You'd have thought she was going to give him an Academy Award the way she escorted him to the box. He certainly deserved one. He'd sat at the defense table all day smirking or looking bored out of his mind, but the minute he hit the witness stand, he was the portrait of a concerned citizen, just there to do the right thing. You'd never have known he was on trial for a felony.

At first Ms. Dorchester asked him what I thought were pointless questions, which gave me time to remember that Preston had probably been prepped as much by his attorney as I had been by Mr. Quintera. That was why he was wearing the tie he would have flushed down the toilet if anybody else told him he had to wear it.

It was dark blue with gold somethings on it, the shirt a lighter blue. The combination kept his eyes from seeming so cold—although they still made a small part of me shiver. He had let his hair grow some, so he obviously wasn't seriously training for swimming. I knew for a fact he even shaved his legs and armpits to create less friction in the water. As he nodded and smiled and said, "Yes, ma'am"—which I had never heard him utter before except to make fun of me doing it. I had a vision of him at a class reunion ten years from now. Everybody else would have matured into an adult, and he'd be the same Preston wearing grown-up clothes. Just like he was now.

Ms. Dorchester folded her hands against her wide patent-leather belt. It was time for the serious questions. But she didn't ask him to give his version of our relationship. In fact, she directed her pointy gaze at Mr. Quintera and said she wasn't going to waste the court's time by doing that. Instead she ran through a series of queries punctuated with sighs, like it was all just a simple matter of clearing up my lies.

"Did you plan to break up with Bryn the night of the accident?"

"Yes. Ma'am."

"Was it because she wouldn't have sex with you?"

Preston shrugged. "Maybe that was part of it. It was more about her being such a drama queen about it."

Ms. Dorchester looked amused. "'Drama queen'? I'm not familiar with that term."

"It's when a girl goes emo over everything," Preston said.

Ms. Dorchester actually laughed. "Clearly I'm going to need a teen dictionary. Can you define 'emo'?"

"She gets all emotional about everything. She's always crying." He said *crying* with the same disgust he'd use to say I was always belching. "She gets off on a crisis, and I got sick of it."

"Did you 'drag' her out of the party and out to your friend's car to break things off?"

His lip curled. "No."

"Speaking of the accident, Preston," Ms. Dorchester said, "what did cause it?"

"I was just driving around trying to calm her down." Preston grunted. "She grabbed my arm and jerked the wheel and I couldn't get control back. She was always doing stuff like that."

My hands were clenched so hard in my lap, pain shot up my arms.

"Did Bryn ever tell you her father hit her?"

"Oh, yeah," Preston said. "She cried on my shoulder about that all the time."

Ms. Dorchester lowered her chin at him. "You didn't think she was just being a 'drama queen'?"

"Yeah—until I saw the bruises."

Mr. Quintera had his hand on my arm before I got my mouth all the way open. I closed it. I liked it a lot better when I was the one up there talking.

"Why didn't you tell anyone—try to help her?" Ms. Dorchester said.

"She got even more emo when I said I was gonna tell the school counselor. She said her old ma—her dad would only do worse to her."

I twisted in my seat. Dad sat with his elbows on his knees, hands clasped in front of his mouth, eyes boring into Preston.

I never said that, I mouthed to him.

I know, he mouthed back.

"One more question, Preston," Ms. Dorchester said. "Did you ever hit Bryn Christopher?"

"No way."

"Grab her?"

"No."

"Push her against a wall? Pull her hair?"

"No," Preston said. "I never touched her except to show her my love."

Why I didn't throw up, I had no idea.

"Your witness, Mr. Quintera," the lawyer said, and swept back to her table.

Mr. Quintera got up quickly and crossed the space to the witness stand in two strides.

"I don't want to waste much time on you either, Mr. Oliver," he said. "So I'll just get to the point. When you were in the car with Ms. Christopher, did she punch herself in the stomach with a flashlight?"

"No," Preston said. His smirk slid into place.

"Did the air bag deploy when you crashed?"

"Yeah."

"Interesting. Because sometime within a half hour of her arrival at the hospital she was hit in the abdomen hard enough to cause a hematoma. You were with her all evening, weren't you?"

"Yeah—but—"

"Was she ever out of your sight?"

"No—"

"Was anyone else with the two of you?"

"It was a party," Preston said, deepening the smirk.

"Did you see anybody hit her?"

"No. Her dad probably did it before she left the house."

"Did she appear to be in pain when she got to the party?"

"No—okay—wait—maybe—"

"Which is it?"

"Who could tell? She was always acting."

"So did she 'act' like she was in pain?"

"I don't know." Preston snapped his head to look over his shoulder for no reason—except the one I knew, which was that Preston never admitted he didn't know something. Everything.

"Josie Lentz has told the court that she witnessed you grabbing Bryn by the arm and dragging her to the front door. Can you explain that?"

Preston gave a jerky shrug. "I guess I was sick of the conversation."

"What conversation?"

"I don't remember. I just wanted to get her out of there."

"Bryn."

"Yeah." The 'duh' hung on his lip.

"To break up with her."

"That's what I said."

"So from that moment you had her by the arm until you got to the car."

"Sure."

"And then you got in the car, just the two of you."

"Yeah."

"You had another 'conversation,' took off in the car, had the accident, the air bags deployed. Is that right?"

"Yes."

"So how'd she get the hematoma, Preston?"

"I said I don't know!"

"She has testified under oath that you rammed a flashlight into her abdomen."

199

"Well she's a lying—"

The five-letter word flew from his mouth and headed straight for my heart. This time I didn't let it in. It was just another word. Another meaningless lie.

Mr. Quintera returned to the table as the judge dismissed Preston and told him to watch his language in the courtroom. Her glare over the top of her half-glasses would have wilted anybody else.

"It's late," the judge said finally. "I'm going to adjourn until nine a.m. tomorrow. We'll hear closing statements then." She gave the bench a stern rap with her gavel.

When we had all risen and she was gone, Mr. Quintera ushered us down the hall, which was almost deserted by now.

"I think we showed the jury his hot streak," he said. "We'll see what happens."

"I wish I was on that jury," Mim said.

Mr. Quintera nodded. "I wish you were too. Bryn—nice work today. You couldn't have been better."

Dad hugged my shoulders and Mim smiled, but I didn't share their enthusiasm. The one thing missing was Mr. Quintera saying this was a done deal.

"Are we going to win?" I said.

His face sobered. "We have a very good chance. But it isn't over yet. Dorchester provided reasonable doubt. It's up to the jury to decide how reasonable."

CHAPTER TWENTY ONE

Dad talked to Mom on his cell on the way home, singing my praises and assuring her that I wasn't upset because she and Tara had to spend the night in Atlanta. I hoped he wouldn't pass the phone to me, because I was suddenly too tired to talk to her. Actually, there was only one person I really did want to talk to.

Dad went to the clinic and Mim, of course, made me a smoothie to make up for the lunch I hadn't eaten. I was still only staring into the glass when she said, "All right, out with it before you implode."

"Is it already all over my face?"

"Your face—your hands—in the way you're pumping that straw up and down."

"I want to see Shaun," I said.

"Of course you do. What time does he get off work?"

"Not until seven."

Mim smiled. "I see your dilemma. It's only five."

I swiveled the chair toward the sunroom window. "I know it's lame, but I want to go to the Surf Shack right now."

She looked warily at the sky. "It isn't lame—but we have another major storm coming in."

"I don't want to surf. I just want to see Shaun." I gave the straw another pump.

"Okay," Mim said. "I'll drop you off there while I go pick up a few things." She gave the angry bank of clouds another glance. "Including flashlight batteries."

By the time Mim left me at the Shack, the trees were bending sideways in the wind, and Shaun was trying to get the boards that were on display on the porch inside the shop before they took off on their own. I forgot everything I'd wanted to tell him.

"I'll help you!" I shouted over the howl of the storm.

Battling the wind carrying surfboards was even harder than fighting incoming waves. Shaun told me to get the shortboards while he took the long ones. We got the last one in just as the rain started to slam us. Shaun had to wrestle with the door to get it closed—and no sooner did he have it shut than somebody flung it open and literally fell into the shop. Shaun stepped over him to grab the door, yelling, "What are you *doing* here, Goof?"

Goof got to all fours and shook his hair like a dog.

Shaun hauled him to his feet. "Dude, you are a moron!"

"You gotta call VBLS."

"Why?"

"Because I'm not the moron. That friend of my brother's is out there surfing—"

"Is he in trouble?" Shaun already had his hand on the phone.

"Probably. But the girl definitely is."

Shaun turned away from us with the phone, a finger in his other ear, and Goof's gaze landed on me so hard I could almost hear his brain click.

"I think it's that girl you hang out with," he said. "That surfer chick."

"Fielding?" I said.

Shaun hung up and grabbed two life preservers off the wall. "VBLS is on their way."

"Shaun—it's Fielding out there!"

"Yeah, I knew it was some weird name." Goof grabbed a ring from Shaun. "It's her and her boyfriend."

Shaun and I stared at each other for a fraction of a moment before he headed for the door.

"The lifesaving service has got an emergency at the other end of the beach and everybody else is tied up securing stuff. He said for us to try to wave them in. Bryn—" he said before he shoved the door open. "You stay here."

I ignored him and snatched a Windbreaker from the rack on the way out. The price tag dangled from the sleeve as I jammed my arms into it and took off after Shaun and Goof.

The wind was coming straight at us off the water as we slanted our way onto the beach. My face and hands and legs stung, and even though I squinted my eyes, they were instantly sandblasted. Through the pain I could still see the ocean, churning angrily and hurling whitecaps at the shore. Not even Preston would be enough of an egomaniac to try to surf in that—not unless it got that way after he was out there. Still…

And yet in front of one of the breakers poised to crash was a person—arms slugging into and out of the surf as he swam. It was Preston.

I didn't see Fielding at all.

By the time I reached the water's edge behind Shaun and Goof, Preston was staggering onto the sand. His chest was heaving.

"Where's Fielding?" Shaun shouted at him.

Preston shook his head.

"Goof—go call again!" Shaun said.

Goof disappeared with the wind. Preston was leaning over from the waist beside him, coughing onto the sand.

"Where is she?" Shaun shouted again.

"She probably came in up the beach—I don't know—"

"You don't *know*!"

Preston twisted his neck to look up, face momentarily stunned, because it was me who was screaming at him.

"You just left her out there?" I said.

"Forget it, Bryn—he's a jerk."

Shaun tossed me Goof's life preserver and we started for the water. Before we got two steps, Preston grabbed Shaun's arm, pulled his own back, and slammed his fist into Shaun's face. Shaun collapsed with his own blood blowing into his eyes.

Preston flung himself on top of Shaun. I screamed a scream I myself could barely hear in the wind, but hair and fists flew until he rolled off, leaving Shaun motionless with the sand whirling around him.

"Shaun!" I screamed again.

I hugged hard on what I was holding and realized it was the life preserver. Fielding. I couldn't leave her out there.

"You really are despicable," I said to Preston. I shot him a scalding gaze and once more went for the water.

I made it one step this time before something grabbed my ankle and I went down. My face planted in the wet sand and a terrified little wave gurgled over me and back out, sucking the ground out from under me. I heaved myself up, and there was Preston, one hand already groping for the back of my neck. I backed out of his reach and cringed.

Almost.

Until I saw the cold, hard look in his eyes. The muscles twitching his face into ugliness. His teeth clenched like it was going to take all his power to hit a girl. I'd seen it all before. It truly was the same old script.

But somehow, I'd forgotten my lines. New ones flung themselves out of my mouth.

"Go ahead, Preston — hit me."

He jerked to a stop with his hands clenched halfway between us.

"It's what you do, isn't it?" I cried over the wind. "*You* screw up but you hit somebody else like it's *their* fault — right? Like a girl — who can't hit back."

It wasn't working. Preston flinched out of his pose and came at me. Six feet of weight-pressed muscle at a hundred-and-twelve-pound girl. It was pathetic.

The wind slapped a hunk of my now-soaked hair into my eye. With one hand I smacked it away. With the other I swung the life preserver into Preston's face. The wind caught it and flung it the other way, but he stared at me as if I'd just delivered him a crushing blow.

"Are you stupid?" he screamed at me.

"I used to be!" I said. "Not anymore. Bring it, Preston — right in front of the VBLS."

He wrenched around to where I'd pointed, to where the VBLS hadn't shown up yet. It gave me enough time to grab the ring again and with wind and spray slapping my face, plunge into the water. It plunged back. Preston didn't. He was too much of a coward.

I tried to ride the ring the way I did my board when I was working myself seaward, but I'd never fought a surf like this. For every stroke I took forward, the livid ocean knocked me back two. I dove straight into the next wave before it crashed above me and tumbled below it for so long I had to gasp for air when I'd clawed my way back to the surface. Another bank of water crested above me, and with it a flash of turquoise.

"Fielding!" I screamed.

The breaker crashed and she came down with it. I ducked beneath it and came up with my head whipping around. Fielding was only a few feet away, arms flailing. Even through the screen of wild foam, I could tell she was wiping out from the inside.

I flung out the life preserver. "Grab this, Fielding!"

Fielding groped for the ring and found it with both hands.

"I'll pull you in!" I shouted.

But she kept crawling—across the life preserver and into my face. Her panicked arms went around my neck, and she pushed us both under the next wave that fell on us like a crumbling building. When I tried to pull us to the surface, Fielding's hands were everywhere, clawing me in terror. I had to let go of her or we were both going to drown. When I did—when I wriggled away and broke through to air again—something hard collided with my shoulder blades. A gasping five seconds passed before I realized it was Fielding's surfboard. It must still be attached to her ankle.

Fielding's face appeared from the foam, and then her head. I was sure she didn't even know where she was anymore. I grabbed the board and pulled it to me. Fielding came with it. I started to panic myself when I saw how limp she was—but maybe that was good. Maybe—

I got myself across the board sideways and grabbed both straps of Fielding's swimsuit. The ocean chopped at us, but I managed to hold on to her as I shifted myself around and pointed the board toward shore. With one arm around Fielding, I shouted at her, "Paddle, Fielding! Paddle like a mad dog!"

Her arms flapped pointlessly, but I yelled, "Good! Keep paddling!"

With the arm that wasn't holding her, I paddled too, and I prayed. *Take us forward. Please—take us forward.*

The wave hit us from behind like a train—and lifted us up. "Hold on, Fielding!" I screamed.

It was all either of us could do. And even then we couldn't do it for long. The board keeled sideways and Fielding and I rolled, still clinging to each other, then breaking apart as the current ripped us one from the other. My face scraped the bottom and I slid on my cheek until I stopped in a heap. There was no more water. Only the wailing wind.

"Fielding!" I screamed. "Somebody help Fielding!"

"We've got her," the wind answered. "It's all right."

I pushed myself up, still shouting her name, but bulky arms came around me.

"She's right there — see?" a male voice told me.

I didn't see Fielding. I only saw Goof, his right arm around me, his left pointing to two figures bent in the wind. One was Fielding. The one holding her up was Mim.

I pushed Goof away and stumbled toward them, the soaked Windbreaker weighing me down. I should have stripped it off before I dove into the ocean. I should also have kicked off my sandals. I had no idea where they were now.

"Let's get Fielding inside!" Mim shouted when I got to them. "Goof, can you carry her?"

"I'll get her."

I flipped around. Preston was holding his arms out.

"Where is Shaun?" I screamed into his face.

"He's fine." Preston pushed me aside with his elbow and tried to pull Fielding from Mim's arms.

Mim delivered a withering look to Preston and handed Fielding over to Goof. "Let's get inside," she said.

They still hadn't told me where Shaun was. I turned my head in every direction, hair whipping into my eyes and slapping my face. I called his name until my voice broke in the wind.

"He's in the Shack, Drama Queen."

Preston's upper lip was curled and swelling around the bloody split that interrupted it.

"They're giving him first aid or something. He's a worse wimp than you are."

I didn't waste a word on him. He was no longer worth it.

And the cold, hard look had lost its power.

*

Back at the Shack, Fielding was sitting up in a chair with Mim wrapping a blanket around her and a lifeguard barking questions at her. I looked wildly around until I found Shaun stretched out on the floor with another lifeguard crouched beside him, talking on a cell phone.

"We've got the paramedics on the way," the guard said across the room. "And the cops."

Before I could get to Shaun, the wind ripped through the doorway and two bodies fell inside, one on top of the other.

"You're not goin' anywhere!" I heard Goof say from the floor.

He straddled Preston and pinned his hands with his wrists. Preston shuffled his feet, but it was pretty pointless.

"Who does that?" somebody mumbled. "Who hits a woman?"

The somebody was Shaun. One of his eyes was puffed closed but the other one shined at me.

"You're okay," he said.

"Yeah—are you?"

He didn't look like it. The few spatters of blood the rain hadn't washed off speckled his face, and his nose was red and swelling worse than his eye. It would be black and blue in twenty-four hours. I knew that well.

Within five minutes there was standing room only in the Surf Shack. Officer Day arrived, which barely left room for the paramedics to squeeze in and stretch Fielding out on the floor.

"Let's see if we can sort this out," Day said as he hauled Preston to his feet by the arm. "Who hit who and why?"

Preston pointed down at Shaun. "I was trying to save my girlfriend and this guy grabs me—"

"Whoa—what's going on here?"

The paramedic lifted Fielding's arm into the light. I gasped out loud when I saw the red finger marks around her bicep. I knew those well too.

"I did that when I was trying to save her," Preston said.

"You didn't," Fielding said. She looked at me, and her face crumpled.

"I want my lawyer," Preston said to Officer Day. "I'm not saying anything without my lawyer."

Nobody else was waiting for legal counsel. While Preston was calling his, Shaun talked. So did Goof. They described the episode of World Wide Wrestling that had gone down on the beach while I was out trying to bring Fielding in.

She herself sat, surprisingly quietly, even after her parents arrived and the paramedics left with Shaun's promise that he would go to the hospital and get checked out. Fielding's mother and father seemed to be in shock. Strange how much we kept from the people who loved us the most.

"The storm's slowing down," Officer Day said when he'd questioned everybody but Preston. "Looks like we can take this to the precinct." The Shack's owner, a man I'd never met before, had also shown up and didn't look happy about all these people clogging up his shop but not buying anything.

Mim patted my leg and whispered that we should go. I nodded, but I didn't want to let go of Shaun's hand where I sat cross-legged on the floor. That was when the door opened again. The wind had finally begun to die down, so that Ms. Dorchester didn't blow in the way everybody else did. Somehow, the hair barely came loose from her bun. Her pumps didn't even look wet.

"You haven't said anything, have you, Preston?" she said.

"No." He gave her a sulky look.

"Are you going to arrest him?" she said to Officer Day.

"For what?" Preston said.

Everybody looked at Day. Everybody but Fielding. She was searching my face like some answer she needed was hiding under my skin. Feisty, so-sure-of-herself Fielding, who never let a wave knock her down—except maybe for one.

While Officer Day went wearily back to his sorting, with Ms. Dorchester barking questions at him like a Jack Russell terrier, Fielding kept her eyes on me and yet turned her back slightly. With one hand she pulled the scooped back of her swimsuit down. I put my hand over my mouth to smother a gasp. Her lower back was striped with three bright-red welts.

Quickly she snapped the suit back into place, eyes still on me. They were filled with questions—the same ones I'd asked myself so many times. Back before I knew the answers. With a nod, I gave her one.

"So you really have nothing to charge him with," Ms. Dorchester was saying to Officer Day.

Fielding gave me one more long look before she said, "Yes, he does. Preston forced me to go out there."

Preston let out a hiss. "How could I 'force' you?"

"By threatening to do this again if I didn't." She turned again and showed her back.

Fielding's mother gasped the loudest, but nobody else was much softer. Even this second time, a wave of nausea pushed my hand to my mouth.

Preston rolled his eyes almost into his head. "Come on — what is this, a conspiracy?"

"Preston, stop."

Ms. Dorchester put her hand on his arm, but he slapped it away. "No, man, I'm sick of these hos making a big deal out of nothing. You can't even touch a girl anymore — she runs to her daddy like you tried to kill her."

"Preston, that is enough. We're going."

"You're going down too," Preston said to Fielding over his shoulder as Ms. Dorchester steered him to the door. "Just like Bryn did."

"You're not getting any help for that from my brother this time."

We turned like one person to look at Goof. His blond bush of hair lay soaked to his head like a wet rug, which made him seem even goofier than ever. But his eyes looked like they belonged to somebody older.

"I just figured it out: Kane stole my key to the Shack and got in here and painted stuff on the walls — for you." Goof did not look like he was "just kidding." "He's not doing any more of your dirty work for you."

"Fine," Preston said. "I can do my own."

"Out," Ms. Dorchester said.

"I want to say something."

This time they all looked at me. I stood up and made my way to the only space left in front of the door where Ms. Dorchester was still trying to get Preston to move so she could open it. No blush flooded my face. No fear muddled my thoughts. No doubt choked off my words. All I heard were the ones in my head—the only ones left to say.

"You can do all the dirty work you want," I said. "But you'll never take away who I am."

I looked at Fielding, and she nodded.

"Who *we* are," I said. "You don't have that kind of power anymore."

Preston gave a hard laugh. "After me, you're never gonna be the same."

"I know," I said. "Thanks to God."

CHAPTER TWENTY TWO

Mim and I went to the courthouse the next morning while Dad headed to the airport to pick up Mom and Tara. He promised he'd get them there before the opening statements.

But when we arrived, Mr. Quintera met us at the door to the courtroom and led us to another room instead. He wasn't wearing his suit jacket, and the tie was loose and the shirt sleeves rolled up.

"What's happening?" Mim said when he got us inside.

"Good news."

Mr. Quintera motioned for us to sit but the lift in his voice kept me on my feet. He leaned on the back of one of the chairs and smiled at me.

"I hear you had an adventure yesterday."

"Yes, sir," I said. "How did you know?"

"Kayla Dorchester and I had a meeting with the judge this morning. Between what Preston evidently spouted off at the surf shop yesterday—"

I nodded.

"—and what he told her on their way to the police station—namely that he 'might have put a few bruises' on you—Dorchester had to tell the judge she unknowingly put on perjured testimony. You know what that is?"

"Lies," I said.

"You got it. The judge declared a mistrial."

Mim, who was the only one who had sat down, frowned up at him. "Doesn't that mean we have to start all over?"

Please, no.

Mr. Quintera looked younger than thirty again. His eyes were dancing. "Preston didn't like that idea either. He took our offer. He's going to spend six months in jail and Daddy's going to pay a pretty hefty fine."

Someone tapped on the door, which gave me a chance to absorb those words. I'd never thought I would actually hear them—and as I stood there staring at the tabletop while Mr. Quintera went to the door, I realized I'd never even wanted to hear them. Preston was getting the punishment he deserved, but I didn't feel like celebrating. He was never going to admit that he had a serious problem. He was always going to find a way to blame it on me or Fielding or whoever else he managed to fool for a while with the person he could be. He was out of my life now—but he was never going to be out of his.

"Bryn!"

I looked up in time to see my mother coming at me, hands outstretched to grab my face and kiss both of my cheeks. She held me at arm's length and took a full survey with her jewel-blue eyes. They looked sun-strained and tired, and surprised.

"You look good," she said. She glanced at Mim, who was hugging Tara on the other side of the table. "Mom, she looks good."

"Of course, she does," Mim said. "She's been taking care of herself."

Tara grunted, her arm still around Mim's waist. "Under duress I'd be willing to bet."

"Then you'd lose," Mim said.

"Yes!"

That came from Dad, who had been conferring with Mr. Quintera in the doorway.

"What did we miss?" Mom said.

"It's over," Dad said. "He's getting six months' jail time."

"He was convicted?" Mom blinked around the room but nobody answered her.

Dad came to me and I threw myself into his hug.

"You did it, Brynnie," he said into my hair. "You put him away."

"I'll catch you folks later," Mr. Quintera said. "Nice to meet you, Ms. Christopher. Tina."

"Tara," my sister said as the door closed behind him. She looked at me and widened her eyes. "He's cute."

"Does somebody want to tell me what's going on?" Mom said.

I didn't. I let Dad do that. I dropped into the chair next to Mim's and put my head on her shoulder.

"Doesn't really feel like a victory, does it?" she said.

"No, ma'am," I said. "What's that about?"

"It's about you being the kind of person who wants everybody healed."

My cell phone rang in my pocket, the sound bouncing off the walls of the tiny room. I fished it out and answered it, because the only person calling me now would be Shaun.

"You think it's over now, don't you?" a raspy voice said. It didn't wait for an answer. "We're not letting it be over—because you ruined Preston's life."

I stood up with the phone pressed to my ear. The room fell silent around me.

"No," I said. "I didn't ruin Preston's life. He ruined it himself."

"Bryn, hang up," Mom said.

"No." Tara snapped her fingers at me. "Let me talk to them. I missed out on all the fun."

I shook my head at both of them.

"It's over for him," the voice said, slipping from its disguise enough for me to know I was talking to Regan. "But it isn't over for you."

"No, it's not," I said. "I'm just getting started. And I hope everything isn't over for Preston. I hope he gets the help he needs. I'm going to be praying for him."

My hand shook as I pressed END CALL and shoved the phone back into my pocket. I looked at Dad, who was watching me. "I need to get a different number," I said.

"Done," he said.

"I can't believe you just did that!" Tara skirted the table with her hand out. "I'm going to call them back and say what you should have said, which is that you've got the big guns behind you now and—"

"Oh, Tara, hush up." Mim stood up beside me. "Your sister is doing just fine without your 'big guns.' "

213

Dad gave me a grin. "Better than fine," he said. "She's even taught me a few things."

"Okay," Tara said. "Who are you people and what have you done with my family?"

*

Mim and I went surfing together the next morning while Mom and Tara were still in bed recovering from jet lag and Brynshock. Mim said it was going to take them awhile to get used to the new me.

I thought about that as we waited together for a nice set of waves, Mim on her board, me on mine. No lessons today, she'd told me. Just the two of us and the ocean we'd shared.

"Are you at least going to stay until they stop looking at me like I'm an imposter?" I said.

"That depends on how smart they are." Mim pivoted her surfboard. "This one's mine," she said.

I watched her paddle and stand up before the wave and angle gracefully down its silken line. She has her waves, I thought. And I have mine.

So it didn't surprise me when I'd ridden to shore and joined her on the beach that she said, "I have to get back to camp, Bryn."

"I know," I said.

"I promised God I would stay as long as you needed me. I cheated and stayed longer." She handed me the tube of sunscreen. "You haven't needed me since the night we talked about the Good Samaritan. I just wanted to hang around and watch it happen."

"The trial?"

"No. You starting down the path." She held out her hand for me to squeeze lotion into it and rubbed my back. "You're on a beautiful journey, Bryn. I'm not going to miss all of it. We'll be together many times."

"With you three thousand miles away?"

"If you want to come visit me, I'll send you a plane ticket. I would love to have you at the camp."

I lowered my head so she could get my neck. "I could always use more surfing lessons. Although—I'm never going to be the surf queen you are."

"You have the potential to be if you want to." She stopped rubbing. "But I think there are other things you want more, aren't there?"

I leaned back against her, gooey back and all. "Yes, ma'am. I just hope some of them I can still have at Prep. I know a lot of people aren't going to want to hang around me after all this. I guess I'm okay with starting over."

"As who?" Mim said.

I tilted my head back and smiled up at her. "As the real Bryn Christopher."

*

The night before Mim left for San Diego, I felt the pull to pick up RL. I'd actually read something in it every day since before the trial, but that evening after everyone else was in bed, I couldn't sleep for it calling to me from the chair. Or maybe that was Copper meowing from his usual curled-up place on its cover. Whatever — the pages waved a welcome as they fanned into place.

They didn't land on a story. The page had only a few lines in the middle of it.

You've discovered why I was left for you, the words said. *It's time for you to leave me for someone else who aches for me. But you are not alone. You will always have Yeshua. You will always have his Word.*

I closed it and let it fall softly to my lap. It had pulled and tugged and dragged me to so many places. Places I needed to go. Places I didn't want to go but had to. I stretched my hand out on the cover and rubbed it. I hadn't been easy on it along the way. I'd dumped it on the floor. Slammed it shut. Yelled at it. Did everything but flush it down the toilet, and I'd even considered that once or twice.

And here I was almost in tears because I had to give it up.

"I know. I have the Bible," I said to it. "You've taught me how to read it — and I will, I swear. But — "

You have me.

I pulled the book to my face and smelled the leather. "I know. And I know everything is going to be okay from now on — what?"

The book was pulling at me.

"I thought we were done."

It pulled again.

I laid it on my lap and opened it, let the pages flip impatiently into place. It gave a sigh that clearly said, "Let's go over this one more time."

"Go over what?"

I let it sweep my gaze to a spot halfway down the page.

One day a big group of people were following Yeshua, and he turned to them and he said, "Anybody who comes to me but at the same time isn't willing to let go of whatever she has to in order to stay with me can't really be my follower-friend."

I—

"Not just once but as often as necessary. You have to be able to let go of anything that separates you from me—and sometimes that will seem like the same thing over and over. It's what's called your cross."

"I have my cross to bear like everyone else," Mim had said.

"You'll have to pick it up and follow me," Yeshua said. "I'll help you carry it, but don't think for a moment it's going to be a piece of cake. I never promised that."

I'd hoped he wouldn't say that.

"If you were going to audition for a play, you'd plan ahead, yeah? You'd size up the competition before you went for the leading role, wouldn't you?"

He was waiting for an answer. I nodded.

"So do the same thing before you make a promise to follow me. Count the cost, because you WILL have to sacrifice for it. Know who you're up against, because there will ALWAYS be somebody who wants to knock you down."

I trailed my finger down the page and it let me. I wasn't going to be tugged against my will. This was up to me.

The answer was the easiest one yet.

"I've already given up being popular," I said. "I gave up the guy every girl wanted for a boyfriend. I threw all my dignity into the ocean and made a complete fool of myself in front of everybody on the beach. I almost drowned saving Fielding." I closed the book and pressed it to my chest. "I did it for you. And I would do it all again in a heartbeat."

I didn't have to open it to hear Yeshua say, *Then you have ears to hear. You can follow me.*

*

Shaun and I took Mim to the airport the next morning, at her request. My mother complained that she had barely gotten to spend any time with her, but Mim just smiled and hugged her and told her to stop whining. She hadn't raised her to be a whiner.

So we piled Mim and her suitcase and the big purse I was taking into the backseat of Shaun's Jeep, and they said their good-byes. Tara, who was still in sleep pants and a T-shirt, whispered in my ear that Shaun was a hot-hottie.

"Just don't let this one push you around," she said.

I didn't even answer her as I climbed into the Jeep.

"I think I know what one of my crosses I have to bear is," I said.

"Your sister will fall off of her ego sooner or later," Mim said. "Just be there when she tumbles."

"Should I ask what you're talking about?" Shaun said. He could still only shine in one eye. "Or is this a family thing?"

"It's a we-have-better-things-to-talk-about thing," I said.

"Let's talk about both of you coming out to San Diego at the end of the summer, before school starts," Mim said. "My treat."

Shaun's good eye bulged in the rearview mirror.

"I think it's a sin that an athlete with your gift hasn't surfed in the Pacific Ocean," Mim said. "I try to wipe out a little sin every day."

Shaun gave me a fading-black-and-blue smile. "I'm there if you are," he said.

That kept me from crying as hard as I might have when we left Mim at the curb in front of the terminal. I was still sniffling some, though, as we drove back toward the beach.

"I'm totally going to miss her too," Shaun said.

"You don't think I'm being a drama queen about it?"

He squeezed his shoulders together. "You know what—I don't ever want to hear those two words together again."

"Okay," I said.

"Did I come on too strong just then?"

"No. Are you hungry?"

"Always."

"I want to buy us Mexican food."

"That's cool with me—but you do know it's eight o'clock in the morning."

"Taco Bell's open."

"I like it."

Shaun pulled the Jeep into the next one we came to. The line at the drive-through went almost to the street.

"Looks like nobody else knows it's only eight o'clock in the morning either," I said.

"We can eat in the 'dining room.'" Shaun grinned. "How do they get away with calling it a 'dining room'?"

"I know. It's not like they have white tablecloths," I said.

It occurred to me when we got inside that Shaun was the easiest person to talk to I'd ever met. Except maybe for RL.

"Will you order for me?" I said, crunching a wad of money into his hand. "I'm gonna go—"

"Got it," Shaun said. "Everything extra hot, right?"

"Yes, and then I'll breathe in your face."

"I was planning on it."

I laughed and made my way to the back of the "dining room" where the restrooms were. A cone outside them said they were currently closed for cleaning, which was fine. I didn't really have to go.

I slid into a booth that was out of sight of the counter and pulled RL from my bag. Two big good-byes in one day.

"But you're going to say 'hello' to somebody else," I whispered to the leather cover.

Before I could let go of it, I had to flip through its pages one more time. As always, they stopped on their own, this time at the very back, a place I'd never peeked at before. Others before me had left their initials, like the ones carved on the covers. Still others had doodled or jotted down verses. But one thing pulled me in just as Yeshua's words had. "If you ever want to talk about what you learned from RL," someone had written, "call me. Meanwhile, I'll be praying for you."

It was signed Jess K. and had a phone number next to it.

Feelings rushed up from it to meet me. Some pain. A few heartaches. A little fear. But most of what wrapped itself around me like one of Mim's blankets was a mixture of hope and anticipation and the first whispers of joy. Real joy. I could almost hear the voices cheering me on, and when I closed my eyes, I saw the vision—of the next girl who would find these pages in the tangle of her doubt and her anxiety and her endless confusion about who she was.

I dug into the bag and produced a pen.

"I'd totally love to share too," I wrote. "And I'll never stop praying. Bryn C."

I added my email address.

And then I wrote Jess K.'s number on a napkin and tucked it into my bag. Maybe someday ...

As Shaun wove his way toward me, grinning and juggling Taco Bell bags, I slid RL onto the seat of the booth and got up to meet him.

"Can we take our food with us?" I said.

"Sure," Shaun said. "How come?"

"Because it's time to move forward," I said.

His grin widened. Shifting the bags to one arm, he put the other one around me and pulled me close to his wonderful healing face. In a magical moment he brushed his lips across mine.

"I like the way you think," he said.

Yeah. I was liking the way I thought too.

I was liking it a lot.

ABOUT THE REAL LIFE BOOK

You might have figured out before Bryn did that when she opened the leather Real Life book, she was reading stories from the Bible. They aren't the actual Scriptures, of course, but they are inspired by what Eugene Peterson did in *The Message*, which was to use modern, everyday language that makes you realize the Bible is for and about you. Jesus spoke in the street language of his day, so it only makes sense that we should be able to read his words that way. In fact, Eugene Peterson was inspired by a man named J. B. Phillips, who in 1947 wrote *The New Testament in Modern English* so his youth group could understand the Bible and live it!

Of course, no matter what translation of the Bible you read, it doesn't actually "talk" to you the way Real Life carried on a conversation with Bryn. Or doesn't it? Scripture is the Word of God and a Word is meant to be spoken. When you really settle in with the Bible,

- *doesn't it make you ask questions?*

- *doesn't it answer the questions that pop into your head?*

- *doesn't it seem weirdly close to the exact things you're going through now, even though the stories were told thousands of years ago?*

- *doesn't it sometimes say something you didn't see the last time you looked at that very same part?*

Reading the Bible really is like having a conversation with God, and I hope the Real Life book helps you open up your own discussion with our Lord, who is waiting for you to say, "Can we talk?" Comparing what Bryn reads to the actual passages in the Bible might help you get started. All of them are found in the Gospel of Luke, who even more than Mark, Matthew, and John, showed the love and sympathy Jesus had for the people who didn't fit, the people who others said were weird, sinful, and not to be hung out with. Luke also shows how much Jesus respected women. It seemed like just the thing for our RL girls — and for you.

THE SCRIPTURES

WHO HELPED?

One of the most fun parts of writing a book is working with experts who know stuff I don't. I mean, seriously, how much time have I spent surfing or practicing law? These are the pros who helped me make *Boyfriends, Burritos & an Ocean of Trouble* feel like real life:

Joseph A. Davidow, Trial Attorney, who helped me sculpt the courtroom scenes and found a way for justice to be served when it didn't look like it could go that way.

Coach Lee Painter and the students of Friendship Christian School, Lebanon, TN, who let me hang out with them and get caught up on current teen vocabulary. I love the way y'all talk!

Dustin Boshart, Surf Station, St. Augustine, FL, who gave me a hilarious surfing lesson and helped me catch both waves in the ocean and mistakes in the manuscript.

Rebecca Ferguson RN, MSN, APN-BC and Benjamin A. Smallheer PH.D. MSN (Master of Science in Nursing), ANP (Acute Care Nurse Practitioner), who guided me through the hospital scenes with their real-life experiences

Phil and Pat Hatcher and Kacky Fell, my traveling-to-the-beach companions and cheerleading squad for my surfing adventure. You'll see Phil's professional photo on the back of this book.

Cory Moore, whose teen-ness and talent as a writer himself made all the details true to life.

The Rev. Gail Seavey, who shared her own visions with me and helped me to see Bryn's.

Real Life Series
by Nancy Rue

A mysterious book unites four teen girls and unlocks the secret that will get each of them through the real-life struggles they face in their lives.

Motorcycles, Sushi & One Strange Book
Book One

While family dinners and vacations to touristy destinations are ordinary events for her "normal" friends, fifteen-year-old Jessie Hatcher's normal life means dealing with her ADHD and her mother's bipolar disorder.

Tournaments, Cocoa & One Wrong Move
Book Three

Sixteen-year-old Cassidy's promising basketball future is threatened when she finds herself a victim of Female Athlete Syndrome.

Talk It Up!

Want free books?
First looks at the best new fiction?
Awesome exclusive merchandise?

We want to hear from you!

Give us your opinions on titles, covers, and stories.
Join the Z Street Team.

Email us at zstreetteam@zondervan.com
to sign up today!

Also—Friend us on Facebook!

www.facebook.com/goodteenreads

- Video Trailers
- Connect with your favorite authors
- Sneak peeks at new releases
- Giveaways
- Fun discussions
- And much more!